THE TREE THAT CALLED US HOME

A NOVEL

Robin Shaw

The Ttee That Called Us Home

Wild American Chestnut Foundation,LLC.
Visit our website, www.TheTreeThatCalledUsHome.com

Produced and printed by Stillwater River Publications.

Visit our website at
www.StillwaterPress.com
for more information.

First Stillwater River Publications Edition

ISBN: 978-1-960505-31-6

1 2 3 4 5 6 7 8 9 10
Written by Robin Shaw..
Published by Stillwater River Publications,
Pawtucket, RI, USA.

Grateful Acknowledgement is made to Deb Gessner for the permission to use her photograph copyright (c) "Saxton's River

For Fred and Nita,
who raised me in the hollow between emerald meadows
and untamed woods, to be in awe of the beauty
and wonder of nature.

SUPPORT FOR THE AMERICAN CHESTNUT

"Where there be mountains, there be chestnut."

—Hernando deSoto, explorer 1540

"This tree was as much a part of our national story, as the Liberty Bell or the Bald Eagle." —Rex Mann, Retired US Forest Ranger

"It's kind of a challenge for scientists, but I have faith in the integrity and permanence of the chestnut tree."

—Jimmy Carter, 39th President of the United States

"Everybody has memories of chestnuts and chestnut trees, I know all mountain people do...You don't want something so great and such a part of your whole heritage, your whole background to be gone."

—Dolly Parton, Singer/Songwriter/Philanthropist

"This movement is about the biology of chestnuts but also about the psychology of people, about the nobility of the forest giant, but also about the nobility of the people who have devoted themselves to its recovery."

—Bill McKibben, Environmentalist, Author, Journalist

"The chestnut tree was just this magnificent giant of a tree, and the fruit that it beared, the chestnut itself, was one of the most important foods for wildlife and for mankind…To see the work that's going on to bring that tree back and to see the success that has occurred, it's just very, very exciting. "

—Chuck Leavell, American Musician,
Allman Brothers and Rolling Stones

"We don't really have a clue of what it was like to have an entire forest floor littered with this mountain of calories. By connecting the history of the past with the stories of the present we want to make sure that we move forward together; stronger, living our ancestors' dream of freedom, prosperity and blessing."

—Michael Twitty, Culinary Historian
commenting about the American chestnuts.

The following novel is a work of fiction, based on true events. While the characters and certain elements of the story have been fictionalized for creative purposes, the underlying events depicted in the novel are based on actual American history.

The author has conducted extensive research and taken creative liberties in order to tell this story in a compelling and meaningful way. However, the novel is not intended to be a completely accurate depiction.

While the names, characters, places and incidents are the product of the author's imagination or used fictitiously, the author hopes that this novel will serve as a respectful tribute, and honor, to those who lived through these events, and continue to do the hard work necessary to recreate the past into the future.

HAYES FAMILY TREE

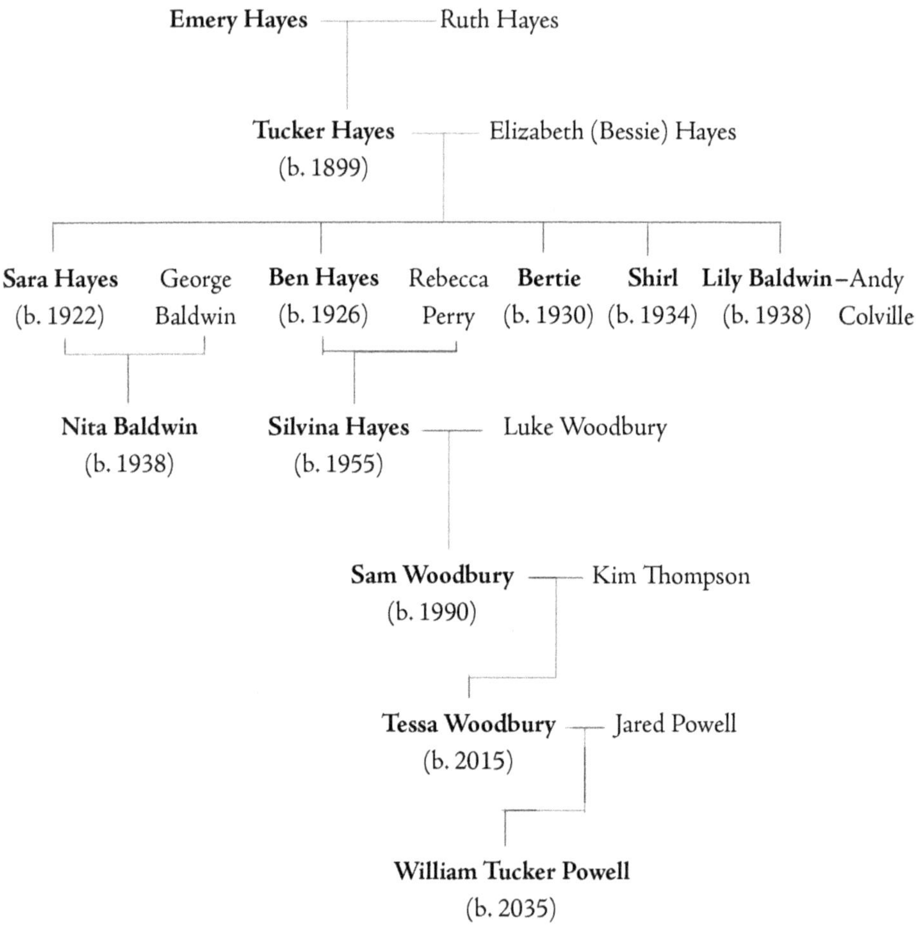

Emery Hayes — Ruth Hayes

Tucker Hayes (b. 1899) — Elizabeth (Bessie) Hayes

Sara Hayes (b. 1922) — George Baldwin

Ben Hayes (b. 1926) — Rebecca Perry

Bertie (b. 1930)

Shirl (b. 1934)

Lily Baldwin (b. 1938) – Andy Colville

Nita Baldwin (b. 1938)

Silvina Hayes (b. 1955) — Luke Woodbury

Sam Woodbury (b. 1990) — Kim Thompson

Tessa Woodbury (b. 2015) — Jared Powell

William Tucker Powell (b. 2035)

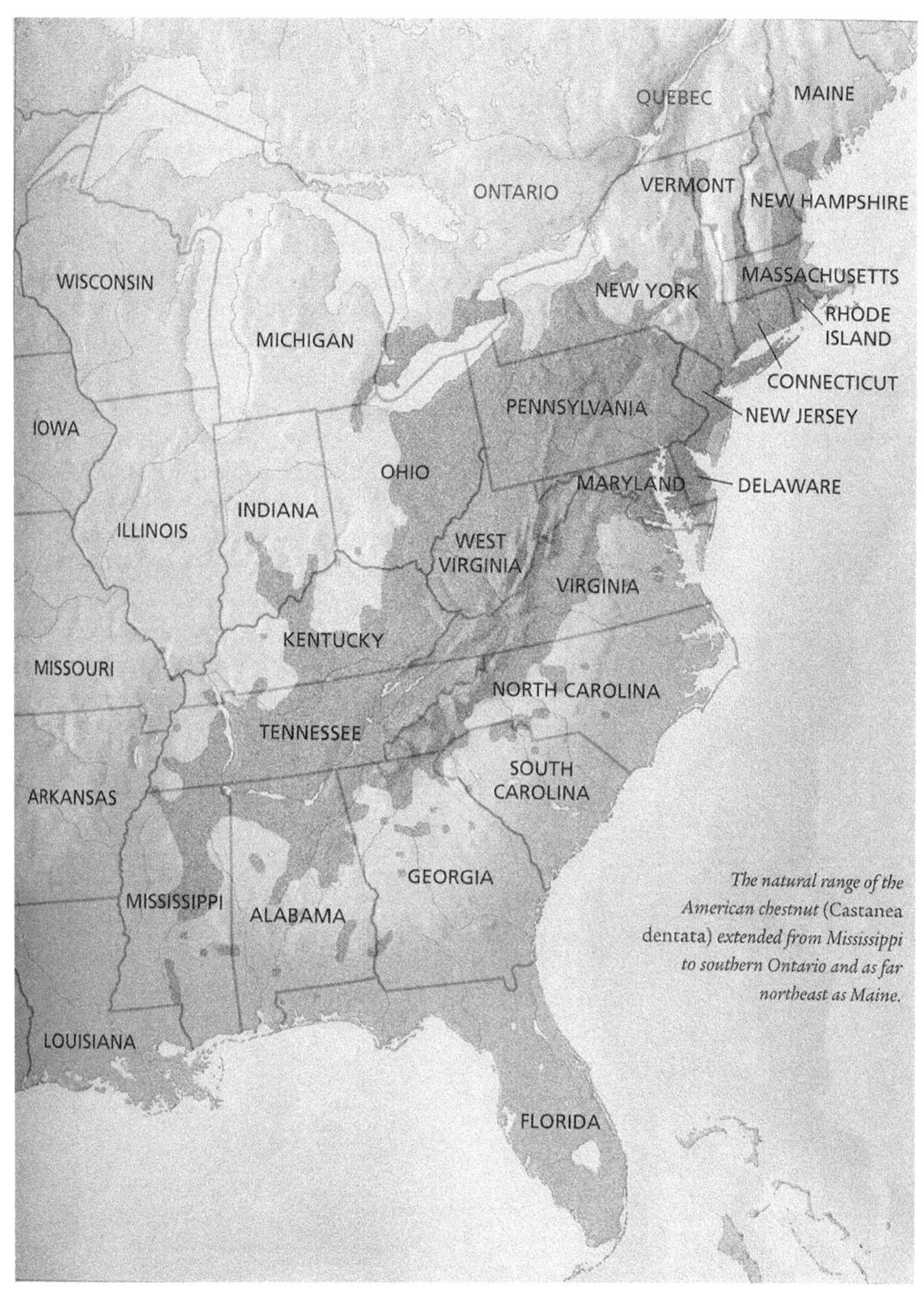

The natural range of the American chestnut (Castanea dentata) *extended from Mississippi to southern Ontario and as far northeast as Maine.*

PROLOGUE

Life in Rural Appalachia
1900

The lands of Alabama, West Virginia, Kentucky, Mississippi, Tennessee and all the other Appalachian states were rich acres and dense forests. The farmers homesteaded a patch of ground, put up barns, cabins and log fences. They tilled the dirt and planted crops and raised families. For generations these men dug deep and had a hunger for the land. They toiled, sweated, and ferociously worked their hands raw. The creeks and rivers crisscrossed swaths in the countryside. The earth under their feet, and the sky over their heads were their spiritual powers. The farmers were the tenders of the Earth and they sang homage to its abundance. Heartbeats pulsed with the pull of the moon. They instinctively lived in nature's rhythm.

It's all they knew, and therefore never complained. Hard physical labor meant they could survive another winter and keep their families fed. The men grew from the land, it was part of their grit. Fingernails were begrimed with dirt in every crack and crevice of their rough, crusty hands. It was part and parcel of who they were. It never crossed their minds life could be different. It was a hard life, but one full and complete. And the women were as connected to the land as their men. Their slim fingers worked the soil and planted the gardens that fed the family. Corn, squash, beans, potatoes, wheat and always flowers were in abundance. This was everything that defined them as wives and mothers. They knew well that they were dependent upon their land.

And they were beholden to its favor.

Summers in the southwestern Appalachian Mountains were warm, sticky affairs usually giving way to billowy clouds and an inevitable afternoon rain permeating the air with a waft of fresh cut grass and honeysuckle. Summer brought the farm's bounty; community picnics, laughter, banjo pickin', singing and food! Tables with red checkered cloths and well-worn wicker baskets were always set and piled high with delicious, deep country fare. Everything was grown or raised on the farms and all the food was made fresh from scratch. Tables were embellished with sky-high apple stacks dripping with apple compote, cut from crisp Winesaps grown in the orchards along the dirt roads. Appalachian sweet cornbread, fire roasted potatoes, spiced pickled beets, copious green beans, and a big spit of country ham were frequently provisions on hand. You could count on Mama's fresh blackberry cobbler, oozing purple stain on everyone.

Camping was a July pastime for pas and their sons. Boys anxiously paced for days with tackle box and rod, sleeping bags and snacks that mamas prepared, "in case they got hungry." This was a rite of passage to be alone in the woods, to be sleeping out together, under the constellation's starlight. Fathers and sons woke to a symphony of bird's song and morning wings, fluttering at first light. The chestnut trees in full bloom, their thick green canopy and long dangling white flowers cascading like a waterfall encompassing the entire world they knew. The sound of pa's harmonica, the humming of old Appalachian songs etched into the minds of young boys for the rest of their lives. They ached for these days to last forever. They wanted life to be this simple. Year after year, traditions were entrenched in their way of life. And then passed on to the next generation.

Boundless summer days in the Appalachian country would find the boys rambling along, fishing on the east fork of Cedar Creek for Walleye or Blue Gills. Or chasing croakers and polliwogs. The mountains were full of azaleas and rhododendron, sarsaparilla, and Queen Anne's lace. Day would eventually turn into dusk as the last of the sun set on another day and the fireflies started their luminous, phosphorescent dance of the meadows. And those boys knew they were late for supper.

As sure as fish swim upstream, autumn followed. Autumn was filled with chopping and stacking wood, brisk nights by a blazing fire and bountiful harvests. Food always took center stage. It was the best time of year on the Appalachian range. It was full and rich. Hovering on mountainsides, the American chestnut trees wholeheartedly embraced the season with bright yellow leaves that would lay bare by winter.

By November, days turned crisp, and enchanted frost patterns fixed to windowpanes. The farmers of Appalachia settled in for a winter wonderland of family and different kinds of chores. The evergreen forests were quiet, and cues were taken from Mother Nature. Gardens lay fallow, brown grass and left-over weeds poked through the snow. Only bunny tracks broke the crust's defiance. Women taught the girls to sew, and make clothes, quilt and cook by the roaring stone fireplace. Boys became men, as they learned to build furniture and tools from the felled wood. It was another rite of passage handed down from father to son, generation after generation. Chestnut was a beautiful and abundant wood; solid, hard, and surviving generations of kin.

As the sun slowly rose higher in the sky, sunbeams tumbled to Earth. They lifted winter blues up to a periwinkle sky, blanketing warmth on yards, as snow turned to slush. Tufts of clouds turned to vapor, icicles melted, dripping off every roof. Eventually the snow melt soaked the green grass below. As days turned warmer and warmer, the mud turned hard and dry. The dogwoods blossomed with small green leaves, hellebores showed their faces and the mountains exploded into magnificent canopies all at once.

Spring had Arrived.

The seeds that had been collected the previous autumn were again planted on the first warm and sunny days. Green carrot ferns popped, and beans split to reveal a pair of leaves that signaled renewal in the garden. Subsistence farming in these parts kept millions of people alive for generations.

They were simple agrarian folk that relied on the forests mast of nuts for their livestock. It was as familiar as a rooster crowing or the sun setting.

Although millions of these people were poor of material trappings, they were culturally rich abounding in the land and nature. Days followed the seasons. They would sit on front porches with neighbors plucking out a tune on the banjo or working together in gardens. Every one of them knew how to grow their provisions, the sustenance of life.

The mountains that surrounded them were majestic. The forest was abundant and provided food for all the animals. Work was hard but they were proud people who had tight family connections and a dedication to a good life for generations of children.

There was a genial comfort, a wholeheartedness on these lands, in their homes and in these communities. Through the seasons, together they thrived. And it was powerful. Some say they were just a bunch of hillbillies, making hootch and educated by the land, and in some way it's true. But they knew things that citified folks who had relocated to urban centers, removed from nature, had lost.

For the millions of subsistence farmers throughout Appalachia there had always been a deep ancestral connection to this land. The land provided for them; the land protected them.

Until the American chestnut forests died.

CHAPTER ONE

Southwestern Appalachian Range, Virginia
Sara Hayes
July 19, 1938

It was a stifling summer evening when life changed forever. The change didn't come all at once, but when it arrived, it was resolute and with abandon. It left destruction and bewilderment in its path. Life as we knew it became extinct for my dad, Tucker Hayes, and our whole family. Dad was the son of homesteaders and hog farmers, in the small rural town of MeadowBrook in the Appalachian range of southwestern Virginia.

July always brought the thick canopy of white blossoming catkin tails on the imposing 100-foot-tall chestnut trees, atop the vast mountainsides, as far as the eye could see. The long creamy whip like flowers formed an encompassing umbrella over the Appalachian Mountains high above the Hayes hog farm. For generations, summer brought an explosion of white on the crown of the forest. It was frequently mistaken for a snowcapped mountain range at the MeadowBrook 4th of July picnic.

But not this year. The flowers did not come. And on July nineteenth, it was 93 degrees at 80 percent humidity as the sun set. Unusual for this area of Virginia. Bedclothes stuck to arms and legs. Rivulets of sweat ran down the crease in our backs, as dampness pooled in the crook of our elbows. The angry rain pelted the roof and the hog shelters, like a barrage of wheat, land sliding out of a rusty grain silo. An old creaking fan at the top of the big log beam in our cabin slowly moved air that clearly had no interest in being roused.

Our cabin had two bedrooms and a loft. The gathering kitchen was open in the center of the main room and a large cast iron pot set inside the towering stone fireplace darkened with soot from decades of nurturing all the Hayes children. This cabin was homesteaded, log by log, stone by stone, in 1883 by my grandparents, Ruth and Emery Hayes. It was constructed of tall strong, straight-grained chestnut wood logs, felled right at the forest edge. The fireplace still perspired the redolence peat of winter. As you passed by, a collection of cinders from the previous winter still lay in a heap, permeating the air like the timelessness of the thousand-year-old chestnut logs.

Tucker Hayes, my poppa, sat a moment on the dank earth and aimlessly stared at the large pigs curled under an overhang fast asleep, as a torrent of rain fell in sheets off the shelter roof.

Minnie was bedside with Momma. All was ready to go, like they had done many times before. Everything was in slow motion but seemed to happen so fast. Momma's groans increased by the minute. Then a short break. Some cool water helped her catch her breath. The moans got louder and faster. At eight minutes apart, she gave forth a low throaty scream as the contractions came faster now, her face scrunched like a prune and her neck flushed burgundy.

"Don't push, don't push yet, Bessie, it ain't time yet," pleaded Minnie.

Poppa was sitting outside on the porch now, watching my little brother Ben, trying his best to stay distracted by the hogs. He always held his breath when the time came. Poppa was useless in labor, and he just tried to stay out of the way. Minnie had been by her side for all her babies.

"Minnie is the best midwife in these here parts. She has delivered more healthy babies in southwestern Virginia than all the doctors in Charlotte," Momma would say.

"Bessie, listen to me. You gotta stop pushin', stop pushin' right now, this baby is turned sideways and if you don't stop pushin' right now, we're gonna lose him. And you!" implored Minnie with her hands planted firmly on her sumptuous hips.

Bessie drew a big breath from deep inside. She was spent. It'd been eleven hours and it seemed this baby wanted nothin' to do with joining the world. Minnie'd done all the tricks she knew. The contractions were coming just two minutes apart now. Minnie gave Momma a shot of the moonshine that Poppa made in the underground cellar. It was hot and burned but gave her a moment to relax and catch her breath. I stood by the doorway in case Minnie needed me. Momma's moaning tugged at my insides, and I wished I could do something to make that baby pop out. She had been in labor since 8 o'clock this morning and I could see, she was exhausted.

Momma was a slim thing, not like me or Ben. We took after Poppa. Momma stood at 5'9" and had steel blue eyes that sparkled like they were plucked from a crystal mine. She had thick, long, silky chestnut brown hair that she wore up in a ponytail most of the time. But at night she would let me brush it. It was like a sleek thoroughbred's mane, and it almost touched her waist.

Minnie knew that baby would not last much longer. It needed to come into the world, and it needed to happen now. Minnie locked on Momma's big blue eyes and said,

"Miss Bessie, I'm gonna try to turn this child around. I need you to take a big breath and hold it while I lean on you and try to grab it." Momma, sweat dripping down her temple, nodded knowingly and took a deep breath.

The sky darkened and the wind howled as the blustery rain blowing sideways now, drove Poppa inside the cabin. Ben was running around out in the mud like a pup rolling in chicken poop. Poppa didn't care. I don't think he noticed. We sat together anxiously fidgeting. Poppa began to nervously reminisce.

The words and memories came fast. I listened intently as he

recalled the old days; "Ahhh Sara, I've known your momma my whole life. By the time we were fifteen we knew we were in love. We were just two kids with messy hair and a sparkle in our eyes. One warm summer day we carved our names into the bark of that big chestnut tree in the middle of the garden. I held the knife steady, and she guided it with her slim fingers on my wrist. We carved our names, Tuck and Bessie, and drew a rough heart around it. We laughed under our breath and whispered, as our heads touched, and she looked up and kissed me for the first time. It was the best moment of my life. By nineteen, your momma and I were married. All the families across MeadowBrook came to our wedding in the summer of 1920. Everyone was there. A light summer rain swept through overnight, and the air was unusually clear and cool. Getting to marry Bessie removed any doubts of my purpose in life. I had loved Elizabeth Jenkins for as long as I could remember, and I could not wait for the time we could be together. She felt the same. All the neighbors came, and Reverend Bradford Stanback married us. Ha, funny I remember it like it was yesterday. The reverend had been there for my birth and all my sisters too. But that day was the happiest one that had come to our little town of MeadowBrook, that I could recall for a long, long time. Everyone said we were born to be together.

Bessie and I made a home in the small barn right over yonder. And we couldn't wait to start our family. It wasn't long before you came along, Sara."

"You were the best baby."

Poppa looked me right in the eyes. "Everyone loved you, even the animals. When you would waddle out to the pig barn at 3 yrs old, the piglets would squeal and come running to see what you had in your hands. It was usually something sticky and delicious. We had a beautiful life, and I was so in love with your momma. I couldn't have been more blessed to have my two girls to come home to every night. Bessie made me a better man and I wanted to give her the world."

Poppa laughed and told me that she always said with a chuckle

"Tucker Hayes, I'd a married ya' even if you weren't my next door neighbor."

"Even after all these years it still makes us burst out loud laughing."

"Every evening your momma and I took a walk in the forest. We always held hands and shared what happened in our day. Or sometimes we just walked arm in arm and didn't say a word. The floor of the forest was so thick with mulch that we literally bounced with each step. The moist, woody scent filled our lungs with a richness that can only be described as the breath of the forest."

"OK, Ms. Bessie, now take a real deep breath and hold, hold, hold...," I heard Minnie say.

I remember being at MaryBell Price's farm when one of their cows was giving birth. Her poppa tried to help the momma cow deliver her calf by putting his arm up inside the cow and pulling. I was imagining that's what Minnie was doing to Momma. There was no choice left. The contractions were coming again, and they were hard. This was the last chance to get ahold of that baby. The closest doc was in Jeffersonville. Minnie said that Bessie wouldn't make it by the time a doctor would be brung out on the farm. And Poppa knew this. This driving rain woulda made it impossible for him to cross the river, so, it was up to us, to Minnie, to get that baby borned.

My younger sisters Bertie and Shirl were at Aunt Rachel's for their annual summer visit to West Virginia. Each summer they would put up raspberry and huckleberry jam with our cousins. Aunt Rachel was our momma's sister, and she always made the trip to MeadowBrook to pick up the little girls. Momma was close to her sister, and they always looked forward to their annual visit. We would have picnics and play up in the forest, picking big heads of rhododendron and long spikes of columbine to bring home for the vase on our mantel.

Then, Aunt Rachel would take our girls to her home to be with our cousins, and then bring them back a few weeks later. They loved having playmates their own age and Momma and I loved the time alone.

Normally, Poppa would take Ben on a fishing trip up in the mountains this time of year, just like his Paw did when he was a boy. They would spend lazy days stocking up on German Brown trout to hold us through winter, with sumptuous dinners. But Poppa knew he couldn't leave Momma alone at this time and decided to do the annual fishing with Ben after the baby arrived, hoping the trout were still running.

And as always, I would stay home with Momma to do a summer cleaning and have a special girl time, just me and Momma. This was my favorite time of year with Momma. We would sing her favorite songs as we would clean the cabin; beating rugs and mopping every corner as clean as the day it was built. Momma taught me to cook and to can summer beans and cherries. At night we'd curl up together and she would tell me stories of what life was like growing up in these parts.

About a week ago Momma says, "You are looking mighty radiant darlin'. How's George?" George Baldwin was my boyfriend since we were 6 years old. We always knew we were gonna get married. He was my best friend, and he was 'round our house more than he was at his own home. Frankly, his home wasn't that fun to be 'round. His daddy brewed hooch and he would get on a drinking spell, and he was meaner than a stri-ped snake on a hot potato. Momma was happy to have George around. He was handsome and proper mannered, helping with lots of chores that Poppa didn't have time for. And she liked him. Poppa wasn't as fond of George because there was always another mouth to feed. And times have always been thin around these parts.

So, when Momma said, "Sara, you have a radiant glow," and somehow observed the gradual but oh so slight softening of my belly, she knew. Momma's just sense things like that of their little girls. It was only time before we had one more baby in the house. I was about four months along. Only Momma would think I was showing yet. I figured we'd need to tell Poppa soon or he would start noticing by the time the big spiny burrs would appear on the giant chestnut trees and the leaves would start turning bright yellow and gold. George wanted to marry me, but I knew if I told Poppa, he woulda killed George before we coulda had that wedding. Momma was tickled about the idea of George and me, and a grandbaby! But I was afraid Poppa would make me go to the girls' home in Charlotte to have this baby and it would be adopted out to some rich family from the city and I couldn't bear that. I trusted Momma would talk sense into Poppa and we would raise my baby as another child about the same age as the one Momma was carrying.

Momma was big and couldn't wait for her baby to come. She and Poppa decided on names, if it were a girl, they would name her Lily and if it were a boy, he would be Jacob.

After having me, she had Ben, then had two more children that were sadly "Miscarried", is what Miss Minnie called it. That is why Ben and I are several years older than Bertie and Shirl. Momma said this baby would be her last. She was done having babies and Poppa agreed. She wanted to spend more time on her quilting, gardening, and her cooking. Momma was an impressive little farmer and felt at home in nature. In fact, Momma loved all of nature; leaves, and nuts and the animals of the forest. Momma had an eye for capturing the beauty in all of nature.

And she did love babies, but after all those pregnancies, she was exhausted and done. And she could feel it with this one. She was tired all the time and felt queasy and sick with morning sickness, heaving, and sweating for months. The last couple of months she was feeling a little better but being summer and it being hot and sticky...she was just never comfortable.

This night was particularly sticky, Minnie was sweating like a pat of butter on a hot biscuit. Her thick, curly dark hair pulled back into one big braid down her back that was matted to her neck. Minnie was short but exceptionally strong and determined, and she never seemed to tire. And on this day, Minnie was not gonna lose this baby.

She yelled for Poppa to bring more towels and hot water.

I couldn't stand it any longer and ran in with the towels. I started shaking like a leaf in autumn when I saw Momma.

"Bessie, breathe, Miss Bessie you stay with me." Minnie groaned as Bessie pushed and screamed out one last time and with one last breath she collapsed. Minnie was able to grab that baby by its head and shoulder with a shiny contraption used to turn babies the right side down. One, Two, PULLLL, it looked like a river of blood coming out of my Momma. I gasped and lost my footing. The baby exploded into Minnie's arms, the cord was wrapped around her neck, and she was turning blue. Minnie turned that scrawny little blob of flesh upside down, smacked her on her pink, puckered, soft baby skin and swept her finger through her airway. Minnie worked fast to get that baby breathing on its own.

Momma's pulse was pounding. You could see her heart jumpin' right outta her ribs. Her breathing was hard, and she was gasping for air. She was bleeding bad, and Minnie called on Poppa to come by her side.

"Hang in there Bessie," Minnie prayed, mumbling her best Baptist prayers, and calling out loud to the Lord to help Miss Bessie through. Poppa stood at the doorway, in a stupor. His feet seemed heavy, he was paralyzed, as if his boots were nailed into the creaking floorboards.

"Sara!" Minnie barked, get your Poppa over here.

I gently shook Poppa. "Poppa, Poppa," I softly uttered, but he didn't move.

"Tucker Hayes!" I hollered, and he snapped out of his bewildered numbness, and he shot to my mother's side and held her hand.

She held his hand and looked him right in the eye. And mouthed, "I love you, Tuck."

Momma's cheeks were like red hot coals under a winter fire grate. She was struggling with every breath. Minnie laid the baby girl right on Momma's chest. She raised her right arm and embraced that baby; she couldn't even lift her head to look at her new daughter. Blood was everywhere, and sheer exhaustion overcame her. Momma's worn-out body could not hold on any longer.

Momma looked right at me, piercing deep into my eyes and she whispered faintly,

"Sara, you promise me, you take care of this baby." My eyes were wide with fear, focused only on my Momma. I nodded my head. With a deep throaty moan, she took her last breath.

And the baby Lily let out a blood curdling wail that you could hear all the way to Jackson Ridge...

CHAPTER TWO

Hayes Hog Farm, 1938
MeadowBrook, Virginia
Sara Hayes and George Baldwin

We all stood in disbelief.

Ben came running when he heard the baby scream. Startled and mouth wide open, gasping when he saw the blood. He swallowed hard and went to Poppa's side. Poppa just collapsed on the floor and sobbed.

The pelting rain stopped. And but for Poppa's tears hitting the sheets, it was silent. Even the percussion of crickets halted as darkness crept over the bed and shrouded the room.

I had never seen my father cry before... And never would again.

Days went by and Poppa would not eat, he wouldn't get out of bed. Ben did his best to care for the hogs but with the chestnut stash dwindling, we knew it wasn't long before we would have no food for the hogs, let alone us. There was no way we could afford to buy feed for them hogs. And with the chestnut trees dying, there would certainly be no mast of nuts to graze our animals on this autumn.

Oh, it wasn't a surprise. Poppa had heard stories coming from up north for 20 years, but our family and neighbors had been spared, until now.

1938 was a hard year. It was when everything changed. Momma died that summer and with her, the entire chestnut forest in

MeadowBrook, Virginia. At once, living off the land, and our simple way of life would never again be the same.

Additionally, at 16 years old and pregnant, and without Momma to talk sense into Poppa, I knew I would be sent to the wayward girls' home and be forced to give up my baby. A baby, of which Poppa didn't even know about, yet.

A few weeks later Poppa started to slowly come around. He was so completely lost without Bessie, the love of his life. We were all trying to pick up the pieces and create some sort of life without Momma.

"Sara, we need to get out of here. And we need to do it before your Poppa realizes that you are carrying my baby. I love you and I will take care of you," implored George.

George Baldwin was my best friend. We always expected to get married. George had family in North Carolina. His uncle worked on a big estate as the stable manager.

"Uncle Joe lives on this beautiful horse property. He wants us to come be with him. He lives in a one-bedroom cottage behind the stable and he said that there is another larger cottage that we could make into a home. The owner gentleman passed away this year and his widow needs help. Uncle Joe got me a job being the chauffeur to the woman of the house. We need to go Sara," implored George.

I knew that I had to decide, and fast.

"Uncle Joe says the widow, she could use someone like you Sara, as she is getting on in years and needs some extra help around the house," explained George.

"I can't leave my newborn sister, I won't leave baby Lily, I promised Momma that I would take care of her," I declared resolutely.

"Of course, we will make it work. You'll have our precious baby, and we can raise Lily there too. We'll have jobs and live near a city. We'll get our baby educated and give these kids a good home," exclaimed George.

"We don't have a choice Sara, now that your momma is gone," George said.

I knew he was right. With the blight having devastated the farm, the Depression nippin' at our heels, and Momma gone, there was no way that Poppa could care for all these kids alone, that is for sure. Shirl and Bertie could probably stay with Aunt Rachel. And Poppa and Ben will do fine between themselves. I said out loud, as if convincing myself more than anyone.

"George, I know it's best for everyone." Through deep sobbing tears, I agreed that there was no other choice.

"George, let's make plans to leave with the full moon."

1938 October

It was the first cool night of October. It was Poppa's birthday, but nobody dared to speak of a reason to celebrate. I made a cake for him, but there were no candles, and nobody felt like singing. Although days were still warm, this was the first night that smelled of autumn. It was the time of year where birds filled the sky on their journey south; cackling and chirping until the sun set and magically the noise and the birds vanished. Quiet replaced the buzz of day.

I stood in the middle of the cabin. The thick eight-foot-long chestnut mantel hung on the stone fireplace. It held a small glass powder jar that Momma kept our baby teeth in. Aside of the jar sat the rusted metal vase that she used for the flowers we would grow in our garden; azaleas in spring, sunflowers in summer. And in autumn, right about now there would be aster and Queen Anne's lace with some branches of wild sarsaparilla.

After what would be my solemn last supper in my childhood home, I cleaned the kitchen and went to collect up the few things I would take on our clandestine journey.

I stared out the window, the breeze pouring through as thick as honey, the smells of autumn leaves filled my lungs, the window frame squeaked as I leaned against the peeling paint on the geriatric sill. I could see Momma in her apron tending the garden. She always wore the same gardening hat and the same cotton apron with its bright red strawberries and tiny white jonquils on the front of it, as she danced under the chestnut tree. Mom loved to dance, and she loved to whistle. She whistled when she was happy, and she whistled a lot. In the pockets of her apron were always treats. Sometimes a nut, sometimes a home baked snickerdoodle.

We kids would collect chestnuts until we had a wheelbarrow full. And then we brought them up to the barn for sorting; most to go to market, and then there were the ones we kept for ourselves.

The laughter always echoing in our home rang out to me in crystal clear voices now. Momma in her cotton apron. There we were, her kids collecting nuts on a large burlap sheet. Ben would throw a large rock against the bark of a chestnut and the nuts would teem down like raindrops on a lake. I got lost in the vision, tears welling in my eyes, knowing life would never be the same, and yet wishing I could change the hands of time. For just one day, I would give anything to sit by my Momma and laugh as we shelled peas. Talking about autumn coming and the holidays we loved so much. The rich smells of autumn; a roasting turkey, freshly picked, end of the season vegetables from our garden and the smell of chestnuts roasting in our big blazing, toasty warm fireplace.

A tear ran down my cheek, as I knew those sounds and smells were just memories now. I was jolted back to the moment. My baby moved inside me; a little kick snapped me back to reality. There was no way that I could give up this baby and there was no way Poppa would let me and George keep it. He'd say, "Now Sara, there is a good family that will raise this baby the right way, a good loving home that will raise this baby right."

I knew he was already sick to let Bertie and Shirl live with Aunt Rachel, but he knew there was just no way he could support all these mouths. And in these past two months after Momma died, he lost his spark and had little ambition to do much of anything.

The breeze blew again through the open window and the wind

trembled as the last of the perfume scented petals filled the air. The sun was setting. I felt a tear sit on my cheek like the dew on a morning Rose. The leaves were starting to turn yellow but there were no burrs on the chestnut trees. Many branches were becoming devoid of life and looking dispirited and arthritic. Normally the thorny chestnut pods would be starting to turn from green to light brown and contemplating a popping explosion of the sweet, brown chestnuts that we loved to make into soups and breads, roast on our open fire or just eat raw, straight from the tree.

I hurried, packing the few things I could take, knowing most of the space would be for Lily and our new baby. I tucked everything under the bed so as not to raise any questions, not that Ben or Poppa would notice, as I made my final arrangements. But there was no room for error. We had to go now. I was starting to show and if Poppa had been his normal self, he might have noticed beyond the loose dresses I had been wearing for the past couple of weeks.

I sat for a moment at the kitchen table and wrote Poppa a note telling him that George and I were leaving, that we're starting our life together but with no further details. "Poppa, I will always love you. Your first born, Sara." I tucked it into his fishing tackle box, I knew he would find it there.

We ate our final meal together. Knowing this was my last meal with Poppa and Ben made me so sad and heartbroken. But I couldn't say goodbye. Poppa would never have let us go. He would have said, "Sara, we will manage." But he didn't know my secret and I just couldn't tell him.

As the sun set, there was a still silence that I had never known before. I sat on my bed, on top of my cotton quilt that momma handmade, a pillow filled with old goose feathers. The darkness glued itself to the window as it seeped across my room and splattered silence where there once was laughter. I sat with wide, damp eyes. As the hours ticked by, the full moon rose.

It was an autumn evening like so many others that would have merged into a lost memory. The dark enveloped the whole of our little cabin. The crackling of the evening's embers slowed like the last popcorn sporadically snapping until there were no more to pop. But I would never forget this night for the rest of my life. Time passed with the haste of a very old hound dog.

I was ready when George arrived. I couldn't tell if he was excited to see me, or nervous. We hugged briefly. It was just after 11:00 pm and I quietly brought George our few belongings, to tuck into the buggy. I went back inside the house knowing Ben and Poppa would be sleeping. I stood for a moment fathoming that I was leaving my home, perhaps forever.

There were several photographs of our family above the fireplace. One of my grandparents, Ruth and Emery Hayes, with Poppa as a small boy. One of Momma, Poppa, me, and Ben. And one with the whole family. I took one last look, and one last deep breath inside of my childhood home. The security of solid chestnut log timbers that sheltered us and protected us. It smelled safe. There was a comfort in this homestead. In that last breath, I grabbed the photo of Momma, Poppa, me, and Ben. My baby brother Ben, I would miss him the most. And I bolted out the door into the dark of night. The stars would guide us now. George and I, pregnant and wildly scared, with baby Lily, stealing away to start a new life. Not sure when I would see my father and my siblings again.

CHAPTER THREE

The Wild Majestic Mighty Giants

The impressive California Redwoods are a sight to behold, standing on guard like noble sentries of the West Coast. They are painted in lavish oil colors and provide a canvas, a canopy for the diverse array of wildlife that call the forests their home. They are known around the world standing tall and proud for hundreds of years, some even dating back 2000 years to the time of Jesus.

Yet this magnificent stand of West Coast giants, pale in comparison to the stately and iconic American chestnut forests of the East. From Maine to the Gulf Coast, Georgia to Alabama to Michigan, hundreds of millions of chestnuts grew. Hundreds of millions of thriving trees, making up a forest. They grazed the clouds; some a hundred feet tall with canopies spread the width of a basketball court. They covered the eastern third of the United States. The forests of New York, Pennsylvania, South Carolina, and Virginia were the playgrounds to men, women and children inundated by these magnificent behemoths. Beautiful secrets were held within their dark brown, furrowed bark; their ridges lighter grey when young. Chestnut trees were the shade of picnics and the shelter of many a shepherd. Life happened among the chestnut forests. Many lovers' first kiss was born beneath its majestic umbrella of dentile leaves with an arm spread, a canopy, wide as the night sky. And many were laid to rest under these giving trees.

But these were not any old-growth forests, as devastating as that might be, this American chestnut was the "Perfect tree". Every October, without fail, they rained down over the entire Eastern Seaboard millions of pounds of nuts. Chestnuts were the lifeblood of the subsistence farmers of Appalachia.

Each summer, high in the hills you could count on a blanket of draping flowers atop the trees with long whiplike tendrils full of white fluff. They smelled musty, like a grandma's old attic, that stored ancient relics, and old leather valises that could've been carried by President William McKinley.

By autumn the green sawtooth-like leaves turned brilliant yellows and shimmered in the sunlight. Being deciduous, the leaves began to drop at first frost. And those grand flowers transformed into large round, sharp, prickly pods as large as a man's fist.

As soon as the air turned cool, the burrs' symphony of bursting began. Opening to reveal dark brown seeds with a slightly furry tip, they were the sweetest, creamiest, most delectable nuts known to mankind. Clawing their way through the spiny burr would leave many a bloodied finger, but well worth the sting to peel into the shiny brown nut and savor the fresh sweet, creamy seed inside. Chestnuts are best roasted... and roasted on an open fire was the proper way. Millions of families had chestnut roasting boxes, rectangular metal boxes, black on the bottom from years of scorching. The lid slid closed after the nuts were sliced on one side and placed inside. And it would be shaken, shaken, shaken over the fire until the nuts popped, and the slightly smoky and sweet wisp of aroma drifted up to their nostrils and embraced their senses.

Unlike the oak's tannicky acorns, these nuts could be eaten raw right from the tree and ripe for the picking. The American chestnut was a reliable source of food, year after year, for thousands of years. They were a veritable annual feast for all the forest animals. From squirrels to bear, to birds and mostly to farmer's livestock. They dropped virtually unlimited calories at our feet.

Millions of American families simply could not survive without them. The nuts were so coveted that they were used as currency. Every Thanksgiving through Christmas, train cars overflowing with thousands of pounds of nuts, headed to the cities across America. People in chestnut country bartered their chestnuts for essentials of life that couldn't be gathered or produced on their own; shoes, garden tools, clothes, sugar, paper. The reliable mast of chestnuts, year after year, decade after decade, century after century, kept these people alive. The trees grew fast. The wood was tall and straight grained, and it was the foundation of the lumber industry for centuries: homesteads, log fences, barns, furniture, telephone poles, cabins, even musical instruments. The chestnut trees built America in the 1800's and early 1900's. They were also rich in tannins which made the wood rot-resistant, logs would last a long time and never warp.

But, as the 20th century unveiled, a disaster struck; a devastating epidemic spread throughout America and, like an impending doom, a spell was cast. Soon the chestnut trees were functionally gone from their natural range.

In 1904, at the Bronx Zoo in New York, on a beautiful summer day, a fungus was discovered on the old chestnut trees. It was novel and there was no cure. The fungus systematically and adroitly killed the trees throughout the park. This blight then spread with the speed of an express train at rush hour across this continent and wiped out nearly an entire life-giving species. Within 40 years, 4 billion American chestnut trees; from the Atlantic Ocean to the Mississippi river, lay barren toppled logs or standing silvery grey ghosts; lingering symbols of death.

This blight, having unintentionally been imported to the U.S. on agricultural Chinese chestnut trees, crumbled the weight of nature. The Asian chestnut trees had natural immunity to the infestation. They had adapted over millennia to survive this infection, but that wasn't true of the American variety. On our side of the globe, the trees had no resistance to this new pathogen. For our iconic American chestnut, there was no protection. The loss was untold, incalculable and it devastated millions of families. Millions of families, in the span of one generation.

There had been so many chestnut trees, all up and down the Eastern Seaboard, that it was believed that nothing could take out this quintessential species. But this invasive fungus did just that. This fungus, *Cryphonectria parasitica,* wiped out almost every American chestnut and the free banquet it provided to countless families and farms.

It was a sad inconvenience to some, mostly city richlings, yet to others, those that lived off the land, the country folk, the heart of Americana, it was an unendurable end-of-life, as they knew it.

The chestnut forests were as American as Apple Pie.

And then one day; To the Appalachian country and all points north and south, this deadly blight moved with the alacrity of a panther with his sights on a lone hog.

But only in perspective to generations to come.

Men told stories about the chestnut trees in New York, then Pennsylvania, then Connecticut and Massachusetts, north to Maine and south to Virginia and Georgia. The women spread the word of the destruction, the devastation, the depression up and down the Eastern Seaboard; an entire forest wiped out by a fungus. This desolation they experienced moved slowly only if you were there living it day to day, but in the rear-view mirror to generations next, it was swift and sure. As unintentional as it might have been, it is certainly the greatest ecological disaster to befall our nation, caused by one species; Man, against another species; The American Chestnut tree.

For the farmers, silver naked ghosts of a forest stood where a vibrant and busy life once was. For the wives waited, watched their men, stood back, held their breaths, and listened silently. Their land lay naked, bare and barren. There was the hush of death in the trees. All the animals of the forest grew silent too.

It was unimaginable, yet denial wore thin, and hunger was a death grip they couldn't ignore.

CHAPTER FOUR

Ben Hayes, in His Own Words

Alone on the Farm

Tucker and His Son Ben

1951

We were lucky that it spared us for a long time, but when it came, the Blight wiped us out faster than a bobcat chasing a white-tail. Momma died that same year and Sara left with our new baby, Lily, in the middle of the night and we never heard from her again. I felt confused, scared, and abandoned. Sara's leaving was the last straw.

Her boyfriend, George, was gone too. So, very quickly there was dead silence in our formerly bustling, busy home. For Pa and me, it felt like our life just fell apart.

The chestnuts didn't produce that year, so there was no feed. That winter we slaughtered the remaining hogs. The money from that ran out fast.

My little sisters; Bertie and Shirl, stayed with Aunt Rachel in West Virginia, as this was no place for them. Pa felt it would be a better life for them. Frankly, I wished I had been sent off with them too.

But over time Pa and I made a life. We didn't need much, and that was a good thing, cause we didn't have much. We lived off the land. We grew the food that we could. The girls used to tend the garden and do all the cooking. But that was my job once Pa and I were alone.

Momma was the love of his life. After she died Pa would sit out under her favorite chestnut tree, just off the porch in the front of the homestead. The branches hung over the perfectly tended garden that she lovingly cultivated every day. Pa would talk to her. He could see her out there. This is where she would dance in her crisp cotton apron and whistle songs of gratitude for her charmed and bountiful life. That chestnut tree died the following year, and Pa felt that he had lost everything; his precious wife, his beloved daughter, his livelihood, the hogs, and the rich abundant bounty of the land. He just lost his motivation. It would be a long time before he found a purpose to living again.

Our life was hard but uncomplicated until 1939. That winter was bad, and we didn't have enough food to make it through. Over the next couple of years, we had chopped down all the chestnut timber that was left. It was good wood, but as there was so much of it across the Blue Ridge, it didn't fetch much of a price, but we were grateful to sell it and get a bit of money to buy basics.

When the blight was raging, we even took down some trees still producing chestnuts in hopes of saving others nearby from the blight. But it didn't fare well, and we lost our entire chestnut forest. The stark nakedness made us feel vulnerable and for the first time I was scared. And I'm sure Pa was too.

Looking back, we made mistakes. Nobody knew what to do, and everyone had their own opinion about how to save their trees. Some were in denial that this devastation could happen and that it would go away on its own. But most grasped at straws looking for solutions from burning the infected trees to witch doctor spells.

In retrospect, there wasn't really anything, at that time, that could overcome a widespread disease that coursed through the United States with a fierce and destructive target on one specie: the American chestnut. In fact, logging those trees during the early years of the blight, destroyed trees which might have survived this disease, ones that might have had natural immunity. We probably made the calamity worse.

After the wave of destruction passed, what was left were oak, birch, and evergreens. Nothing to sustain a family and no reliable food source for pigs. It was devastating.

Thank the Lord, Momma was not here to see this horror. Pa and I barely survived. I grew up very quickly that year. It seems I went from a boy to a man in one season. We went to bed many a night hungry and we realized something had to change. After the lumber was gone, Pa begrudgingly went to work for Westmoreland, the mining company. But as the Depression was full on and everybody was hungry, he was just happy to have work no matter how much of a pittance it paid. Men had no jobs, and families were starving. We heard the whole country was in a bad way.

I was tall like Pa, so a couple of years later after barely making it through another bad winter, nobody questioned me when I lied about my age, and was lucky to get a job with the CCC; The Civilian Conservation Corps. This back-to-work program for hundreds of thousands of men working on conservation projects around the country was a lifeline. And it was right up my alley, as it put me smack in the middle of nature, where I was most at home. Plus, I was able to send money home to Pa. They gave me a roof over my head, a paycheck, and meals. It was during this time that I gained a deep appreciation of the outdoors and for our natural resources, and I realized I wanted to spend my life at the U.S. Forest Service. After living through the devastation of the chestnut blight, I knew that there was a need for the protection of our natural resources, especially our forests. It was said that millions of trees were planted during the CCC. But, I can tell ya', none of them were American chestnuts.

I was stationed at Camp Roosevelt and felt blessed to have this job, along with thousands of young men that were able to not only work but to help send money back home when things were so rough. I served at Camp Roosevelt until I returned home in 1943, when our country needed us in WWII. I was deployed to Camp Pendleton where I did my basic training and served in the Navy until the end of the war. I came home in the fall of 1945 and joined the U.S. Forest Service and spent my working career overseeing the natural resources of our land.

After the war, Dad remained working for the coal company until he retired, and I was transferred to the U.S. Forest at Lyons Falls in the Adirondacks in Upstate New York.

I missed the Appalachian range; the sounds and smells were different. You don't notice the noises of life until they change. Waking to the hundreds of different birds in MeadowBrook, the turkeys and grouse, the falcons, the hawks, the eagles, even the occasional flycatcher or the wooting of a whip-poor-will. I also missed the community of MeadowBrook. We had lifelong friends and neighbors that were really the only family we had once Momma died, and Sara and Lily left.

One night as I pondered my aloneness, I took up a pen and wrote Pa a letter. It would be the first of many letters during my days at the Forest Service. Pa was alone in Virginia, at MeadowBrook. I was in the New York wilderness, places at the Forest Service where our uniform was a flannel shirt and a pair of khaki pants, or overalls. I felt blessed as these were special places where Nature is the boss.

I got to work every day where there was a long list of threatened and endangered species, not unlike our precious American chestnut. It is a place of solitude and a place where people with a wholesome spirit can find adventure alongside respect. Respect for the awe, that is the wildness for all generations to come.

It is a formidable task but one so critical to our survival as a nation, for the world. I was cursed with witnessing firsthand the devastation of a species.

Watching the death of a forest changes a man. But it gave me purpose. I knew what it was like to take for granted the forest in autumn, the crunching of leaves underfoot, the smell of mulch as you breathed the crisp fresh air, the soft blanket of green moss clinging to tree trunks. In spring the buds exploding into canopies of green and summer abounded with sounds of nature's animals scampering amongst the shrubs, talking to each other tweeting and twittering high up in the branches overhead.

I vowed to spend every day of my life upholding the charge of the

Forest Service to protect and preserve. Not only against epidemics of insects and disease, but against wildfires, and to manage a clean watershed for my children, grandchildren and all the generations of children to come.

It was my honor and my life's work to be a part of this team. I loved my long hard days because at the end of the day, I knew that I made a difference to this planet and the people who live on it. Every day I got to wear overalls, flannels, boots, gloves, and a ranger hat. I got to spend my days with likeminded people who respect and appreciate the wilderness. Those of us that get to walk among the world's most pristine trees and breathtaking scenery in the world.

May 1953

It was a Thursday in late May 1953. We were in the forest near Logan, off county road 4, working on an oak tree that was hit by lightning. Most big trees can't be saved with these kinds of damage, but with the right treatment some can recover. We knew it was important to tend to it as soon as possible, so time is of the essence. We trimmed and removed all the injured or cracked branches and tried to patch with tar any damage to the bark, so insects didn't settle in the pulp and create further disease from the inside. It's back breaking, tedious work. I was exhausted, and at the end of the day, I stopped by the ranger station at the Finger Lakes Field office.

My boss, Sam Perry, who was an old veteran forester was training a young gal that was recently hired to be a visitor information assistant for the summer season. She was the most beautiful girl that I ever laid eyes upon. She was petite and she had short blond hair with a smile that could derail a train right off its tracks. I walked into the office and practically fell over her.

"Um, excuse me ma'am. I need to watch where I'm walking," I floundered. She cast her gaze down and then just her eyes looked up at me. They were mesmerizing, without saying a word.

"Um Sir," I said to my boss.

"I um, just wanted to let you know we are done with that big oak and will have the fire block finished tomorrow."

I backed up, nodded, and said to her, "Nice to meet you ma'am."

And walked out the door. And gosh dang it.... "I was a bumbling idiot. She must have thought I was a buffoon," I said under my breath. I stumbled down the old moss-covered wooden steps onto the dense pine needled forest floor and realized just then, this golden-haired beauty had stepped out the screened door. I heard the thwack of the door close behind her. I swung around and saw her. She was standing right on the front log entryway, watching me mumble to myself.

"Hi, I'm Rebecca," she reached toward me to hand me my gloves that I had set down on Sam's desk.

"Thank You, nice to meet you, Rebecca." There was an awkward moment of silence.

"And what is your name?" this lovely face said.

"Oh, I'm Ben, Ben Hayes," I blushed.

She stared at me, I walked toward her and extended my hand. "Nice to meet you," I stuttered again.

"Will you be working at this ranger office?"

"Yes, through the summer, before heading back to Syracuse in the fall where my mom is a teacher at the normal school," she said.

She went on, "I'm hoping to become a teacher too."

I learned later; her name was Rebecca Perry. Oh, for Pete's sake, she was Sam's daughter!

I made a habit of stumbling by the visitor center often that summer and found myself staying late meandering under some old growth conifers, sitting with lunch or a cup of coffee, far too shy to approach her. Eventually, with my heart pounding in my ears, I got up enough nerve to strike up a conversation with Rebecca. That season flew by, and I looked forward to getting up early each day and was excited to go to work.

Rebecca was as beautiful on the inside as she was on the outside. Being with her made me feel like the luckiest man on earth. It felt like the love that I know my Pa had for my Momma. For me, it was more than love at first sight. It was a mutual love and trust that I had never had before. Meeting Rebecca was like finding a missing piece of life that had fallen from the heavens right into place. After losing Momma and Sara in one year, there was an emptiness that I couldn't fill. It was a deep hole in my gut that was my constant companion. Sure, I could have fun, and enjoyed my friends and co-workers but the hollowness left at the end of the day was certain.

After the summer season, Rebecca stayed in Upstate New York working for the Forest Service. We couldn't wait to see each other every day. It was easy to be with her, we laughed and shared intimate moments, she was my kindred spirit. And when we were not together, the anticipation of spending time with her sent chills down my spine, thoughts of her filled me with joy and desire. I couldn't get her off my mind. We were drawn to each other like the stars of a constellation. She always remembered the smallest details and looked directly at my eyes whenever I spoke. She was a veritable feast for the senses... ah the sweet, sweet feeling of new love. As each day passed our feelings grew stronger, more intimate, and authentic. I only wanted to hold her tightly and never let her go. I knew in my heart Rebecca and I were meant to be together for a lifetime. I wanted to commit to that and protect her and care for her every day of my life. Just like my Pa did with the love of his life, until the day she died.

That autumn, the forest in Upstate New York was particularly colorful. Mid-November, Rebecca and I took a walk after dinner in the crisp evening air, as we frequently did. We built a fire in one of the stone campfire rings and we were roasting marshmallows on sticks.

"Ben, Let's drive down south to MeadowBrook for Christmas, I want to meet your dad."

"Ah, ha-ha," I laughed out loud. "I've been trying to figure out a way to ask you if your mom and dad would be okay giving you up for the holidays, Rebecca. I couldn't be happier to take you home to meet Tucker. My Pa is going to love you."

I leaned over to kiss her, and she licked the sticky toasted marshmallow off my cheek. We laughed. I was elated and giggly.

A year later, I put a ring on her finger. Rebecca and I didn't wait long to have a baby, and she was as beautiful as her mother, but she was a real Hayes. She had the features and coloring of my mother; Bessie, the wonderful woman we lost in childbirth so many years ago. Our baby had long, silky dark chestnut hair and those piercing steel blue eyes. We named her Silvina and her middle name Elizabeth, after my momma.

We were blessed and beyond ecstatic to bring a new life into the world, our girl: Silvina Elizabeth Hayes.

And we couldn't wait to go back to MeadowBrook for Pa to meet Silvi, his first grandbaby.

CHAPTER FIVE

The Journey to Start a New Life

North Carolina

Sara and George

October 1938

Over 300 miles of dusty, dirty roads and the old Chevy farm truck puttered for what seemed an eternity. Pregnant Sara, her new husband George Baldwin and her new sister, baby Lily had left MeadowBrook, Virginia in the shroud of darkness and finally made it to North Carolina. Sara's legs were swollen and her back hurt from sitting so long. They hadn't taken much to eat in their haste to leave, so they were also starving. They dared not stop as they drove through the night with only the full moon to guide their journey. Blessedly, baby Lily slept most of the way. Sara and George were mentally and physically exhausted, but excited to start their new life, full of anticipation.

They drove through the night and most of the day. As the autumn sun began to set, they arrived. They were just a couple of teenagers, barely old enough to be married, with almost nothing but the clothes on their back. They were young and frightened, yet so grateful to be somewhere safe.

George had arranged everything and was relieved when they found the address. He stopped the truck at the magnificent stone wall and heavy iron gates and wondered if they were at the right place. Sara was a bit punchy after the long drive. She looked at George in disbelief, their mouths agape.

"George are you sure this is the right address? I've never seen anything so beautiful in my whole life. That heavy stone wall goes on as far as I can see."

"This is the address that Uncle Joe gave me. Oh, Sara, we don't belong here. Did we make a big mistake leaving MeadowBrook?"

They were tired and hungry, and Sara was physically and emotionally uncomfortable. But they had nowhere else to go. Just then the gates very slowly and magically started to swing open.

George said, "There is no backing out now, my love." Sara squeezed George's hand, and they slowly started forward.

They drove their old farm truck through the gate as a wave of golden light rolled down the tree lined driveway announcing their arrival. As they approached down the long drive to the manor house, Uncle Joe Douglas appeared as a mirage. The estate was like nothing Sara had ever seen. At the end of the drive sat an antebellum manor house. Off to the left was a beautiful, massive, pristinely white stable. In the distance was a riding arena and several small white cottages. The expansive lawn was deep green and manicured. Deer meandered across the grass as afternoon turned to twilight. The white fences seemed to go on for an eternity.

Uncle Joe came toward them and said, "Welcome, welcome children, it is so nice to see you." They stepped out of the truck and Uncle Joe embraced the two of them.

"Sara, look at you. You're all grown up and radiant. And George, my boy, I cannot tell you how happy I am to have you here. You are going to love it in North Carolina. I came for a summer and never left going on twenty years now."

Sara lifted baby Lily out of the truck and Uncle Joe smiled and kissed that little baby right on the head.

"You kids must be terribly tired after driving through the night. Let's get you settled and get you something to eat."

He directed them to a cottage at the east end of the property. It was small, dank and had remnants of use scattered about, but Sara could already see how she would make it a home for her new little family. It had a stone fireplace with a peaty smell that reminded her of MeadowBrook, and a tear fell onto her cheek.

"I think you have everything you will need for tonight. Why don't you unpack your things and I'll come get you in an hour for some dinner," said Uncle Joe.

"And then tomorrow after you've had time to clean up and rest a bit, I know the others will be anxious to meet you, especially, the lady of the house, Mrs. Marshall Bradham."

Sunday, October 18, 1938

After a good night's sleep, and Uncle Joe's warm welcome, Sara and George were feeling a lot more comfortable. Lily slept through the night, which was a huge blessing. She was such a good baby and Sara adored her. Her baby sister, who she would 'mother' for the rest of her life.

That afternoon Uncle Joe came by, "Hey are you kids ready to meet everyone else?" He took George around the grounds, and he set up a meeting for Sara with Mrs. Bradham.

Mrs. Bradham was exceedingly kind. She immediately made Sara feel at home. She was petite, but stately and obviously came from a long line of folks with a proper education and upbringing. She had a cook and a butler.

"Sara, it is so lovely to meet you dear. Your coming here could not be at a better time. I could use a personal companion and someone to help in the kitchen, as my long-time cook will be retiring soon."

Mrs. Bradham and Sara went off to a formal parlor. The butler brought in a shiny silver tray and backed out of the room. Sara felt like a country bumpkin and was embarrassed at her long-sleeved cotton dress that had belonged to her mom. But, it was the best she had. Mrs. Bradham had tea and biscuits ready. She wanted to know about all about Sara and her family, and how they ended up in North Carolina.

Mrs. Bradham had a genial way about her. One of those people you instantly felt comfortable with.

"I am thrilled to have a baby at the property again, Sara. My children are all grown up and have flown the coop. And they've all moved to the city and have busy lives and don't come around very often anymore."

She took a liking to Sara, and baby Lily right away.

"Sara," she said. "That is my name too, but ever since I was a kid everyone has always called me Charity."

She was exceptionally warm and embraced this new family with open arms. After a while, Uncle Joe walked into the parlor. Mrs. Bradham said to Uncle Joe, "We will get on just fine, Joe."

Mrs. Bradham wanted to know everything about Sara. And it brought her to tears when she heard the story about Sara helping her Momma birth Lily and the promise that she made her mom to raise Lily. Mrs. Bradham understood why Sara wanted to raise Lily as her daughter and she promised to keep her secret. Sara was grateful for that, as she didn't need anyone gossiping about how she had kidnapped her baby sister and took her across state lines.

That second night in North Carolina, after dinner, Sara sat at a tiny desk in their new cottage. She had cleaned the place immaculately, and finally took a deep breath. Sara wrote Poppa a long letter and included a note to her brother Ben. She told them that she and George were married, that she had the newborn baby with them, and that they were all safe and healthy. She told Poppa how much she loved him and how she and George felt that leaving on their own was best for everyone, given the Depression and the blight of the chestnuts. She also told him that she was pregnant, and that she and George were having a baby.

Sara felt guilty about abandoning her dad and her brother Ben, in their time of need, but he never would have understood about her being pregnant. She didn't feel there was any other choice but to run away.

Sara told her poppa how sorry she was and that she already missed him but that he didn't need to worry, and she asked for his blessing for their new baby, and baby Lily and the new life they were creating in North Carolina.

Then she got ready for bed. Sara, George and the baby, Lily all slept.

As the weeks went by, Sara grew restless of pregnancy. She was big and uncomfortable and exhausted much of the time. The letter she wrote to her dad and Ben, addressed to Tucker Hayes, MeadowBrook, Virginia, sat on the desk for a long time. And after much procrastination, Sara never got up the nerve to mail it. She and George had started a new life, and she couldn't take the chance of complicating that.

Sara birthed the baby right about Christmas; a beautiful, healthy baby girl. They named her Nita.

Nita Baldwin.

The baby didn't have features of George or Sara. She had the complexion, the long silky brown hair and those steel blue eyes of her blessed momma, Bessie. She really looked a lot like Lily. They definitely looked like sisters with dark hair and piercing blue eyes that sparkled like pools of liquid turquoise. It was strange to imagine that Lily was actually Nita's aunt. Something everyone agreed to not ever speak of. They were sisters; Lily and Nita Baldwin.

Uncle Joe and Miss Charity agreed that it was simpler.

Over the years as that baby grew, she looked more and more like Sara's momma; tall for her age, slender, and had the most engaging laugh. The two girls were best of friends. Sara so missed her momma. Bessie would've loved her first grandbaby. And Sara would've loved to share the pregnancy and the new baby girl with her. She missed her mom every day of her life.

Life in North Carolina was a dream. It had all the natural beauty of Virginia, but it had a decadence neither Sara nor George ever knew existed. They loved to explore the estate. It had perfectly manicured, deep forest green grass, for as far as the eye could see. The riding arena was large and the stable of five horses were cared for immaculately by Uncle Joe. The stables were nicer than most people's homes back in Virginia. There was enough room for 20 horses, with a beautiful paddock they would graze in all day. At one time that stable was full, but now the five horses more than fit the lifestyle of Miss Charity.

Uncle Joe loved his life there. He couldn't have wished for a better job tending the horses, and now having family living on the grounds was a dream come true. The white fenced farm, rolling green hills and manicured stable looked like a page right out of a coffee table book depicting life on a majestic southern horse farm.

Sara thought this place was 'highfalutin'. There were even flushing toilets in the garage and Miss Charity owned cars. Not one, but four cars. One truck for the estate workers. One big fancy car for her chauffeur. George drove that one. And one small sportscar that Miss Charity used to drive to the countryside for picnics and special outings with her daughter Mary, or just to escape to be alone with a book and a shaker of cocktails. And then there was one old vintage car that nobody seemed to drive but they kept it looking really pretty.

Quite soon after arriving, George built on to the bunkhouse and Miss Charity put in running water and flushing toilets for them as well. Every night they all ate dinner together in the main house, George, Uncle Joe and all the girls. After dinner Sara would clean up and Miss Charity would read to the girls at night before they went back to their cottage to sleep.

Over time the girls blossomed as they grew. They went to a proper school and got a good education. And Miss Charity became Sara's best friend. She was truly like a grandmother to the girls. And she loved having them around and the girls loved to be with her.

Miss Charity's children were grown and married and came around on holidays, but they had their own lives up north. So, they rarely came back home to the farm. Miss Charity embraced the Baldwin girls like they were her own.

Miss Charity gave the girls riding lessons and they became quite good at it. The four of them; Sara, Miss Charity, Lily and Nita were like family, and they built a life together.

The girls grew into lovely young women. They were both tomboys and loved the horses and adored being in the great outdoors. Especially her daughter Nita who was always running in the woods surrounding the property, finding all sorts of trinkets from nature on her long horseback rides. Everything in nature fascinated Nita. She would get lost for hours upon hours exploring the forest and watching how the animals and plants gave each other life.

Lily spent her free time with Sara in the kitchen and became a very good cook and eventually did much of the cooking for the family. Lily loved the smells of the kitchen and became fascinated by cooking and especially baking. She loved to make the family special desserts and pastries. And the family was happy to oblige and critique each new experiment with food.

The girls called Miss Charity 'Grandmama' and she taught them everything she knew. She really took them under her wing.

Sara never thought she would recover from losing her Momma, but they were blessed beyond belief to come into the life of Grandmama Charity.

Miss Charity took good care of this family during those years. And they cared for her deeply too. As the girls got older, and Miss Charity got older also, she made out her last will and testament. She naturally left all of her property and possessions to her own three children with Mary as the custodian.

But one day she sat Sara down for a heart to heart.

"Sara, this pendant belonged to my mother." She lifted the necklace off her chest. "And I want you to have it." It was a beautiful gold horse with a diamond eye.

"It means a lot to me. I've worn it every day of my life since I was 13 and I know you have admired it over the years. It would make me happy to see you wear it." Sara was stunned and couldn't find the proper words to say, as Miss Charity placed it around Sara's neck. But she didn't need to find words at that moment because Miss Charity went on.

"Additionally, I have established a college fund for Nita and Lily. It is important for women to be educated to make their way in the world these days. Things were different in my time. We found a good husband to take care of us. And I was blessed, as you are Sara, with George. But the world is changing, and these girls are bright, that's easy to see. I want to be sure they get a good education. I want them to be strong voices for issues that affect the world. And I want them to be prepared with a proper foundation to do whatever they choose in life."

Sara's mouth dropped open, and she was seriously at a loss for words. She never expected this outpouring of love and generosity and didn't know what to do or say.

Her eyes glazed over. Miss Charity's thoughtful and generous gesture was overwhelming. She hugged Miss Charity and simply said with tears streaming down her red streaked cheeks,

"You will never know how you saved our lives taking us in and giving us a good life here on the farm. Thank you Miss Charity. I will cherish the pendant my whole life, and a college education for the girls," Sara shook her head and cried.

The gift was beyond measure. She wanted to run and tell her momma. She wanted to assure her painfully frightened seventeen-year-old self, who arrived that autumn day at the farm so many years ago, to trust in the universe, and that everything would turn out ok.

"George and I can never thank you enough, for this, and for all you've done for us."

When Miss Charity's husband died, prior to Sara and George moving to the farm, she felt lost with no purpose or direction, not unlike this young family. In some ways, it seems they saved each other.

The girls grew into fine young women. They graduated from school. And with a combination of tears and excitement, they went off to college to pursue their lives and careers.

Thanks to Miss Charity's generosity and love, they each went off to follow their dreams. Lily went to the School of Culinary arts in Boston and loved being in the kitchen. She learned to cook professionally but, baking was her real gift. She was creative and she designed cakes, pastries and desserts that were unique twists on classics and some innovative new ones. She loved to put her own flair on old flavor profiles. Lily graduated at the top of her class and then apprenticed at a charming Inn in Upstate New York, in the Catskill mountains. She became an accomplished chef and opened a boutique gourmet food and patisserie shop, and she published several cookbooks.

Nita went to Upstate New York, to Syracuse University, where they had bachelor's and master's degree programs that were unique in the country. Nita was more than a lover of nature; it was in her DNA. The lifeblood of the forest coursed through her veins. She fell in love with the forests of Upstate New York too. They were different, alive with a density of animals and plants that fascinated her. Nita got a dual degree in botany and forest management and then went on for her doctorate in plant genetics. During her time on the Syracuse campus, she was hired at the College of Environmental Science and Forestry and worked on mapping the gene sequence of certain threatened species of trees. Every day was new and exciting for Nita, and she was doing important work for the balance of man's existence with the natural world.

Miss Charity grew old and frail over time. She needed more and more personal attention and assistance. And of course, Sara and George were there by her side. They stayed on the farm tending to her and the estate until the day Miss Charity died.

They wouldn't have had it any other way.

It seemed like another lifetime, but Miss Charity stepped in to become the mother Sara needed as a lost young girl, and Uncle Joe filled the big void Sara created by abandoning her own father, Tucker and her brother Ben, at such a young age.

And as for the girls, Miss Charity was the only grandmother Nita and Lily ever knew. They were wholly unaware of the life Sara and George had left behind on the hog farm and forests of MeadowBrook, Virginia.

Miss Charity's daughter Mary inherited the estate and moved into the manor house. She kept Uncle Joe on to tend the horses. But she had no need for an assistant. She had her own housekeeper and cook and didn't require a chauffeur.

With both daughters in New York, and Miss Charity gone, George and Sara decided to move to Upstate New York to be close to the girls and their families. They briefly discussed going back to Virginia. But after all these years, they were embarrassed and still in denial about what they had done. And had convinced themselves that those they abandoned would never forgive them. So, they closed the chapter of raising their daughters in North Carolina. And with great anticipation for what lay ahead, they said their goodbyes to their wonderful life and headed North to Upstate New York to start the next phase of life with Nita and Lily.

CHAPTER SIX

Silvi Grows Up

Silvina Elizabeth Hayes

January 3, 1955

Ben Hayes, Tucker's only son, and Rebecca Perry were married a year after their first awkward encounter in the visitor's ranger station at Finger Lakes in Upstate New York, during Ben's sixth year at the U.S. Forest Service. It was a case of love at first sight, not unlike Ben's mom and dad... Tucker and Bessie. Ben had grown into a strapping young man but had a warmth about him that made everyone feel as if they were his best friend. He also had a maturity that was far beyond his years. It probably came from having to be everything to Tucker once Bessie died. Likely compounded by Sara abandoning them to go off with George when the chestnut blight ripped apart their family and life. Losing his mother in childbirth was devastating, but losing his sister, his best friend, that was a pain that cut him deeply.

Ben desperately wanted a family of his own and after he and Rebecca were married, they wasted no time starting one.

Silvina Elizabeth Hayes was born on a snowy winter night at 10:32 p.m. near Syracuse, New York. She came from humble Appalachian rootstock.

Ben and Rebecca were a happy young couple and were ecstatic to be parents. Rebecca never did go back to school like she intended, but she became a devoted mom to Silvi.

Ben's love of nature was imprinted in Silvi's heart, and she developed a love of the outdoors, mostly the wildlife and the plants of the forests. The smell of freshly fallen summer rain, the glistening of icicles dripping off fragrant Ponderosa pine needles, the essence of dogwood trees that blossomed to the call of spring all imprinted on Silvi's heart. And of course, the distinct smells of autumn, when leaves turned spectacular colors in the Upstate New York old growth forests. Silvi loved the mulchy smell of fallen leaves as they crunched under foot. And the plunky sound as acorns fell and were scurried away by well-fed squirrels for winter.

Silvi was a beautiful child. She took after her grandmother, a woman that she would never know. Like Bessie Hayes, Silvi had high cheekbones, long, silky, chestnut color hair that glimmered with golden red highlights when the sun caught it just right, and piercing steel blue eyes that were captivating, with long dark eyelashes that curved up at the ends. Her skin was as translucent as pink rose petals. She was not a fair-haired maiden like her mom Rebecca, but she was beautiful and striking in her own way. She took after the Hayes side of the family. As Silvi grew up, she was embraced by everyone she met. She always had a sparkle in her eyes, a bright smile, a keen intellect and would connect with people the way cheddar does to cheese.

As she grew into her teenage years, Silvi made friends easily but preferred the intimacy of a few close people in her life. When Silvi spoke to you, you felt as if you had her full attention and that you were the most important person in the world. She naturally knew how to make you feel special. She had a calm demeanor, and infinite patience. The only time Silvi stood up loud and clear was if she perceived someone she loved was being threatened, then she would protect them fiercely.

Every year at the end of school, Silvi spent her summer at her Grandpa Tucker's family farm in Virginia. She looked forward to this family journey. It always started out with her mom and dad driving her down to Virginia for a week. They would spend that time together at MeadowBrook visiting Grandpa Tucker, and all the old neighbors who would come around to see Ben and Rebecca.

They would swim in the creek, and ride horses, pick berries and make lots of great farm fresh southern meals out of the freshly picked produce and fruit in Grandpa's orchards and gardens. And as Silvi was settling in to spend the summer with her grandpa, Ben and Rebecca would go back to work, in Upstate New York, and she would spend the rest of summer learning how to be a hillbilly.

And she loved it.

Silvi was very close to Grandpa Tucker, and she shadowed him around the farm, hanging out with the neighbors, learning to garden, fish and be a steward to the land.

Deep down Ben loved coming home. The place was core to his roots. He fondly remembered the carefree, joyful, and loving years when his mom was alive and when the forest produced abundance for all life. And in retrospect, he came to embrace the difficult years, after his mom died, because he became very close to Tucker. Furthered by their heartfelt correspondence through the letters they wrote back and forth during his years at the CCC, and while he was at the Forest service.

Each summer Ben and Rebecca looked forward to their family vacation at the farm. They relished spending time with his dad, and his childhood friends, most of whom had never left MeadowBrook. And it was the best time of the year for Silvi. She could not wait for school to be over and head south for a summer filled with nature, pristine forests, sparkling rivers, relaxing days of fishing and hiking in the woods, growing a bountiful garden, and being loved like a princess by her Grandpa Tucker.

She knew this is where her daddy was born and raised, and she appreciated the down to earth life of her people. But if the truth be told, she was happy to have not been raised in this homestead house where her dad toiled on a hog farm in his youth. She realized it was a hard life and a constant effort against nature.

Silvi heard all about the harsh times, the poverty and struggle that these Appalachian people had endured since the turn of the century. Especially when the farm fell into chaos with the arrival of the chestnut blight that wiped out an entire way of life, and the livelihoods of millions of families. As Silvi got older, she asked questions about what life was like in MeadowBrook at that time.

"Grandpa, I know this must be hard to talk about, but I'm really curious how it felt when the chestnut trees started to die? What was it like for you?"

"Silvi, my love, it was a really sad time. Back then, the forest provided everything we needed to live. The forest was abundant with food for us; nuts, mushrooms, and small animals. It provided all the food for our hogs, and it was the currency we used to barter in town for essentials that we didn't have out here. When we lost all that, I've gotta be honest; I was terrified. It was a hard, hard time. And I had no idea how we would survive."

"I can't even imagine how scared you must have been. And I'm sure all the people you always counted on in hard times were suffering too; the Burnhams, the Perkins, the Winslows. They all must have been going through the same thing on their farms," she said, riveted at her grandpa's every word and shaking her head.

"You know Silvi, I've lived my entire life in these woods. The blight that took out the chestnut trees was... devastating. Everything good was gone. The food, the income from selling the nuts, the lumber, that wood, oh Silvi, the lumber that built our cabin, our home, the fences, and our barn. Watching those trees wither away and die was like a part of me dying."

Silvi was still shaking her head. She leaned in and hugged her grandpa and put her head on his chest.

Tucker took a deep breath and said, "First losing your grandma, then the chestnuts, I felt hopeless and lost, as if my entire world had crumbled. Life was never the same in the forest. It was once filled with life and animals scurrying everywhere. But the forest of silvery dead stumps became eerily quiet, and they were a constant reminder of the tragedy that surrounded us. I had lost everything that I had known and loved. I can only say it left me with deep grief and despair. It was a dark time, my love. It was a dark time."

Tucker stared off into the distance, his eyes moist, his expression sallow. Silvi kissed his cheek while she cupped her tiny hands around his. "I'm so sorry Grandpa, I can't even imagine how alone you must have felt."

"But I'll say one thing, I was blessed to have Ben with me. He gave me a reason to get up in the morning. And eventually, your dad was able to get a job with the Civilian Conservation Corps and he sent me part of his paycheck. That helped me get back on my feet. And he wrote to me every week about life outside of MeadowBrook. It's what kept me going, waiting for those letters and the bit of money he was able to send home. I'll be forever indebted to Ben for those years. He stood by me and kept us alive. He's a good man."

Because of her roots, Silvi learned to be a steward to the land, and she learned the responsibility that comes with it. She also learned to respect people of all kinds, and to see their goodness and worth in society, even if they were different. She didn't tolerate disrespect from anyone and even though she realized most of these people were uneducated farmers, loggers and coal workers, they wanted in life what every other parent wants for their children, and their lives; simple security, respect, healthy food on the table, hard work and love.

As she grew older, she became intolerant of incompetence and greed. She learned from the people of the forest, and she learned how to live within the rhythm of nature.

Silvi was the first in the Hayes family to go to college. Her parents, Ben and Rebecca were enormously proud of her. She did well in school and immersed herself in her studies. She chose to attend the College of Environmental Science and Forestry, near her home, close to Syracuse.

Silvi lived in the dorm and made friends easily, but she didn't have a boyfriend until her junior year. That is when she met Bradford

Spalding at a concert in Haven Hall on the Syracuse campus. They were a local sensation, the Stomping Suede Greasers, performing jazz and classic music of the 1970s. The piano player, Charlie, was incredibly talented, and all the girls loved to listen to him.

Brad had been nursing the beer keg for the better part of the night and making his way through the crowd as he turned and splashed an entire red Solo cup of brew all over Silvi. He was a sloppy drunk, and he fawned all over her with intoxicated apologies, like he had ruined a cashmere sweater or silk gown. Silvi was not flattered by his slurred, insincere pleas for forgiveness. She was sure he would not even remember the incident. Silvi and her friends left the concert, but not before Brad got her name and the name of the dorm where she lived. She went home to change out of her sticky, wet clothes and just called it a night.

On Monday afternoon when she returned from her botany lab, there was a beautiful bouquet of mixed flowers by her dorm room, with a sincere note of apology requesting a real dinner date. A real dinner date, at a restaurant, was not something that happened often in college, and it never happened to Silvi.

She reluctantly accepted. Brad picked her up, right on time, on Friday night. He was driving a bright red Aston Martin sports car with a convertible top. She had never even seen a car like this, let alone ride in one. She giggled under her breath. Brad was from Boston and his family were aristocrats with a long, wealthy, blue-blood line. He had boyish good looks and dressed preppy. He even had pennies in his polished brown loafers. Brad opened the door for her, and they drove to a cozy little restaurant called "Josie's Italian Kitchen." It was authentic Italian home cooking. The smells of caramelized onion, garlic, peppers and fresh oregano struck her as she walked through the door. Oh, Lord, it smelled amazing. Brad obviously had been there before because the waiter knew his name.

"Welcome Mr. Spalding, ma'am," said the waiter as he held the chair for Silvi to sit. Brad was interesting, fun and he was a perfect gentleman. She learned about life in Boston, that he wanted to be in politics and was majoring in political science. He had a dream of becoming a D.C. political analyst or a New York politician. He was curious about her and wanted to know about her goals in life. Before they knew it, the restaurant was closing, and the staff were cleaning up the tables. Brad and Silvi were still obliviously laughing and chattering as the waiters loosened their bowties and hung out at the bar.

He got her home after 1:00 in the morning. She had to admit, she had a genuinely fun night. She saw Brad almost every day after that. They became inseparable for the remainder of that school year.

Brad was always the life of a party. The opposite of Silvi's more reserved, soft-spoken demeanor. They dated all through senior year and started discussing what they would do after college. He was an extremely outgoing, social guy, with a thousand wild friends. Some who were not exactly Silvi's cup of tea.

It was the 1970's and drugs permeated college campuses. When Silvi and her dad went on a tour of the college as a high school senior, they were shown all the highlights of the campus by an upper classman. Ben asked the student guide a question at the end of the tour.

"Is there a problem with drugs on the campus?"

The young man jokingly and without hesitation said, "Oh no Sir, there's no problem with drugs, you can get anything you want."

That did not impress Ben, but everyone else laughed.

Silvi found his answer to be quite accurate. It wasn't her thing, but many a night Brad stumbled home to his dorm room not quite remembering how he got there. Silvi looked past his wild side, believing that he would settle down and grow up once they graduated.

Silvi was working on a Bachelor of Science degree in Botany and Horticulture. She planned to follow in her father's footsteps and go to work for the U.S. Forest Service. She loved being with people, close to nature, and loved the science and preservation of the forests. She believed strongly in the perfection of nature and that man didn't need to tamper with God's creations by genetically modifying plants beyond hybridizing as they might occur on their own in the natural world.

She learned the big difference between creating hybrids by cross-breeding plants with their own species, versus, altering the genetic makeup of different species that would never naturally occur in nature. She was adamantly opposed to genetically modifying a plant with a gene from a completely different species. Even if the result would be similar to cross pollination, it was the process in the laboratory that was unnatural. And it set her resistance to genetic modification technology.

She found that these maneuvers were generally done to the benefit of big agricultural businesses to promote capitalist profits and not what was in the best interest of the species, or nature, nor particularly the health of humans.

She did, however, find the process fascinating, and learned a lot from her professor in the laboratory where she did research on a work-study program. Silvi applied for credits and was accepted to work as an assistant to a Dr. Nita Baldwin. The woman, she learned, was a PhD in plant genetics. Dr. Baldwin and Silvi hit it off at once. Silvi was her intern for the second semester of her sophomore year, and she looked forward to her days in the lab with Dr. Baldwin very much.

She found the process of identifying individual genes and mapping genomes of all sorts of species fascinating. The technology was cutting edge and she followed Dr. Baldwin's lead, and soaked up the knowledge like a giant sponge.

Nita Baldwin was thirty-six and Silvi was twenty-one when they met. Nita had been working at the College of Environmental Science and Forestry ever since she went to Syracuse University for Undergrad. She was now the head professor and researcher in charge of genetic studies and was working on all kinds of projects that improved the lifecycle of trees and plants throughout the forests and heartland of North America.

Mapping the genes of organisms was a monumental task. And it had been in the works for many years. In fact, since before Nita herself was a college student.

Silvi learned how the technologies have changed and advanced over the last decade, and they were nothing short of miraculous. From the simplest breeding of produce, such as crosspollinating to make a tangelo between a tangerine and grapefruit, a limequat between a lime and a kumquat, a pluot between a plum and an apricot.... And, on and on. Silvi found it all fascinating. She soaked in everything, and she was a quick study.

Under Nita's tutelage, Silvi learned how science made a difference in everyday lives of Americans. Nita taught her about hybridizing plants and what genetic modification was and the difference between the two.

Nearing the end of the semester, Silvi spent a weekend at home with Ben and Rebecca. She couldn't wait to tell them about her research assistant position with Dr. Baldwin. And how she was learning so much fascinating information about real life science. Ben and Rebecca enjoyed seeing Silvi so passionate about school.

Silvi gushed to Ben and Rebecca, "So my mentor is a brilliant researcher named Nita Baldwin. I was really lucky to get this assistantship with Dr. Baldwin, she's a nationally renowned plant geneticist doing groundbreaking work on DNA. And she's very nice, I like being around her."

Rebecca asked, "What kind of projects are you working on honey?"

"Well, Dr. Baldwin has grants for several different research studies, mostly from the government. We spend a lot of time mapping the DNA for trees that are being threatened by pests in nature. But what I like best about working for her is that for any challenge I bump up against, she finds a way to ask me questions that help me figure out my own answer. It's made me think and gain confidence in myself. I've realized that it helps me navigate other issues in my life, not just in the plant labs."

Ben thought that was perceptive of her and was gratified that Silvi was thriving at college.

Ben and Rebecca could see how fascinated their daughter was about these projects. They had never seen her so spirited and excited about anything before. She was fully animated when she talked about plants and trees and the genetics of it all. Ben could already see Silvi heading up a national park conservation program and was so proud of her and all she was learning. He had high hopes she would follow in his footsteps.

The whole weekend Silvi talked shop with her dad. They discussed how he got into the Forest Service and what the job was like. Ben could not be happier to think Silvi might work side by side with him before he retired. It was a much needed break for Silvi; being embraced by mom, in her childhood home, with some good home cooking by Rebecca. It rejuvenated her energy to go into finals.

The next Monday was the last week of the semester and the school year. Silvi was anxious to get back to work with Dr. Baldwin. Her mentor had gotten used to having Silvi there and realized how much she appreciated the work and dedication Silvi did at the program.

"Silvi, you remind me of myself at your age. Your thirst for knowledge is insatiable. I've read some of your papers and your deep knowledge of forests is far beyond your years."

"Aw thanks Dr. Baldwin, I look forward to this part of my day. I can't wait to get to the lab and do real life work. You have inspired me. I've realized that in natural science there is always something more to learn. And it seems just not enough hours in the day. But my quest for uncovering the answers of life has certainly blossomed with your encouragement," Silvi laughed.

Clearly the respect was mutual. Silvi applied to work again with the doctor through her junior and her senior years. They became great partners in ecology, botany, environmental studies, and genetics.

Silvi found herself spending more and more time at the lab. She and Nita were becoming friendly and would frequently meet up at the laboratory on a Saturday afternoon to putter around and work on their plant projects. Whether it was the breeding program to document best practices on choosing features to get a certain trait on a cantaloupe, or just shadow Dr. Baldwin on some other exciting and cutting edge project.

The more she learned, the more she wanted to know.

Dr. Baldwin assumed, and hoped, that Silvi would follow in her footsteps, and she encouraged her to stay at the Forestry school and get her PhD to do research in these advancing times.

Silvi had a different idea. She knew she did not want to work inside a lab for her whole career, although she recognized it was very important work for the planet. She was committed to furthering the voice and knowledge curve of mainstream America, so that everyday people would benefit from the impact of this work. Silvi knew this was the foundation of education that she needed and couldn't find a better place than the College of Environmental Science and Forestry in Syracuse. It was exceptionally first class.

"Dr. Baldwin, I'm so grateful to you, and I've learned so much over these past few years, being able to work side by side to learn from you. I feel that I have grown and developed a voice for the preservation and protection of our natural resources."

Silvi always had questions, and she so admired Nita and her team at the lab for the strides they were making every year in the understanding of who we are, and how our genes guide who we can be in the future. Silvi, surprisingly, even came to respect what genetic modification could do for an overpopulating society.

She learned however, that one byproduct of genetic modification was greed! The manipulation and patenting of these "Novel plants" created in the lab, could now be called property of whomever developed the new breed. And usually, it was not for anything other than profits. The more she learned, the more she stood against the concept. Being a scientist, she was torn between her fascination of the science, with its technological breakthroughs, and the continued loss of important heritage and heirloom farm produce, due to proprietary new breeds.

She and Dr. Baldwin bantered about the pros and cons of tampering with genetics and man's need to control his environment.

Silvi looked up to Nita. They became more than coworkers, they became friends. And occasionally they got together after work to share dinner at the Varsity Pizzeria or go down Marshall Street to "The Orange" for a glass of wine. Their conversations were always around plants, healthy forests, and grasslands. Even over lunch they never ran out of subjects to chat about regarding nature. They became close in a student/mentor sort of way. Silvi looked to Nita as someone who really understood her, where a lot of girls her age, were more interested in an MRS. than a PhD.

Silvi started reading about, and hearing stories of, the manipulation by large agricultural businesses producing genetically modified plants. They were creating food that could be dangerous to the health of humans, and the land it was being grown on. And even though she could appreciate the benefits of technology, she became an activist against GMOs creeping into our produce aisles. She was articulate and spoke with the confidence that comes from having firsthand knowledge of how GMOs worked. She learned about the herbicides that were being sprayed on entire farms to rid fields of weeds. Herbicides that would kill unwanted plants, but not kill the crop, like corn. Although some might feel it's clever science, she was profoundly concerned about the toxins and poisons that stayed on the corn that went to market and reached family's tables for dinner! It terrified her to think how physiologically damaging it would be to ingest all those chemicals and pesticides.

Silvi felt strongly that moms and dads be informed. "They have the right, the duty, to know what is in the food they put on their dinner table, especially if poisonous and toxic substances are being sold in markets and grocery stores across America."

Silvi felt that this sort of abuse of genetics must stop. She exposed the names of companies that were filing ownership patents on new varieties of food. She spoke out against large agricultural businesses who were successfully manipulating America's food supply. These agribusinesses created monopolies to own and control most of seeds available to farmers throughout the country.

Silvi became a voice in her community standing up to these corporations. She led demonstrations against GMOs and led the charge to have GMOs labelled on food packages, so people could make informed choices.

She became identified as a troublemaker in biochemical circles. Yet, she intensified the conversation. She motivated people to ask questions, and to raise the consciousness of everyday Americans, to the detrimental effects on health of some of the farming practices she had witnessed. Silvi became defiant and led boycotts of brands that used particularly toxic chemicals in the farming or processing of their products.

In her free time, she raised the collective awareness of industry violations and the good ole boy network behind the scenes. She wrote papers. She got published nationally and her op-eds in newspapers across the country were gaining traction.

On her urging, people were forming organizations for the preservation and protection of heirloom seeds, along with safe, healthy farming practices. They fought for complete GMO disclosure on every farm that was using poisonous chemicals, and toxic pesticides on crops that would be transported to supermarkets throughout America.

Silvi Hayes caught the attention of lawmakers and corporations that profited from these products, and the monopolies they were creating. She was creating a name for herself, and depending upon whom you asked, the name was frequently TROUBLE.

CHAPTER SEVEN

Breeding Hybrids vs. GMOs

In high school gymnasiums, church basements, and makeshift nonprofit "holes-in-the-wall", dedicated activists gather to strategize and plan for their cause. Led by community organizers who rile and galvanize the troops, they bring poster boards, large colorful markers, ribbon, glitter, and glue, to make signs and banners. At rush hour, hundreds of supporters stand on busy corners chanting catchy rhymes, and enthusiastically waving at honking cars as they thump slogans through megaphones to get attention and spread their message. The louder, the better. Wearing bright costumes, carrying balloons, they circulate petitions and hand out bumper stickers. They march through the streets of America, as they speak to reporters with fuzzy microphones and cameras rolling. Excitedly a proud husband cries, "Hey, hey, kids, look at this, Mom is on the 5 o'clock news."

People march for a cause they believe in. They give up family time and relaxing weekends to join forces with likeminded folks who have created a movement to protect, preserve, defend, and champion their ideals. These grassroots efforts often garner media attention and are the driving force behind social and political change.

The Anti-GMO movement is one of these more passionate groups, driven by a belief that genetically modified organisms (GMOs) are dangerous. They believe that man's tampering with God's creations is wrong and detrimental to people and the planet. Coordinated and passionate, they inspire the masses and raise consciousness as well as money for their cause.

Recently, science has advanced to the point where genes of animals and plants have been mapped, decoding the DNA that makes up their genetic material and isolating individual pieces of life. Genetically Modified Organisms are living plants or animals that have had their genetic material, or genes, modified by humans in a laboratory. DNA are the building blocks of our genetic material. It's the matter inside each cell of a living organism. The study of DNA and genetics has led to significant technological breakthroughs, including the ability to map and manipulate the genes of different organisms. The study of genetics is an exploration as important as man's quests in conquering outer space. Stretching our boundaries to the world's mysteries around us. While science has the potential to save lives and eradicate disease, it also carries the risk of exploitation and the alteration of food, plants, and animals, for the benefit of a few at the expense of many. This tension between the potential for doing good and the potential for resultant harm is not new. Many well-meaning, intelligent people struggle.

That's where the environmentalist groups come in, working to protect our climate, food sources, and the ownership of these newly created organisms. GMOs, or genetically modified organisms are derived from plants and animals that have been altered in ways that would never occur naturally, usually through the introduction of a gene from another organism, with the help of man. This scientific process allows scientists to take genetic traits from one organism and implant them into a completely unrelated one. But messing with Mother Nature can have devastating consequences.

The very beginning of our understanding of genetics goes back to a garden in Austria, in the year 1865, where a botanist, Gregor Mendel, did experiments on pea plants. He discovered that he could predict with accuracy how characteristics of shape, size, and color of flowers were passed down through generations. He found that he could create flowers for specific qualities that he chose by cross pollinating them. The resulting flowers had completely different characteristics from either of the parent plants.

This can and does happen spontaneously with lots of fruits and vegetables in gardens. Hybrid fruits and vegetables are conceived by pollinating two different varieties of similar fruits or vegetables together. Although many hybrids are cross-pollinated by man, this happens quite frequently in nature by wind blowing pollen or bees or birds brushing up against one flower and cross fertilizing another flower. New hybrid fruits are created by man, the same as the bees. The result of intentional crossbreeding of similar fruits gives us hybrids.

Controlled cross-pollination between two stable varieties happens all the time to get fruits and vegetables we've come to love.... Oranges for instance, are hybrid fruits of crossing a pomelo and a mandarin. Many familiar fruits and vegetables that we commonly eat today come from hybridization. There are many apple varieties like the Pippen, Anna, or Baldwin, and of course, Seedless watermelons are hybrids.

So, there are good reasons to selectively breed plants for specific traits.

This cross-pollination is the natural sexual reproduction between two different flowering plants within the same species, even if assisted by man. It happens with many varieties of bushes, and flowers too. Breeders can use this type of cross-pollination to produce hybrid plants that are more vigorous, productive, uniform or stress-tolerant than the original parents. Also, with different tastes.

What Gregor Mendel discovered with his pea plants, was the fundamental laws of inheritance of genes from sexual reproduction. And this applies whether it is a simple pea plant, a chestnut tree, or a human being.

When we intervene and put the pollen of one plant onto the

organs of a similar plant, we call it selective breeding. And we can predict what the new offspring will look, feel, and taste like. This is all very innocent and innovative.

However, (and this is where the story changes) as technology in the laboratory advanced, we were able to identify and locate the genes in each cell and surgically snip a gene out of the DNA of one species and insert that gene into a wholly unrelated animal or plant. It is a fact that genes from one species don't mix with genes from a different species, the process of genetic modification in the laboratory uses science to overcome this natural barrier. This kind of genetic modification never happens in nature. It would be impossible.

So, this is where the conflict starts; we have the technology to surgically manipulate these genes and create organisms that would never occur naturally. This has the potential to revolutionize medicine, agriculture, and many other fields, but it also has the potential to do devastating harm.

As we know, messing with Mother Nature can have disastrous consequences that the Anti-GMO crowds work passionately to avoid. They show up with bullhorns and slogans, and work to raise awareness to protect the planet from the potentially negative consequences of human tampering of the natural world. They've taken up the cause of protecting our climate, food sources, and against the ownership of these genetically modified organisms.

Many times, greed became the goal of those in charge. For instance, through genetic modification, one large agribusiness created a species of corn that was unaffected by weed killer. A farmer could spray a toxic herbicide on his entire field, killing all the weeds, yet leaving the corn unharmed to grow to maturity. Clever, perhaps, but the question begs; how safe is it for humans to eat corn sprayed with toxic chemicals? These are the issues that keep activists up at night.

And they realized that when the ones that had the scientific knowledge and equipment started to ply the natural world and shape it for their financial benefit, they had to get loud, very loud!

On the other hand, what if genetic modification is used for good? To save lives, cure diseases, or replenish a forest? Whether one believes in the potential of GMOs or the dangers they pose, there is no doubt that the subject elicits strong emotions and opinions. As with any important issue, it is crucial to approach the topic with an open mind, considering all sides and evidence, and to act with care and consideration for the well-being of ourselves and the world around us.

CHAPTER EIGHT

Washington, D.C. to New York City
Silvi and Brad

FINALLY, GRADUATION ARRIVED. BEN AND REBECCA WERE SO proud of Silvi and all she had accomplished during her four years. She and Brad were still together. They had grown to be best friends as well as lovers. They talked about everything; his political career, her work in nature and science. They could hardly wait to start their lives together.

Silvi graduated from college with a Bachelor of Science in Ecology and Botany. She and Brad talked about getting married. They got engaged before Silvi and her family met at Grandpa Tuckers farm down in Virginia for their annual summer get away. When Silvi returned, they started making plans to move together to New York City where Brad would be working on a political campaign. But, life got in the way, plans changed, and they didn't quite get around to setting a date for the wedding.

Silvi wanted a bigger voice in the community. She believed she could do more. She thought long and hard about it, and then talked to her dad about applying to law school.

"Silvi, you know we can't afford to send you to law school. Your mom and I completely support you following your passions and dreams. We will help you any way we can," Ben said.

"Dad, I feel that I could do far more, be taken more seriously, and garner respect, if I had a law degree with a focus on environmental law," said Silvi.

"As much as I love the science, I feel the legal side of environmental science and technology is more to my calling than going to work for the Forest Service. I feel that I can be a more powerful voice, a grander force for change."

Her dad understood, and only wanted his daughter to be happy.

She and Brad discussed their future, and although he was disappointed, the wedding was put on hold as she got accepted at Georgetown Law School in Washington, D.C.

Georgetown Law School, Washington, D.C. 1976

Silvi was always mature for her age but, in 1976 when she moved to D.C., she was hitting her stride. She had already made a name for herself in environmental circles, which had given her great confidence with public speaking and community organization. She wasted no time at Georgetown meeting the movers and shakers. They introduced her to the people she needed to know. Washington, D.C. was full of influential men, and women, and she made a point to know who they were.

Silvi was a stunning young woman. She was tall with long, dark, silky hair, and crystalline blue eyes. She definitely stood out in a crowd. You couldn't help but notice her. And that certainly didn't hurt. Silvi's interest was not self-serving. She networked with people who were likeminded, and those that could help her reach her objective for being there; to make a difference in the natural world. She spent her time laser focused on the goal of moving the natural and organic farming movement forward.

Silvi was at the forefront of organic gardening. She started the "One Thousand Urban Gardens" program, which promoted homeowners across America, to create their own backyard edible gardens.

She fought for a ban on poisonous chemicals and pesticides on food crops. She fought against the big boys owning patents on seed, and on food. She was at the helm of promoting permaculture and heirloom seed collection and seed swapping. All this while working her way to the top of her class through law school.

She routinely would be seen in the hallways in Washington, D.C., lobbying Congress on preservation issues. She built relationships up on Capitol hill and hobnobbed with the movers and shakers in the areas of conservation and environmental regulatory law. Her networks were impressive, and her credentials were remarkable. The work was captivating and intoxicating to her. She truly made a name for herself, due to her activities and accomplishments in the organic, and permaculture communities.

Silvi was an articulate voice being picked up and noticed on a national level in the areas of environmental and patent law. She became known as a reformer and champion for the conservation movement. This movement was in its infancy, but quickly becoming mainstream. Silvi frequently was interviewed on national nightly news programs. In her later years at Georgetown, she was called on to testify in lawsuits involving the issues she was most passionate about. She was articulate and incredibly knowledgeable in science and law.

Silvi loved the fast paced world of Washington politics and policy. She thrived there, and people were drawn to her like a magnetic field.

When she first arrived in D.C., she and Brad talked every night. They shared their days' activities and their dreams. Brad moved to New York and was building a name for himself with high powered political teams. He grew up fast in New York and became a workaholic. His successes matched Silvi's. He was proud of her and wished they were closer. As time went by, the nightly calls turned into Sunday afternoon catch-ups of the week. They were both extremely busy and they knew that this was the time to build their careers. There would be time for them later. They missed each other, but were steeped in their lives and were able to compartmentalize work from social life, at least for now.

After Silvi graduated from Georgetown Law School with honors, she was offered several jobs, one in D.C., where she had spent three years networking a tightly knit community of high-power lawyers and cutting edge law firms.

She hated the idea of leaving D.C., but she was also offered a job in New York City, at Hancock, Taft, and Allen. The most prestigious environmental and patent law firm in New York.

Additionally, she was heavily persuaded by her still fiancé, Brad. He was now senior managing consultant at a political relations firm in Manhattan. He was working the reelection campaigns of New York's Senator Moynihan and New York's governor Hugh Carey's race. But more importantly, Brad was taped to be on the team for the high-profile presidential race next election cycle of an actor out of California, named Ronald Reagan.

Silvi took the job with Hancock, Taft and Allen.

Silvi started her job in New York right after the 4th of July holiday. She graduated law school in May and spent her annual summer visit with Grandpa Tucker in MeadowBrook, Virginia. She knew this job in New York would be intense and she decided to spend the whole month of June at the farm. Her mom and dad spent a week with Tucker and Silvi. Then, when her mom and dad left to go back to Syracuse, Grandpa Tucker and Silvi spent three glorious weeks together relaxing, talking, hiking, fishing, tending the summer garden, visiting old neighbors, attending potlucks and being best pals. Being with Grandpa was always like coming home. She was sad to leave on the first of July, but excited to get on with her new life in the 'Big Apple'.

Grandpa Tucker loved that girl with all his heart.

She reminded him, in looks and personality, of his beloved Bessie.

New York City, Silvi and Brad

Silvi and Brad quickly became a power couple in New York City. It was a bustling time. They were each hitting on all cylinders. They rarely had time off and were rarely alone. They struggled to create getaways as their lives were full of events, networking dinners and entertaining clients.

They couldn't have been much more geographically distanced and still live in Manhattan. Brad worked down on Broad Street in the financial district and lived in SoHo and Silvi's job was on the Upper East Side where she found a small, four-hundred square foot studio in Lenox Hill. Her place was overlooking the iconic Central Park. For Silvi, waking up and seeing the lush and verdant copse of timber and sage, the wildness of the park, it nurtured her heart's need for greenery and the backwoods forest that were so imprinted on her childhood memories in Upstate New York, and her summers in Appalachia.

Neither Silvi, nor Brad, dated other people, but their personal time was so limited. They had to schedule dates through each other's secretaries just to be together and those times usually involved other high profile, strictly business obligations. They were either in the political world or hobnobbing lawyers, and those frequently overlapped. They understood that they had important careers and would have time together soon. Silvi and Brad connected as much as possible and talked by phone most every night. Brad wanted to live together but with him down on Wall Street and her way up by the Park, the commute for either of them would be overwhelming with their schedules. So, they decided for that year to stick close to their respective offices and they would start looking for something together once the presidential election was over next January.

New York City, 1980

The 1980 campaign for President was grueling. And Silvi barely saw Brad. This was his first presidential campaign, and it was demanding and exhausting. Although Reagan won in a landslide on electoral votes, he barely got over fifty percent of the popular vote and in many states he won the electoral votes with just 1-2%. But many swing states, where the winner takes all the electoral votes, Carter just couldn't quite squeak it out, and in his four years as president, he couldn't pull the U.S. out of the super high double digit inflation rates that spiraled this country into a deep recession. Reagan stood for change. And he was charismatic. Silvi got to sit with him at a fundraising dinner that her law firm hosted where he was keynote speaker. He had a sportive, amiable, folksy charm in a polished cowboy sort of way. And he was handsome. He commanded respect yet was soft spoken and gracious. When he spoke, people listened.

Needless to say, from 1979 until November 4th, 1980, Silvi didn't see much of Brad. And although they spoke frequently while on the road, he was in his element and completely focused on this race.

No matter how busy or intense life got, the one sacred time that Silvi set aside was visiting her Grandpa Tucker at the farm in Virginia. She spent time with him each summer and at Thanksgiving. The visits were occasionally shorter than she wished, but there was at least one long weekend to reconnect to her roots, and be with her beloved Grandpa.

There were traditions that were cherished and one of them was chestnut stuffing. She always looked forward to the smells of Thanksgiving on the farm...it was like coming home. And Grandpa Tucker was happiest when he had the family around. The stories, the reminiscing, the love, it was palpable. She would never miss a family thanksgiving, not for anything. She treasured her time on the Farm. It was like medicine, a time and place that always had soft memories of a wistful childhood full of nature, and love, and never-ending curiosity.

Even though she was raised in Upstate New York, close to Syracuse, she always felt "Home" at the Farm in Virginia. The people were simple, and they had been neighbors and friends to Grandpa for a lifetime. Through good times and bad times, they were always there for him. It was funny how Silvi's dad always wanted to protect her from the 'hillbilly' roots. The ones that defined him. But somehow, Silvi always gravitated back to the farm, and felt most at peace in that old homestead, where her dad grew up through tough times. It was her legacy. She felt connected to the place where her grandpa grew up and where her great-grandparents, Ruth and Emery Hayes homesteaded and settled this land. It was a place of memories. A place in which the family was raised and had a history rich in Appalachian culture.

Silvi's dad said that after Grandma Bessie died, the neighbors never left Grandpa alone for long.

"Pa was never without a meal, or someone to sit with on the front porch, to whittle or play banjo or harmonica. Pa always knew he had someone looking out for him," said Ben.

And when a neighbor came to visit on the farm, you had their entire attention. You always felt that you were the most important person in their life at that moment.

Life didn't feel that way in the city. People were so busy. They had so many obligations, and so many commitments. Brad and Silvi had been engaged for almost five years and they still didn't find time to get together for more than a day or two, let alone time for the nuptials. But there were burgeoning careers, and as they say, "You strike when the iron's hot." So, they worked hard and played hard in their world and knew that soon they would be able to settle down and have a life together. They were not in a rush; they just knew the other one would always be there. They were truly best friends.

Silvi always said, "Brad was like the brother I never had."

Being a corporate lawyer anywhere is intense and grueling, but in New York City, it was all consuming. Silvi was hitting stride at her firm and became the foremost patent lawyer representing the biggest environmental and patent lawsuits coming into the state of New York.

It was that year that she and her team were to finish up a monumental case involving a small corn farmer on Long Island whose family had been farming, generation after generation, the same heirloom corn for decades. The farmer was being sued by a large agribusiness who had bought the neighboring land to grow their own GMO corn. This large multi-faceted corporation sued a small farm family for patent infringement! They were claiming that this small farm was illegally stealing and growing their patented genetically modified corn.

It had been a tumultuous and long road. Silvi felt it was the pinnacle of everything she believed in, and took it on personally. Plus, she and the National Farm Bureau knew the outcome of this case had the potential to permanently change the face of farming in America. She, as a lawyer, and the nation's food providers, had a lot riding on how she presented this case.

She knew she had to be absolutely on point.

CHAPTER NINE

Silvi and Farm Life

New York City

1987

Silvi sat in the old dark wood paneled courthouse. She had been in this well-worn chair facing the judge's bench so many times before. She had some impressive wins for clients over the years but today was different. Today was the culmination of years of work that affected not only her client and his family, but an entire nation of food growers; America's farmers. This case was different. The verdict could change farming into the future.

She had meticulously prepared her final arguments to the jury. Her legal pads and number 2 pencils, her loyal friends all these years, neatly tucked away as she meditated, reliving her closing argument to the jury. It had been a long journey to this day. Yet, unbeknownst to her, at this moment, her journey was just beginning.

Questions abounded of this young, skilled lawyer. Who was Silvi Hayes? They wanted to know her. Who was she, really? She was impressive, articulate, and mature. She presented herself differently than most lawyers and expressed herself exceptionally well. When Silvi spoke, people listened. She had the wisdom and skills that generally come with age and experience. Lots of experience. It came naturally to Silvi. The buzz about this woman intensified with the notoriety of the case.

Journalists investigated and found the public resume of Silvi, but nobody really knew her, not unless she wanted them to. The common knowledge about Silvina Elizabeth Hayes, was a slender, fit, blue eyed, brunette who graduated from the College of Environmental Science and Forestry with a bachelor's degree in botany, horticulture and plant sciences. And went on to Georgetown Law School in D.C. to pursue Environmental and Patent law. Anyone searching could find that she was an advocate for environmental issues, preservation, and conservation. She was a mover and shaker in New York's society circles. She was on prestigious museum boards, served on cutting edge corporate boards and many philanthropic organizations. Her life as a lawyer was steeped in a fast-paced, hectic world.

What people did not know about Silvi was her private life. Where she was most at home in an old growth forest, and flyfishing on the banks of a river. They did not know that she seamlessly traded her high heels and designer suits for flannel shirts and overalls. People didn't perceive her instinctive connection to nature, having been raised summers in Appalachian Virginia and the Upstate New York forests. This would have surprised, perhaps shocked, people that only knew her New York City or D.C. persona. She could slip from one to the other seamlessly and often did.

Silvi, as a child, was bright but shy. As she got older, she understood the dichotomy of her East Coast New York upbringing with her Appalachian country roots. Although she loved the time that she got to spend with Grandpa Tucker every summer, she appreciated her parent's commitment to education and a cultured lifestyle. Even though at his core Ben would always be a country boy.

Silvi loved her dad's stories. His telling of what life was like when he was a kid growing up in Virginia. He was expected to help on the farm from the time he wore his first pair of overalls. The Hayes family owned a hog farm, and it was her dad's job, from the time he was 8 years old, to feed the pigs before he went off to a one room schoolhouse where he, and his three sisters, attended all their years of schooling. Except at harvest time, when his Pa needed them on the farm.

It wasn't so much that Ben was embarrassed by his roots; his hard life, his homemade clothing, his thinly educated upbringing, or even a lack of indoor plumbing. His motivation for leaving the farm was simply a life with more security. He knew that this desperate life on the farm was rough, and he wanted more. He simply wanted a better, more stable life. He was determined to give his wife and family a comfortable future. One that was impossible on the farm after the chestnut blight hit rural Virginia. He could see the handwriting on the wall. There was no way to make a living. Those that stayed had two choices; starving in poverty or the dangerous, impoverished, begrimed life of a coalminer. And that is not what Ben wanted.

Silvi, loved the stories of her Grandpa Tucker. They were dearly close, she and her grandpa, but she was grateful that her dad left Virginia to pursue a career in forestry in New York. Otherwise, she too would have been raised in that cabin or certainly somewhere on that rural patch of Appalachia.

While spending summers with her grandpa, she heard stories about what life was like before the blight; doing tasks, fishing, church gatherings, trips into Abingdon, and of course holidays with family and friends bringing together wonderful home cooked foods and treats. Grandpa Tucker would go on with boundless stories about his life as a kid. His fish stories were endless.

"There was this one time, me and my two best friends, Charlie Burnham and Tom Winslow went fishing in the creek right over yonder. Every year we had a contest to see who caught the biggest fish each summer. One year Charlie caught a thirty-two-pound catfish, which shoulda won him the prize, but Tom caught a seventeen pound German Brown trout. They each got the award that year because catfish can weigh as much as a heifer, but a seventeen-pound trout was like finding a diamond in a coal mine."

In Tuckers youth, autumn meant collecting nuts in the forest after school. The chestnut leaves were a brilliant yellow, with saw-like edges. Shimmering in the sunlight, they were sublime beauty, a sight to behold. The illusion was heightened as Silvi would only know of this recollection through other people's memories and stories. "The spiny burrs burst open and the smooth, rich autumn smells filled the air," her grandpa would say.

Silvi listened intently to her grandpa's stories...."Oh mind ya, country life on a farm is never easy, even before the Great Depression and the death of our forests. Back then, there was no electricity or indoor plumbing. There were long days and not much money. Everything revolved around the seasons. And everybody in the family had chores; tending the hogs, gathering eggs, cleaning the house, planting, harvesting the gardens, washing clothes, and supporting neighbors when there was an unexpected accident or illness that always happened. But it was the connections between us people, yup, that's what made life rich, the shared experiences, the stories of friendship that formed our community, and how community cemented us into one big family."

Life in Appalachia tested even the most hardened and seasoned of men. Most were farmers that barely made it from year to year when things were bountiful. What they could afford to buy came from the plentitude of their access to chestnuts. These men would barter the nuts for things their wives and children needed, a pair of shoes, some tools, some fabric.

When the chestnut forest died, lifeless hundred-foot-tall shimmering ghosts of trees stood in their place. Many families were swindled by large logging operations buying the rights to log their land for a pittance, like a horse and barrel of flour. These high-powered corporations would come in and harvest the trees, dead or alive, because the American chestnut was the best wood for building almost anything, from cradle to coffin. The companies made millions off these private lands.

Tucker Hayes, as it turned out, was one of the lucky ones. When he had been approached to sell his logging rights, his beloved Bessie had just died. Bessie loved that land, and Tucker knew she would have rather died of starvation than let them strip their farm to a dusty tread-laden wasteland, like had been done on so many neighbors properties. Tucker was torn because he and Ben had nothing left but their old homestead. He was desperate, lost and felt perilously alone. The money from the loggers would have fed he and Ben through the winter. But his sensibilities were to protect everything just the way it was when Bessie was alive. He knew she would have been incensed and probably would have chained herself to the big chestnut tree in her garden. Tucker was paralyzed.

For a while he did nothing. But before long, Ben convinced him to let the loggers come in and clear the land of chestnuts. Unfortunately, along with the dead chestnut trees, some healthy chestnuts were timbered, thereby completely wiping out any chance of a resistant chestnut surviving and reforesting the land over time. The American chestnut was gone on MeadowBrook farm.

It was that moment that set Ben on a mission to create a better life.

And Tucker went to the mines.

Silvi was an easy-going kid, kind and helpful. She felt a strong responsibility to leave the world a better place. As she grew older, she had little patience for incompetence or disrespect, and she deeply loved nature. She became opinionated about "genetically modified organisms," GMOs, and food safety. She feared her world was slowly but certainly suffocating the life out of nature and the forests she grew to respect, through the stories of those who had come before her.

Silvi was happiest being with family. And being on the farm felt safe and comfortable and a world away from the stressful life she created for herself up North. In her real life, as a prominent lawyer, she routinely stood up to the big agribusinesses that preyed on small farmers. She felt she was doing Mother Nature's work, fighting the profit-driven big corporations that had to meet a bottom line for their shareholders and cared only about profits, even at the expense of people's livelihoods or health. She was proud that she was winning cases for preservation of nature and open spaces, but it felt like eating a dragon, and every day was a fight.

And that was the image she wanted the world to know.

The rest was her private step across a threshold painted in golden sunlight, washed in greens and grasses, and abundant in wild silence.

CHAPTER TEN

Coal Mining and the Great Depression

Appalachia

On bent knee, the men across the Appalachian range could be heard saying, "Why, why, why. What did I do to deserve this? Why is this happening to us? I've poured my heart and soul into caring for the land that my ancestors homesteaded, I've nurtured the family and the children, and the ground. Every day of my life I've worked my fingers to the bone. I've been a good neighbor to our community. I've tended the livestock and gotten out of bed in the cold and dark of winter to be a keeper of our land. Why, dear Lord, why has everything been taken. With the chestnut trees dead, how do we survive?"

"How do I feed my family? How do I care for the children that need clothes to keep warm and food to fill their bellies. Oh God, I ask you, I am pleading with you. How do we do it? What do I do now? I'll do anything you ask, if we can just have our lives back."

On hands and knees, grasping at the dusty dirt, they wept.

The owners of the land, the owners of the farms, they gathered in the forests, shaking their heads in unison. They stood looking at the bare silvery stumps that the blight left behind, as it barreled through the hillsides. Death, where a vibrant, verdant, strong tree of life once stood.

Wide eyed and barefoot, the women and children shivered from the cold. But they were silent. Fear was etched in their faces; they'd go to bed hungry again. There were no tears left, only desperation. The fields were vacant, and so were their pantries.

Winter was upon them. The barns once full of animals, long empty. Rusted farm equipment that belonged to parents and grandparents still hung on hooks and cluttered the straw scattered floor of the barns and sheds. The great wooden doors drifted open and shut in the wind. Nothing to sell, 'cause nobody had money to buy. In the anger of the moment, the memories were all that was left. And those memories only caused sadness. What would they do? Where would they go? Bitterness lingered, but that wouldn't put food on the table.

Those with means and transportation left Appalachia. And when I say "Means", I'm talking just enough money for gas to make it to Georgia or Florida. They would have a chance at a new life. Maybe. Knowing nothing of what lay ahead. Not knowing is sometimes a blessing. The unknown awaited them, but at least they would be out of the chestnut range, off the land that had died right before their eyes. Maybe they would find a way, they didn't know. But the uncharted, far away mystery at least gave them hope.

As the Great Depression was full on, the drought of life, and loss of opportunity was compounded. Fear and loss permeated the totality of the country. And the loss of the 'well of sustenance' was the final blow for many. The President instituted a back to work program that a lot of young men signed up for. They had work, a roof over their head, a pillow to lay their heads at night, and a paycheck they sent home. They left everything familiar. They left by the thousands; in some cases, theirs was the only money entire families relied on for years.

"Mine Workers Wanted" became a way of life for generations of Appalachians. As the sun began to set, the men trudged wearily up the long winding path that led out of the coal mine. Their clothes covered in soot and sweat; faces blackened by the dust that permeated every inch of the underground tunnels. Exhaustion weighed heavily on their shoulders. For hours on end, they'd toil deep underground. Grueling work, using pick and shovel to extract the coal that powered the countryside. Donned with helmets and spotlights, goggles, steel toed boots, carrying drills, explosives and wheelbarrows. Dangerous, grimy darkness paired well with their state of mind and going underground almost felt like an escape from the annihilation above ground. If they could get a job in the mine, it paid a pittance. Barely enough for food. Mice ate better, much better, and more frequently. But the men were grateful for the job yet. Better than some, that had no choice, no job, and nothing to live for. Hunger and desperation their constant companion.

By the time spring arrived, weeds grew, a garden could be planted. Vegetables would grow and neighbors would share their crops. At least they wouldn't starve. Fish would run upstream and with it came a crumb of hope. Spirits lifted at least for the moment.

The chestnut canopies never returned. And the shimmery remnants of desiccating stumps were a steady reminder of what they lost. Like a pair of shoes that are too small, after a while the pain becomes indistinguishable. A new life unfolded but a hole the size of Texas was imprinted in the hearts of all that remembered and relied on those trees to provide.

CHAPTER ELEVEN

The Court Verdict—Monsynta vs. Meyers Farm

The dark brown gavel laid sideways upon the judge's mahogany desk. A bible perched on the desk just above the witness chair. Each important seat was clad in worn leather; the judge, jury, the defendant, plaintiff and their legal counsel. White-knuckled, apprehensive concern was suspended in the air. The courtroom had seen its share of truths and lies. Justice and inequity have had their day behind these massive, carved doors which swung out to liberty, or death. The florescent lights added an imperceptible background hum to the tension which hung in the room.

Silvi took a deep breath. She sat alone in the courtroom during the recess. Inexplicably, there was peace in her isolation. She needed a few minutes to think. The redolence of the room was distinct; dust, dank, leather, and old cigars, wafting from the private offices behind the bench. She patiently waited for a verdict on the largest patent infringement case in her career. Outside the press was on standby with minute by minute commentary and opinions.

The wet marble of the courthouse steps was dark and slippery against the muggy, dreary, drizzly day. A low mumbling from the gathered crowd grew in anticipation of the verdict. It was 2:00pm as Silvi Hayes finished her closing arguments to a jury in the Southern district of New York. Their decision would be landmark in the Case of Monsynta Corporation vs. Meyer Farms. Monsynta, a powerful, large, multibillion-dollar agribusiness company held the patents on genetically modified field corn.

Jim Meyer and his family farmed the 1200 acres off Woodbury Road on Long Island since 1814. It was farmed by his great-great-great granddaddy Joe Meyer, his great-great Grandpa Peter Meyer, his great-grandpa Peter junior, his grandpa Pete Meyer III and now for over forty years by Jim. The Meyer farm is known for the best heirloom sweet summer Long Island corn that money can buy. Their orchards of apples; Winesap, Baldwin, and Newtown Pippen are sweet and juicy with just the right tang. These apples told the story of transition from summer corn to crisp autumn days. But mostly, the Meyer's were known for their award-winning, Long Island, sweet summer corn. People would come from far and wide to go into the fields to pick their own bushel of corn in summer. In autumn, baskets of sweet, crisp apples could be carried up to the barn to be pressed into fresh apple cider. Of course, the height of corn season is July, and apple season starts in late October, right through Thanksgiving. This farm had sustained the Meyer family for five generations. They were proud farmers and wonderful stewards of their land. Their farm was flanked by Saint Mary's Catholic church on the North and to the South, a large 2000-acre property owned by LILCO, the Long Island Lighting Company.

And it had been so, since the turn of the century.

Until fifteen years ago, Monsynta, the multinational, multibillion-dollar agribusiness purchased the utility land adjacent to the Meyer's property. They were looking to compete in the livestock corn market with their patented, GMO, proprietary corn, and the utility land was a large plot with perfect soil and weather for growing corn.

The Realtor and lawyers from Monsynta approached their neighbor, Meyer, to purchase their land too. But the Meyer family explained that it was their home, it was their livelihood, and Jim had no interest in selling their land.

"Jim," said Bobby Reardon, the Realtor for Monsynta. "We are offering you above market price for your land. It would behoove you to sell, you'll never get a better offer."

"Look Bobby, the offer is very generous. That's not the issue. This farm has been in my family for almost a hundred and seventy-five years. My father entrusted me to run it and I will entrust my son to run it. We have no interest in selling; it's our lifeblood, it's our livelihood, it's our culture and it's our history."

The representatives from Monsynta assured Jim that they had no interest in competing with his farm's sweet corn, and that most of their product was for shipping overseas to be used for feed, primarily chicken and hogs. The Meyer family appreciated the offer, but declined. Jim didn't feel a threat at all. And for several years there was barely any interaction btwn the two farms. Besides the three hundred Monsynta employees that would frequent the farmstand to buy some corn to take home for the family or a jug of fresh pressed apple cider around Thanksgiving.

"Best cider this side of the Mississippi," they would always say when they saw Jim.

Until 1980, when Jim received a Cease-and-Desist order from Monsynta. They claimed that the Meyer farm had stolen their patented corn and were growing it within their corn fields. The patent infringement suit against Jim's family was for $60 Million dollars. Jim, of course, denied having any interest in their corn and if there was any growing in their fields, it was due to Monsynta's patented GMO pollen blowing into his farm in the areas that were closest to the South fields. And further, frankly, he was pretty upset that it was hybridizing and contaminating their award-winning organic heirloom corn, that the Meyer family had been growing for two centuries. Jim decided to go see the big shots at Monsynta. He planned to just pay them a visit and work this out man to man, or at least to try to understand what happened, and how to resolve it like gentlemen.

Jim drove his old 1942 red farm truck with a flatbed littered with corn husks and silk. The seats were thread bare, but it did the job. Jim, in his worn denim overalls, a light grey plaid flannel shirt with the sleeve's half rolled up, walked right into the lobby of their big, modern glass building. He removed his old straw gardening hat, but he didn't get past the gatekeeper.

A pleasant enough woman, in a navy dress, was seated behind glass at the reception desk. She had a matching navy bow in her hair that held up a bun on the top of her head.

She said, "May I help you, sir?"

Jim explained he needed to talk to Mr. Sheridan and showed her the letter.

She clarified, "Mr. Sheridan is indeed one of our corporate lawyers, but he works in the Manhattan office. Please have a seat Mr. Meyer ,and let me get someone to come down to see you."

She buzzed to someone upstairs and then motioned for Jim to have a seat.

Jim waited, shuffling his dusty old brown work boots on the shiny grey marble floor. He may have been weathered and worn, his calloused hands a testament to years of toil, yet his eyes had a spark of determination and steadfast resolution. One way or another he would work this out. He had an unbreakable spirit for he knew the value of hard work, and he just wanted to get back to his corn. After several minutes, a flinty man with a forbidding look emerged from an elevator.

"I'm Giles, Joseph Giles," he curtly introduced himself. He was a junior lawyer at the firm.

"I'm sorry Meyer, but there is nothing we can do at this level, as the lawsuit has already been served upon you. It would be best to have your lawyer contact us. If you don't have any further questions, I'll bid you good day sir."

He stared at Jim for a moment, tipped his head and he then turned on his heels and vanished into that steel box from whence he emerged.

Jim never said one word, and he never had a need for a lawyer. He didn't even know one, let alone a corporate, patent infringement lawyer. Jim had read about other farmers that were being sued by big agribusinesses with unlimited funds. He sat for a moment and did not know what to do.

"What kind of joke is this?" Jenny Meyer asked her husband.

"Apparently no joke at all," Jim stammered.

"We are being sued by bottomless pockets for $60 million for something completely out of our control, something which we had no involvement, nor interest in."

Jenny was clearly beside herself in fear. Jim knew it would do no good to scare her with the knowledge he had.

"It's all just a big mistake, don't you worry sweetheart, I'll call the Farm Bureau in the morning and get this all straightened out."

Jim thought to himself, this nightmare can't be happening.

Clearly, they had been farming on this patch of land for going on two centuries. The lawyers at Farm Bureau will get it sorted out… Jim tried to sleep but had a fitful night. In the wee hours of the morning before the sun rose over Long Island, when everyone was still fast asleep, he walked out to the fields, took a deep inhale of fresh summer air, and laid on the earth under the moonlight, lost between the rows of their personal gold. He had heard the heart wrenching stories from other farmers. He suddenly felt a tear run down his cheek, and he cried.

The trial went on for two years. Collecting depositions, testimony, and legal fees, it practically bankrupted the Meyer farm. Devastatingly, the court sided with Monsynta. They upheld the patent and claimed that the Meyers had no rights to grow the GMO corn on their land. It was property of the corporation, and they needed to cease and desist and make restitution.

Jim Meyer had no money left to fight. It would mean not only bankruptcy, but having to sell the farm to pay the legal fees. It was a horrifically bad nightmare. It affected the whole family and the stress shown on Jim's face, and his newly grayed hair.

The Farm Bureau understood this case was a devastating blow to all farmers across this land. From the Heartland to the Southwest, from Michigan to Georgia. There was an emergency conference of every branch, in every state's Farm Bureau. They consulted every legal mind to delve into how to stop this attack on the American people. They needed answers on how to crush this decision, a legal decision that would affect all farmers way of life, all farm families, all over the country. The Farm Bureau, and every farmer in America banded together to appeal this decision to the Southern District Court of New York. Everything the Meyer family had built, everything our nation's food supply stood for, not just a farm product but a lifestyle, the history of America, the heritage and the very source of food of this great country was under attack. They hired the firm of Morrison and Hayes. The best legal defense team in the country against corporate greed.

Seven long years since this nightmare started culminated on this day, with Jim and Jenny Meyer, and Silvi Hayes sitting in Judge Addison's court awaiting the verdict.

It was a case that the entire country had been following. Monsynta, with its bottomless pit of money was systematically ridding America of its small farmers, and slowly taking control of the ownership, through patents, of every bit of produce that Americans could buy at supermarkets. It had a death grip, and monopoly, on what every grower of food across our land would rely on to produce the nation's food source.

At the same time, these same agribusinesses were buying up all the seed companies. Buying up small seed companies and large ones, across America. They built a monopoly of the seed supply, that even backyard gardeners had available to plant, and grow in their own little raised garden beds.

. Silvi had come a long way. She had left the big Manhattan firm and started her own with Peter Morrison,. They were focused solely on agricultural patent infringement and had more work than they could manage. She had become a highly sought after, successful, and polished environmental lawyer. Silvi had a lot of wins against corporate biochemical companies. She was sharp as a thistle, and smooth as ice. Silvi's greatest strength was "gentle persuasion, relentlessly applied."

"You can't get a better advocate in environmental law. Silvi Hayes has a conscience and empathy, which garnered everybody's admiration," Jim was told.

She was simply the best of the best in the country, in this field of law. She had a command of the English language that could persuade a penguin to run a marathon in a desert.

On this day, long in coming, as Silvi waited, she knew that news outlets from across America, and across the globe, would be gathered on the steps of the courthouse awaiting the verdict that had the potential to change America's food source, supply, and quality forever. Nine long hours the jury deliberated. The court then recessed, and the apprehension and suspense were palpable. Deliberation would carry over until tomorrow. The decision was expected the next morning. She finally went home and tried to rest. It was pretty much useless. Nothing distracted her.

The sun came out sporadically the next morning, but it was still hot and muggy, even for July. The chattering, nervous crowd outside the courtroom grew louder as each hour passed. Every news outlet had a camera rolling and reporters all talking to their camera at once. There was great anticipation to see if the appellate court would overturn the lower court's decision for the corporation.

Silvi was confident that she presented a solid case but, she knew that a jury was completely unpredictable. It would be a landmark decision and it would have long range ramifications across the nation. This jury would not be swayed solely by one farmer's emotional journey.

The jury finally re-entered the courtroom at four o'clock pm. A verdict had been reached. The two attorneys rose, along with the plaintiff and defendant. The press with passes poured into the crowded lobby from the hot, muggy day. They anxiously awaited the verdict.

"Counselors, ladies and gentlemen of the jury, you have been charged with setting our course for the future," said Judge Addison.

"This has been a long trial. Your verdict will set the course of the future of America, her legal interpretation, and rights, under law. We've all grown older during this investigation. But it has tested our resolve and our wisdom. It has tested our fundamental democracy. Forman, may I have the verdict?" Judge Addison read the verdict.

And then spoke: "On the count of patent rights: Monsynta's rights to the patents is upheld in this court of appeals." The gasp in the room was palpable.

"On the issues of fraud and liability: the defendant's culpability is overturned. Contamination was caused by nature. The creep of proprietary GMO pollen into defendant's property is to be curtailed. Plaintiff will leave a clear cut adjacent to all neighboring farmland of no less than 200 yards, and place impenetrable barriers along same property lines to protect against drift, and to ensure the protection of the defendant's heirloom crops. Damages will be paid to the defendant, Meyer Farms, in the sum of Seven million, six hundred thousand dollars, plus legal fees." Judge Addison turned to the jury.

"Thank you, jury, you have honorably served your country today. With nothing further on the docket, this court is adjourned."

Jenny and Jim's pent-up emotion exploded, and they wept. Their hearts exploded with relief; the weight of the world lifted off their shoulders. Justice had been served and their spirits soared, as the judge declared their long and hard-fought battle over. They could close this chapter of their life with renewed hope. With tears of joy streaming down their faces, they hugged tightly, and uncontrollably laughed, and hugged even tighter.

Silvi didn't realize that she was holding her breath as she stood with her calves pressing hard against edge of her chair. Her heart was pounding as the verdict was read. She had so much invested in this case. It had far reaching consequences and would change how farmer's rights would be viewed in America. Her heart and soul, everything she believed in, was embodied in this core right vs. wrong, David vs. Goliath, of this case. Silvi worked hard to procure a positive outcome to this momentous day. Plus, she knew this outcome would catapult her to a new level of notoriety. She had never before felt this emotionally tied to a client, nor what they stood for.

When Judge Addison read the verdict, it was a win! Silvi instinctively raised a fierce, clenched fist of triumph, and under her breath murmured "Yes!" Tears of joy welled up in her eyes. Before she realized what happened, Jenny Meyer turned to Silvi and wrapped her arms around her. She almost knocked Silvi off balance. Jenny was still crying, almost sobbing. It had been an ordeal the likes of which, a gentle farmer's wife had never experienced in her life. It was as if Jenny took a deep breath for the first time in several years. Jim reached over, to Silvi and shook her slim hand with both of his thick farmers paws and looked her right in the eye. "Silvi, thank you for everything you've done for us through the years. We are forever indebted to you, and your team." Then he stepped closer and hugged her too. And shed a few more tears of joy, and mostly relief.

When they finally composed themselves, they headed toward the door.

On the way out, Silvi touched the opposing counsel's shoulder, leaned close and said, "Best of luck to you", as she stared him in his eyes and sharply nodded her head. She rejoined Jenny and Jim, and the three of them stepped out of the courtroom.

Outside, the massive court doors flew open, the verdict was reported across the country, and around the world. A reporter from the Boston Globe, the New York Times, the Wisconsin Sentinel, and the Kansas Daily Star shoved their way toward Silvi. There were untold numbers of newscasters. Almost in unison they reported live;

> *"We are standing outside the Southern District of New York as a jury handed down a strong message and verdict in favor of America's farmers. This was a fatal blow to leading agricultural businesses that are in pursuit of mass-producing proprietary crops and creating a monopoly on the country's food supply. This effort was thwarted by America's small*

farmers and the Farm Bureaus all across the country. These large agri-businesses lost a landmark case in the hijacking of America's legacy and heirloom food sources. This case sets a precedent protecting diversity and preserving centuries old heirloom varieties of produce and heritage crops for generations to come."

Silvi Hayes and Jim Meyer emerged and were clamored by hundreds in the press for a statement. Jim was shaking. He was a little disoriented by the flashing bulbs of the paparazzi. It had been a long journey, and he aged through it. They all had. But now with this win, Silvi felt proud, and relieved that right finally prevailed.

Silvi stood on the courthouse steps, facing west, the direction from which the colors of sunset would soon illuminate her face, as it ended the very long day. And, it ended one of the most controversial and impactful decisions in modern legal history. Silvi solidified her place on the national stage as a voice for justice.

And the discernible voice for preservation of Nature.

CHAPTER TWELVE

Respite with Grandpa Tucker

Hayes Farm, Meadowbrook

1987

After a well-deserved celebration, Silvi's thoughts turned to her family farm. She needed a break from law and from New York City. She wanted to go see her grandpa. She thought about life in MeadowBrook and the beautiful countryside of Virginia. She also wanted to know more about the devastation of the chestnuts. What caused the blight, how it happened and what caused the death of an entire chestnut forest.

Ring, Ring, Ring....You have reached Doctor Baldwin, sorry to have missed your call. please leave a message at the beep:

"Hey Nita, It's Silvi Hayes. It's been too long. I'm in Appalachia with my Grandpa Tucker for a little R&R on the farm. Maybe you heard, we just won a landmark case for a small farmer on Long Island. I've been working day and night, and just needed to unwind. So, I decided Virginia was the best place to escape for a bit. Call me when you have a minute to talk. I've been poking around up here on the history of the American chestnut blight and wanted to share something that I think is right up your alley. Hoping for a little advice. Look forward to catching up."

Silvi remembered that years ago, at Dr. Baldwin's lab at the College of Environmental Science & Forestry, they were doing research on the chestnut blight. When Silvi was there, she had worked primarily in the gene mapping project. But she knew that Nita was the lead PhD on that research too. She left the message for Nita in hopes of getting answers on what caused the blight, what physiologically caused the tree to succumb to the disease, and what, if anything, could be done to mitigate the damage.

Silvi didn't sleep that night. Her mind was in full gear, not unlike nights preparing to try a case. Only this time, it wasn't for a client. She found herself feeling the emotion, and pain, of her family's village, its townspeople and how life had changed for them when a generation ago, the fungus destroyed not only their forest but also their lives. She particularly had motivation to get answers for her grandpa whose life was never the same after 1938, when Grandma Bessie died, along with the chestnuts on MeadowBrook farm.

Silvi decided to take a few more days before returning to Manhattan. She was so enjoying being with her grandpa and she was still so exhausted, that doing nothing but relaxing with her favorite person on Earth, was just what the doctor ordered.

It was always a joy to spend time with the families down here in Appalachian country. Brad was now campaign chairman on Vice President Bush's presidential run. He was still traveling with the campaign so he wouldn't even notice she was gone an extra week. And she knew they had no commitments coming up this next week, so she decided to take a little longer respite. Besides, Grandpa had just lost his best friend, a hound named Pal. Pal was Grandpa's constant companion over the past 15 years, so, he was feeling a bit lonely. It was good karma to stick around a little while longer.

She knew that the Burnhams down the lane had a beagle that would give birth in a few weeks, and would be weaned right about the time of Grandpa's birthday in October. She thought that she'd surprise him with a puppy. Someone to love and keep him company while he whittled away on his front porch or chopped wood or took a walk. Someone to become his new best friend, help him do his chores, someone to talk to when he was fishing, and a companion to sit by his side while he ate dinner.

She hated that he was alone. Tucker Hayes never remarried after Bessie passed away. He just couldn't imagine being with anyone else. Bessie was his North Star and he loved her for eternity. And he wasn't about to leave MeadowBrook. Where would he go?

Tucker always told people,"I was born in this cabin, and I will take my last breath here."

Nothing would get him to move from this land. It was home. Through good and bad....it was the only constant in his life, he loved this shack that he was born in, and he loved this land. It was truly the fabric of who he was. He was comfortable here.

There is nothing cuter than a beagle puppy. They are full of love and loyalty. Silvi arranged with Martha Burnham, Charlie's wife, to save a male pup. She would give it to Grandpa when she came back in October. Silvi knew he would love that. And she would be comforted to know that he had a companion to be with and to love.

Grandpa Tucker relished having Silvi around. They were like old farm hands together, working the garden, feeding the chickens, collecting eggs each morning, and going on long hikes through the woods. She loved listening to his stories of this land, and its people. He painted a picture for her; of life when he was young, and when he was first married to Bessie and how happy they were. He didn't talk much about life after Bessie died, just to say, "the love of my life died, the chestnut died, and life was never the same."

His memories and stories were of his childhood on the farm with his parents, growing up, having lifelong friends, and the joy of his children.

Silvi learned that in addition to her dad, Tucker and Bessie Hayes also had other children, whom she never met, nor ever heard about before. They had two younger girls who went to live with Bessie's sister in West Virginia. Aunt Rachel always blamed Tucker for her sister's death. Rachel told her sister not to have any more babies, that she was too old, and they couldn't afford any more mouths to feed. But Bessie was determined to have just one more. After Bessie died, Rachel stopped coming to MeadowBrook and she kept the two girls, Berta, and Shirl from Tucker. In fact, she adopted them, and she gave them a nice life in West Virginia. They grew to call her Momma and her husband Daddy. She and her husband raised them as their own, along with the two kids they already had. Tucker didn't have the means to fight her, and he knew in his heart that they would probably have a better life than he could give them.

Grandpa Tucker also told Silvi of another daughter named Sara, who was older than her dad, Ben. He said that she ran away as a teenager with her boyfriend and never returned home. It made him sad to talk about Sara, he loved her dearly and just prayed she was safe and living a happy life somewhere, and would someday come back. He showed Silvi the note that Sara wrote the night she left. He said he found it in his flyfishing tackle box. It said,

> *"Poppa, I hope you can understand why George and I feel we need to leave home. We are getting married, and he has found a steady job that will provide for us. As I promised Mom on her deathbed, I will take care of the new baby every day of my life. You need not worry about us. We will be fine. With the chestnuts gone, no hog farm left, and the Depression weighing heavy on you and everyone in MeadowBrook, we feel that we are doing what is best for the family. I hope you can forgive me for not talking to you about it, but I know you would have said, stay and that we will manage. George and I have loved each other our whole lives.*
> *Please give Ben my love, tell him I'm sorry.*
>
> *Your first Born,*
> *Sara*
>
> *PS: I will Always love you.*

Silvi cried when she read that note. It had been decades since Sara left, yet Tucker still held out hope that one day she would return.

Tucker did not mention anything about the baby Lily, and Silvi did not ask. She felt it might be too painful for her grandpa to talk about. If he wanted to, he could bring it up.

The cabin was the same as Silvi remembered it as a child. Over the years, Ben told her many stories of growing up there, and all the fun it was during the days as hog farmers. He talked about the neighbors and his childhood buddies. He told of how he worked on the farm practically before he could walk. He shared what life was like once his mom died, and how it was just him and his dad for the years before he left to work for the Forest Service. Not much had changed on the farm, except the hogs and the chestnuts were gone. The cabin looked the same, nothing had moved in all these years. The wood pile would be bigger or smaller depending upon the time of year. The house always smelled the same. It had a peat quality that hung like a morning mist over a mountain lake. It just felt like home.

Even for a highly educated, high heel wearing, city girl like Silvi, it felt like coming home.

Whenever Silvi was there, she would always pick flowers. There was an old metal vase on the fireplace mantel that she kept filled with fresh flowers that she'd pick on her hikes with her grandpa, or out of Grandpa's garden. It brightened up the place and gave it a woman's touch. And she thought Grandpa liked it. He told her that Bessie used to keep flowers in that very kettle when they were newlyweds.

Last summer, Silvi was invited by the local ladies to help make a community quilt. She had never quilted before. The ladies in town insisted she join them. They told her it was quite easy once you got the hang of it. Silvi enjoyed the time she spent with them.

Most of them knew her Grandma Bessie and would tell stories about her, and about what a little devil her dad Ben was growing up. Silvi loved the time that she spent in the quilting bee. They told her many times that she looked just like her grandma; tall, with long silky chestnut brown hair and piercingly blue eyes. And she absolutely loved that they took her in, and made her feel like family. They were all older women; Clara Pinchot, Anna Collins, Martha Burnham, Florence Perkins and Julia Winslow. The one exception was Aliza Thompson, who was the granddaughter-in-law to Florence Perkins. She was pregnant and spending the summer in MeadowBrook, as her husband was working in the city, and he could only make it out to the farm on the weekends. Spending time with Aliza made her reflect on her own life. She loved her life and was proud of her accomplishments, but this girl was going to have a baby and had a husband that she still prattled on about him like he was decadent French toast smothered in real maple syrup. It made Silvi think about the kind of love her Grandpa Tucker had with Bessie. In a way, Silvi found Aliza's life simple and servile. Yet, in a way she was jealous.

As they each sat and worked on their little corner of the quilt, they gabbed about everything under the sun. Frequently the conversation turned to life before the blight. How rich life was, and abundant in the Earth's bounty. Aliza and Silvi reveled in the stories. There was no shortage of reminiscing. The chestnuts were so much a part of these family's lives. They painted rich pictures of how the trees would produce an abundance of nuts every single year. And how this deep mast of nuts fell on the forest floor starting in October.

Clara Pinchot told the girls, "You know, collecting chestnuts was serious business. Not only did they feed the farm animals, but they also fed the entire Appalachian area with foods like chestnut stuffing and chestnut pudding."

Julia chimed in, "Yes, and chestnut soup, collard with chestnuts."

Each lady adding her own favorite recipe.

Anna recollected, "Oh yes, and bacon wrapped chestnuts, and chestnuts with wild boar."

Martha chimed in "Don't forget desserts; chestnut tarts, chestnut cookies and candied chestnuts, oh and chocolate chestnut cake."

The ladies all agreed that throwing chestnuts into any meal made it better. They laughed and giggled and swooned remembering the smells of their kitchens in the days before the blight.

Memories, wonderful, rich, sweet memories of a lost era that are in vivid, living color only in the minds, and recollections of those who lived it. No description of these abundant and tasty nuts could recreate those days, but the stories lived on generation to generation.

Kids loved collecting these smooth, round nuts. It was the boys' job to collect chestnuts for each family to take to Abingdon to trade for other items they couldn't grow on the farm. They traded nuts for the essentials they needed to sustain independent lifestyles.

Julia shared one funny story, "so one chilly autumn day, Tommy and Tucker went out into the forest equipped with a large burlap tarp and picked up all the chestnuts on the ground under this one-hundred-foot-tall chestnut tree. When they had cleared the forest floor, they took to whacking at the tree with a large branch to make the burrs that were still hanging on, rain down more nuts. Well, it worked. Nuts started flying everywhere. But unfortunately, they also woke up the beehive that was settling down for winter and it was a sight to see those two boys running home, swatting, and screaming and dancing and screaming, hopping up and down and moving like they had drunk a growler of hootch on a bed of nails. Those bees swarmed them, and they ended up with vinegar patches from head to toe."

Julia laughed, "It was not funny, but the way they were dancing around you woulda thought they was crazy. It took a bottle of calamine, a couple days, a whole lot of whining with a weeks' worth of welts in places you don't mention in proper company."

Through laughter, Clara went on, "But a few days later, they were back out there with a good life lesson under their belts. From then on, they learned to always check the tree before you go swatting at it." We all laughed. "It never happened again," said Clara.

Anna chimed in "We all got a good laugh at the boys' expense. I am so sure they were embarrassed more than anything to be walking around with pink spots on their entire body and itching, itching in places they couldn't even reach."

How the ladies retold their stories gave Silvi and Aliza a glimpse at a bygone life. The way they described those chestnut trees was like a magical, fairyland forest. Their words painted a picture that you could almost smell; of summer flowers and autumn nuts immersed in a faerie world.

Those trees reaching up to the sky with canopies practically as wide as tall, Silvi could almost see them dapple sunlight on the ground below.

The women all giggled like schoolgirls when Clara told the story about getting her first kiss from her husband under a chestnut tree, and how they carved their names in the bark of the young tree that day. When the tree got infected with the blight decades later and it had to be taken down, they went into the woods and sawed a cross section of that tree where they had carved their names so many years before. They saved that piece of the tree. William turned it into a tabletop that still sits in their living room by the fireplace.

Everyone had a life story about chestnuts, and how the loss changed their lives. No one escaped the devastation of the blight. For some, their land was bulldozed, but many families sold their mineral rights to the coal miners for pennies and a pig.

Luckily, these families managed to stick together and survive. Most husbands went to work for the coal mines. It was dirty, hard, dangerous work. But it was all they had left. The women heard stories of those without jobs, destitute and were reminded daily how very much they appreciated the work their husbands did have.

They knew they were the lucky ones, with a roof over their heads. The Depression left so many, tens of thousands of families, homeless and living on the streets, under bridges and in cardboard boxes in Hoovervilles. They were completely depleted and penniless. Certainly, life was not easy. They went to bed hungry many a night. But they were able to stay together. These families had a bond. They were there for each other when they needed a helping hand. The chestnut trees were a gift from Heaven that had been there for thousands of years until greed and poor regulation on imported plants took away everything familiar, everything they took for granted.

The stories of everyday life with chestnuts moved Silvi. Everyone's story was different, and they were all beautiful descriptions of full, courageous, and vigorous lives. They were spirited and intrepid and it bonded these folks as one people, contracted by nature and Earth. A love for the land, and all the living beings that inhabited it under their care and watchful eye.

The ravages and desolation that the blight left behind, the catastrophic loss of the American chestnut tree, it was life changing. There was no answer, the loss was enduring. There was no path to mend the forests to their pre-blight majesty and splendor. People had to learn to move on. But they vowed to never forget the adored and treasured days of life in the chestnut forests.

As the summer sun gave way to the crisp fall air, Silvi cherished her time with these "Old Broads", as they called themselves. She learned of a simpler time, a hard life to be sure, but a simpler way of life. It was rich with memories and deep intimate friendships. These things she found were hard to find in the fast-paced city life that she had chosen. But these were real friendships that lasted a lifetime in a simple place they all called home. And she was embraced into their sphere because she was family. She belonged there.

It was a Friday, and Silvi's last night before going back to New York City. The ladies had a big day in the quilting bee. They were still working on that very same quilt from last year. Silvi suggested that all the ladies get together for dinner at Tucker's house. They thought that was a wonderful idea. Everyone kissed goodbye and went home. Each made a potluck dish and agreed to meet at six pm, just as the sun spilled across the horizon, as a glowing bright ball of red touched the western sky.

Tucker was thrilled to have his friends over. Charlie and Martha Burnham and Tom and Julia Winslow. The Pinchots also came and brought a grand nephew of Clara Pinchot's called Luke Woodbury.

Luke, who was passing through MeadowBrook visiting his family near the Rappahannock River area in northeastern Virginia, was a couple of years older than Silvi but she had recalled meeting him many years prior, when she was about eight years old. She vividly remembered him because at that age, he was a botanical Einstein on the trees in the forest.

Their families went on a hike up the mountain when they first met. She distinctly remembered him because he knew, and taught her, the names of all the trees and most of the shrubs. It was the very thing that got Silvi interested in her pressed leaf collection. Something that she had saved and added to her whole life.

Silvi was pleased to see him again, all grown up. He turned into a nice-looking man, with a kind, easygoing smile. He was someone you instantly trusted. He had a comfortable laugh. He was about 5'11", with dark brown hair and he wore glasses, which he always removed when he was looking up close at the leaves. It was nice to reconnect with another naturalist.

During dinner, the conversation, as frequently happened around there, turned to life among the chestnut trees. It turned out that Luke had been living in Virginia doing research on the blight. Much research had been done over the decades since the blight hit, but there was no cure yet, or method to save the trees. Many treatments were tried, some even turned to praying, saying they angered the Gods. But so far, nothing had worked. It felt hopeless. Most people had chosen to move on. They didn't like to be stressed over the past. They chalked it up to ignorance and bad luck.

What was known, however, was that the blight killed the tree trunk and limbs, but it did not affect the roots. So, the roots would continue to give life to the tree and routinely form new saplings which would grow out of the dead stumps. It had been decades, and most people thought bringing them back was a lost cause. They held memories, and that would have to be enough.

But there were some that were still determined to unearth the secrets of science, to bring back the iconic and unique American chestnut tree. And Luke was one of them.

"We've had so many scientific, medical and technological advances that a small cadre of researchers still held out hope against hope," he said at dinner.

Luke Woodbury was working at the University in Virginia on a new treatment, something that was recently discovered on some of the existing small chestnut trees.

He explained, "After the four billion trees had died, new baby chestnut trees kept popping up all over the natural range, but as soon as they would get to be four or five years old, just when the tree might be producing flowers and viable chestnuts, the fungus would attack again. The all too familiar lesion that turned into an orange canker, that would again encompass the girth of the bark, suffocate, and kill the new baby tree."

He went on "However, we noticed that some of the trees seemed to form a scab over the canker and survive much longer. That's when I was hired at the university to figure out why some trees had this apparent immunity, and most did not."

Silvi asked Luke, "So, if they could identify what was different about these trees, then perhaps they could repeat it and breed for the resistant trees?"

"Correct," said Luke. "We identified a virus, that had the ability to render the fungus harmless. We are working on how to repeat that virus to potentially save the new chestnut trees."

She listened intently and found him engaging. They sat together talking for much of the evening. He schooled Silvi on his work.

Silvi told him about her work as an environmental community organizer, and then going to Georgetown for law school to fight for the preservation of our natural resources and against corporate greed. Luke was a fascinating man, and the night just seemed to fly by. They had a lovely dinner with the neighbors. And most importantly Grandpa had a wonderful evening.

After dinner, the men sat out on the old wooden porch and played their harmonicas and banjos. They laughed, swapped stories, drank Grandpa's homemade hootch and sang old country songs.

Silvi felt embarrassed that she had ever referred to these folks as simple hillbillies.

For her it was a much-needed vacation. And being with her grandpa on their historic farm opened her eyes, maybe for the first time, to her roots; to her family's heritage and deep roots. There was nothing to be ashamed of by being part of this culture and history. It was a gift.

The night wore on, and the science also fascinated Silvi. She couldn't absorb enough about the plight of the chestnut. She grasped to the far reaches of her memory, back to her biology and horticultural days, to imagine what it might be that confers resistance to the fungus in Chinese chestnuts, not present in the American chestnut? And she wondered how to scientifically, or genetically make those trees resistant to the fungus? She was captivated by the story, and she couldn't get enough conversation on the research methods already tried over the past 50 years to save the chestnut trees.

Silvi was becoming obsessed. Every waking hour she pored through the history, the personal stories, the work still going on throughout the chestnut range. And she came up with more questions than answers. But she knew exactly who would have some answers, her old mentor, Dr. Nita Baldwin.

CHAPTER THIRTEEN

The American Chestnut Blight

New York City

Summer 1904

THREE MILLION EXCITED, GIDDY CHILDREN PASS THROUGH THE massive, hand-worn, oxidized iron gates each year on school field trips. A day out from classroom claustrophobia, into the world of tigers, elephants, mythical oryx, and of course, gorillas. The childhood adventure they would remember their whole life. The cacophony that is New York City; horns honking, and steam rising around manhole covers, cabbies cursing, and the aroma of roasted chestnuts wafting from every street corner vendor. In the park, few even notice the natural landscape; lichen covered granite boulders, rolling grass hills, the flora of this zoo is simply a backdrop to the animals they've come to see. As they hop off the bus, the children are buzzing. Teachers shooshing and corralling them into line by the entrance to the New York Zoological Society Park; the Bronx Zoo, as it's known around the world.

Bill Craddock had been curator of botany for over 29 years. He'd seen it all. The world was his playground. He and his team of wildlife botanists scoured for specimens of magnificent botanicals to bring home to the zoo. He was the foremost authority on management and maintenance of over three thousand species; from towering red maples to Chinese elms. He knew the process to import and the best methods to manage these specimen trees.

And Bill, he knew a tragedy when he'd seen one. And this was one of epic proportions.

In the sweltering summer of July 1904, the caretakers noticed a stately 200-year-old American chestnut whose leaves were curling and turning a brownish nutmeg color. It was fatigued and cascading dry, desiccated leaves, like it was autumn. The wound on the bark near the base was a course, rugged lesion the color of a bright Halloween squash. Bill knew this was not good. The spotty orange blemish spread around the bark, swelled, and got papery around the edges. The injury crumbled under a light touch. He knew something was very wrong. This was out of his league. Craddock took a sample to the mycologist, Dr. John Murry at the forestry lab.

Murry sat at his small desk; his threadbare chair squeaked every time he moved. His desk and the floor around it were cluttered with decades of old journal findings. He thumbed through every publication that he could get his hands on. His dimly lit office was connected to the lab. The young botanists that worked for him were science geeks. If there was any literature on this fungus, one of them would have heard about it. Not much passed through his lab that he couldn't identify.

"Bill, I've never seen anything like this before. This chestnut is infested with a fungus. It is killing the tree. It appears the tree has no immunity to this infection. I don't have a clue how to treat it."

Neither John nor Bill was certain how the fungus worked to damage the tree, yet they could see it was contagious, because by autumn, most all the chestnuts at the Bronx Zoo were infected and showing orangy cankers and distinct symptoms of the disease. They were stumped. Panic set in as they watched the death of some of the oldest, largest, and most recognizable trees in the zoo.

New York City has long been the gateway to the world. When you come to America, you pass through the ports of this town, from Italian pasta makers to Asian rice merchants. New York was the melting pot of trade; Africans, Asians, Indians, Aussies all coming to test the American experiment. The American dream brought all sorts of "New" materials and problems to our land.

Importation regulations at the turn of the century were lax. This plague was brought in on commercial Asian chestnut trees that grew in harmony with the fungus. The effects of the attack on the Chinese chestnut trees were minimal. Their small cankers would self-heal and wouldn't critically harm the tree or curtail the tree's lifespan. The Chinese trees easily grew and flourished to produce flowers in summer and chestnuts in the fall. The nuts from these trees lacked the flavor and sweetness of its American cousin. And the trees, well they were very different. The Chinese had a spreading, branched trunk, not tall, straight, massive, nor canopied like the American variety.

Within a couple of years, most of New York's chestnut trees were infected with the blight, which spread easily from tree to tree. With no way for the tree to fight off the spores, which dispersed through air, it was impossible to stop the spread.

New York's governor formed a task force. Congressmen from Pennsylvania, New Jersey, Connecticut, and Ohio drafted bills to throw money at the pandemic affecting their forests and farmers. Environmental groups held conferences up and down the Eastern Seaboard. But each attempt seemed to have little effect on the disbursement of spores, further and further in all directions. The expansion of the blight was assisted by the wind, and by animals. Many people attempted treatments and antidotes to heal the infected trees; scraping the wound, applying pesticides and fungicides, treating the trees with lime and salt, blowing sulfur fumes into the canker, scrubbing the fungus off, packing the wound with mud, binding the wound closed, even cutting off infected limbs. But none of those treatments worked. And particularly what did not work was clear cutting swaths of healthy trees in an effort to stop the spread.

All these strategies failed. In fact, some may have contributed to the demise of the forest because the healthy American chestnuts, with possible resistance to the fungus, were chopped down along with the infected ones. This virtually wiped out any hope of trees that might have contained natural immunity, from surviving to repropagate the forests. And to make matters worse, the government encouraged people to "use the wood, before the blight made it worthless."

Soon, death raced up toward Connecticut, then New England, carried by wind and rain for dozens of miles a year. The tree of life., the perfect tree, that fed families, provided lumber, nourished livestock, and sustained the forest and fauna. It disintegrated into oblivion, for a generation that relied on it.

And, sadly, for all generations to come.

This chestnut tree was most reliably harvested in the countryside, and on farms. It provided priceless chestnuts on Thanksgiving and Christmas tables across America. But more importantly, due to the hardness of the wood, with completely straight grain and its resistance to rot, it was the perfect wood for so much of commerce. America was built using this chestnut lumber. These chestnut logs were used for railroad ties and telephone poles, the crafting of fine furniture handed down generation to generation. It was used by artisans and amateurs alike for farmhouse tables, pianos, lumber for barns, cabins, and churches across America. The chestnut tree was the heart of the entire rural East Coast lifestyle and livelihood. And it had always been there, since before man had recorded history in America. One chestnut tree could provide an entire truckload: thousands of board feet of beautiful straight-grained long planks of lumber.

And of course, the nuts were coveted. They were the livelihood of millions of families, as the autumn harvest of railroad cars filled with chestnuts made its way from the East Coast across the continent during the holidays.

Unlike the acorn, it was reliable, every year. You could count on this tree to produce an abundance of chestnuts to feed not only people's wildest kitchen creations, but also the mast of feed for the wild forest animals like bears, squirrels, deer, and birds.

And economically, it was the food source of farm animals; farmers counted on the nuts to graze their livestock in the wild. The sights, the sounds, the smells of the crowned head of the forest, vanished from Earth in an instant.

One in every four trees in the range would succumb to the disease. Within 50 years, the species was functionally extinct. Four billion trees were functionally dead. Millions of dead stumps, a dirge hanging in the air, like a symphony of silence, was all that was left behind. That, and tears.

As the years passed, life changed. Farm memories morphed. Something new took up life without the majesty of the American chestnut. The only things left were the stories told by those who remember the years of bounty. But, those who would remember, the men and women old enough to have memories of the massive trunks and outstretched arms of these giants, they have mostly passed away now. And just a few black and white photos that have survived from the era.

In the laboratory, Dr. Murry worked diligently. He discovered that the blight fungus produced a toxic acid. This acid worked its way through the bark and attacked the vascular system of the tree. The fungus then continued to grow and surround the girth of the tree. It strangled the tree, until food and water could no longer pass up and down the entirety of the trunk. That, he figured out, was the mechanism that suffocated and starved the tree. They become necrotic; leaves turn brown, it stopped producing flowers and nuts, and it ultimately died. It was a sad sight.

As this fungus rapidly annihilated chestnut trees throughout its range in the first half of the 20th century, farmers stood by and felt helpless. Men shook their heads in defeat. Women saw their strong, hard-working men break down. Stress and worry became their constant companions. Devastation, destruction, and fear brought desperation. The Great depression hit at the same time, and many simply lost hope. Tens of thousands of people lived on farms. The farm families depended upon the chestnuts, and there was no choice but to wither in place or pick themselves up by their bootstraps and persevere in a new way of life. It was devastatingly bitter. Those that could, donned a hard hat and went to the coal mines.

But for others it was a test of life. There were no choices for some men. Women and children starved; their men couldn't bear the defeat. Those families with means moved north or west. Thousands of farmers, migrants, unemployed workers migrated south and west in search of work. Many ended up homeless, living in abject poverty.

This was more than the loss of a tree, or a life. This loss echoed far beyond. A way of life, now extinct, a culture's breath now heavily checked. All that was known, now memories, lifted by the wind. A sadness permeated the land, it was the death of a subsistence way of life. A culture snuffed out in one generation.

CHAPTER FOURTEEN

Helpless in Appalachia

Their large, rough hands stroked the trees they knew so well. The dark brown bark rugged with deep ridges and furrows. The height and width of these giants were incomparable. Men ran their fingers down the crevice's and around the clefts in the tree's hard shell. They inspected them, up and down. For thousands of years these large, self-pollinating trees went into hibernation each winter. Always awakening again to spring with a massive explosion of green canopies, summer's long white draping catkin flowers, autumn's reliable, frenzied burrs erupting and dropping copious and bountiful chestnuts.

American chestnuts, of the Beech family, were natives of Eastern North America; *Castanea dentata,* as they were called, dominated the East Coast of the U.S. and they were among the largest, tallest and fastest growing in all of America. But something was wrong, something was very wrong. The men knew it, they could feel it in their gut. And they heard the stories coming down from the north but hoped, prayed that they would be spared. They prayed that the tree that rained down provisions and sustenance for their families, and their livestock, would reliably continue like it had for millennia. It was a part of their core beliefs. It was their reality, like the sun rising or the turn of seasons. They couldn't comprehend life without the majestic, mighty chestnut tree. They couldn't fathom or comprehend how life would change, until reality upended truth…

The speckled orange canker was visible on more and more chestnut trunks. The farmer removed his glasses and got close. He'd never seen anything like it before. He touched it. The fungus invaded more trees every day, wrapping its deathly grip around the girth of the tree. The papery orange pellicle collapsed beneath his fingers and spores from the mold scattered everywhere in madness. He brought his fingers to his nose and took a sniff, looked at them again and then wiped his hand on the back of his overalls. Farmers of southwest Appalachia had never seen anything like it before, and they didn't have a clue what to do. This fungus was clearly sapping the very life out of the forest. They stood confounded, pondering theories and prophecies to save the chestnuts. They gathered by fireplaces sharing stories they had heard coming down from the North. "Nothing had worked", they said. "The Gods must be angry," claimed others.

But there must be something to kill off the fungus that's snuffing out these massive life-giving trees. These tired farmers wouldn't give up, they couldn't give up.

Gravel crunched under the tires of the old faded blue farm truck. The cab bench was threadbare, and the flatbed strewn with straw. Frank and Jack lumbered out with their boys in tow. The government men said that any hope of saving the chestnut forest would be to get the infected trees out and to salvage any decent wood to sell to the lumber mills. They shuffled up the front stairs that creaked with each step. Paint peeling off the handrail and floorboards, reminding them what took priority on the farm. The screen door thwacked behind them. Everyone mumbled good mornings, and the wife handed the men a mug of hot cider.

The men and boys all headed out with saws and chains, to fell as much wood as they could. Frank had already tried the fungicide on several trees on his land, and it didn't help any more than slathering it with pudding. Some men put acid on the cankers, and some cleaned out the cankers and packed them with mud and wrapped them closed. Most resorted to praying. The blight was oblivious to these efforts and advanced to the next farm, and the next farm, and the next state. They would try anything, as reality set in and with it panic and desperation. They were broken and overcome with exhaustion and stress. But they wouldn't give up. Not until they were plumb out of ideas, defeated, lost, and broken. Because only then could they accept that everything they knew as life would soon unravel.

Women stared from afar. They stood guard on their well-worn, wooden wraparound decks, heads cocked trying to read their men's expressions. They stood vigilant, leaning against the solid posts that held up the deck cover, and the weight of the world. This was their land, their home. This was all they knew how to do. The women stood by, watched their men squat on their hams, reflect, and speculate on how to save their beloved chestnut trees. Children gathered around their mother's feet, clinging to the modest cotton dress that was made of the fabric exchanged for chestnuts last fall.

The women, as they watched the trees, one by one, die and turn to crippled, bare ghosts of their former selves, beseeched the power above, that their husbands would not follow suit. They knew there was nothing they could do, but "pray like hell" that their families would survive the death of these trees without too much suffering. They braced, and cried out, "Please don't let this be the undoing of our men." The women and the children relied on them. Relied on their strength, stability, and tenacity against the odds they faced through the seasons of their challenging lives. The men, the farmers of the land, were the anchor and security that allowed homesteaders to survive. But they too were mortal and there was a point that even they would break. And the women knew this. The women stood vigil; pleaded and bargained with the heavens and God to just let them get through this plague, this devastation. And find a way to carry on, here on their land. The land that was their home.

CHAPTER FIFTEEN

New York City
Silvi Hayes
1987

Silvi arrived back in New York City, after her extended farm visit and was already missing her Grandpa Tucker. She stayed in Virginia far longer than she intended, but relished the diversion from her hectic life. As she dropped her bags the phone rang.

"Hello?"

"Hey, lil missy, it was good to hear from you," said the voice on the other end.

"Hey, Nita. Thanks for calling back. I literally just walked in."

"Do you need some time to get settled?" Nita inquired.

"No, No, I'm dying to chat with you," said Silvi.

Nita caught her up on the people she used to work with and what they have been up to at the lab.

"Silvi, you've been on my mind lately, so I'm thrilled you reached out. What is going on with you, and what are you up to now? Your message sounded intriguing," questioned Nita.

"Well, I just spent two weeks in Virginia at our family farm. And I met a guy that is at the University of Virginia, Dr. Luke Woodbury. He is working on the chestnut blight problem using viruses to counter the damaging effects of the fungus that infects and kills the American chestnut.

We were with a group of older neighbors, and I didn't have a chance to completely understand what caused the blight and physiologically how the blight killed an entire forest of trees.

But, I remember years ago you were working on a project with the chestnut blight and thought you might fill me in? I'm simply fascinated by the ecological devastation that this blight caused and what, if anything, can be done to bring back the chestnut to its native range?"

"Well, Silvi, this is going to take more than a Sunday afternoon phone call. But yes, you remembered correctly. We have been working on these exact questions and looking for answers to explain the death of the American chestnut."

She thought for a moment about how detailed she could get with Silvi, then went on, "For years we have been trying to identify the mechanism that strangles the tree and a possible pathway to interrupt it so the chestnut could once again live in the wild."

Nita took a breath and went on, "What I can tell you is that we have learned a lot since you've been gone. Let me give you a little history."

"First, what we know from years of research is that the disease was imported somewhere just before the turn of the century. It came over quite by accident, carried on Asian chestnut trees. Research done at the New York Zoological Park found a parasite that quickly kills its host. It was a fungus. But, having never seen this fungus before, the majestic American chestnut had no resistance to the disease that the Asian trees seemed to be able to fight off. They found that deadly spores from this fungus propagated and spread quickly. We estimated at least 50 miles a year," Nita hesitated a moment.

"Are you with me so far?"

Silvi said, "Yes, yes, I'm jotting notes, please go on."

Nita continued "The American trees hopelessly capitulated, like dominoes, one by one across the Eastern Seaboard. For thousands of years, they were the most dominant of all trees in the eastern half of the United States, and in a blink of an eye were gone."

"Did all the chestnuts in its path die?" asked Silvi.

"Most all eventually did," said Nita.

"As the epidemic marched from state to state, farm to farm, forest to forest it left in its path ... nothing. Nothing but shadows of former giants, high above the forest canopy. They are a bitter reminder of a gentler time, an abundant time when the forest sent it's blessing of prosperity to the Earth to carry on life with yet another windfall bounty and sustenance for millions of families for another year."

"I can only imagine how devastating it was to these people. No wonder my father moved off the farm for a better life," Silvi thought.

"This blight was probably the world's greatest environmental collapse in the history of mankind. And, as unintentional as it might have been, we, in reckless pursuit of capitalistic evolution, cut off the hand that fed us and created a functionally extinct tree of life," shared Nita.

"That is an incredible story," Silvi muttered. "When I was at the farm in MeadowBrook these past two weeks, I heard a lot of stories from the women who lived through it. They talked of how their lives changed, how they had believed those chestnut trees would always be there with their bounty. They are old now, like my grandpa, but telling stories about the blight still brought tears to their eyes."

"Is there anything that can be done to bring the American chestnut back from the brink of extinction?" asked Silvi.

Nita went on, "Perhaps not all is lost, as the fungus doesn't attack the roots of chestnut trees. Although the fungus is everywhere in the ground, it doesn't seem to harm anything below ground.

To be more specific, the orange fungus secretes acid. The acid breaks down the tissue and blocks the pathway of food and water and eventually it creeps around the girth of the tree under the bark and simply chokes the tissue above the canker. The tree can't survive that. It literally starves to death."

Nita took a breath, then she continued, "For the American chestnut to come back to its rightful place in the Eastern United States, we would need to find a way to mitigate the effects of the fungus, which to date has not been successful, although not for lack of trying."

"So, you see, this is what your friend Dr. Luke Woodbury is working on. I believe they have found a strain of a virus, called *Hypovirus*, that entwines the fungus. It literally neutralizes it, and thereby gives the tree a chance to heal the damage from the blight and survive."

"I see, so that is something very different than what you have been working on to alter the DNA gene that confers immunity in the chestnut tree?"

"Yes, there are a several other methods too.

One uses basic genetic science to crossbreed an American chestnut with a blight resistant Chinese chestnut, with the hope of conferring the blight resistance to the offspring trees.

So, far it has not been successful, but the idea is it would take several crossbreeding's, over years, to keep the desirable characteristics of the American chestnut, such as; tall, hard wood, straight timber with no limbs for dozens of feet, the rot resistance, the fast growth, and the smaller, sweeter nuts. And at the same time, breed for the gene in the Chinese chestnut that confers resistance to the fungus without including the other undesirable traits like shorter height, branchier, less reliable mast of nuts, and less tasty nuts," Nita explained.

"It's a long-range challenge, but idealistically they believe it's possible," Nita stated matter of factly.

"Nita, it's fascinating to me, how can I learn more?"

"Ahhh Silvi, we here at the Environmental College labs are identifying the genetic code of the American chestnut and attempting to insert a gene from another plant that neutralizes the acid that kills the tree. Simply put, we genetically modify the chestnut to include the immunity genes that will naturally confer resistance to the blight for the American chestnut."

Silvi stopped and realized that the work Nita was doing in her lab was what she vehemently fought against in her younger years… Genetic Modification! Tampering with nature by stealing a gene from one plant and inserting it into a completely different plant. She gasped at this realization. She felt torn between restoring nature with its simple life that had been stolen from her ancestors, and that of today's technology to accomplish just that, through modern science. Her brain was whirling.

"Nita, how is that research going? Where do you find the gene that neutralizes the acid?"

Without saying so, Nita could sense the wheels turning in Silvi's head. She could feel her friend balancing, vulnerable, on a highwire, about to tumble into a vast abyss without a net.

She wanted to be there to catch her. And knew it would be best to name the elephant in the room.

"Silvi, you may not know that many edible plants carry this gene already, so we know it's safe. But, as you are aware, it is an uphill battle for some folks who are against using Genetically Modified Organisms in farming."

Silvi vividly recalled all her years leading community activism against GMOs, since before she came to Syracuse. This was a real dilemma for Silvi, as she was battling her demons between strongly held philosophical beliefs against genetic modification, and her real-world truths about science's capability and its potential role in saving an iconic life from extinction.

She was struggling. This realization snapped her back to the nights of hand-made signs, and all the demonstrations she organized. The lobbying she did in Washington, D.C., against GMOs. And yet the science of it still fascinated her. The push and pull of her environmental heart, duking it out with her scientific brain.

Changing the subject, Nita said, "The last method to save the forests would be to find the very few American chestnut trees in the natural range that survived the blight. These few trees for some reason seem to have a natural resistance to the acid that the fungus produces. Those trees theoretically could be bred with each other to attain as many of them as possible to reproduce and reforest the population. However, this would take many, many hundreds of generations and its unlikely this method alone would ever succeed at repopulating the four billion trees that died out."

Nita continued, "It's unlikely any one single method will be successful. It is entirely possible that all four of these methods, and maybe others yet to be discovered, will need to be integrated to bring back the grand wild American chestnut of your dad and your grandpa's youth."

Silvi didn't say a word.

"One thing is for sure; the road is long. It's hard to be optimistic in the face of all the challenges and obstructions that will undoubtedly come our way. So far, the vision of your grandpa's American chestnut forest, it's a pipe dream."

Silvi was discouraged at Nita's overwhelming explanation. She was tired from her travels and needed to unpack so she could get back to work the next morning.

Nita was right about one thing; this wasn't a Sunday evening telephone call. She would need time to research and to think.

"Let me leave you with one thought, Silvi. For Americans to ever see chestnut trees growing again in places that possess its name, one thing is for certain. We will need capable people willing to do the work, to understand the challenges. We will need an organization whose sole purpose is to promote the rebirth and reforestation of the American chestnut. Someone with the scientific and legal background to take on a 100-year enterprise and be passionate enough to dedicate her life to understanding the effects, the positive and negative, of taking on such an endeavor."

Silvi was silent. Her brain was spinning so fast. She heard everything Nita said, and she was processing it in slow motion. She felt something she had never experienced before. She didn't know if it was excitement or fear. Maybe it was… Purpose.

She just knew that an entire culture, a way of life, millions of families hopes and dreams were snuffed out in one generation and almost nobody alive was left to tell the story of the nation that was changed in a nanosecond of time. An ecological community of billions of kindred spirits turned into lifeless and hopeless ghosts in a fraction of a heartbeat in time.

What came to her in that instant was; how is it that there haven't been angry protests, a massive uprising to this desecration. It's a ravaging travesty, a wrongdoing that needs a voice. It's an affront to the natural world that cannot just be swept under the rug and forgotten. Someone must stand up for what's right. It is a disgrace of humanity that needs to see the light of day. We need to face the consequences of our decisions, even if they were unintentional.

Silvi needed time to think.

"Nita, thank you for explaining this to me. It is so much to comprehend. Far more questions now that need answers. But for this moment, there is one thing that baffles me… How is it that so few people know about this devastating travesty of American history?"

"That's a great question, Silvi. I've asked myself that 4 billion times."

The two friends said goodnight. And promised to reconnect soon.

Silvi called Brad as soon as she hung up with Nita and told him all about her trip. She rambled on so that Brad didn't have a chance to get a word in edgewise. But that was okay, because he really wasn't looking forward to having this conversation. Brad met a woman working on the campaign, and she swept him off his feet. He was smitten with her. He felt guilt, and was embarrassed, but his relationship with Silvi seemed to be going nowhere, and his heart and head were no longer in it.

He wanted to tell Silvi in person, but he was leaving again the next day on the campaign trail and wouldn't be back in New York for three more weeks. She asked if they could meet tonight and grab a quick dinner at their favorite little Italian place. Mama Marchi's was at 231 E 31st street, midway between where they each lived. She loved how there was no menu, but an old Italian grandma that cooked in the kitchen every night and brought out course after course of food. Dinner always ended with homemade tiramisu or homemade cannoli and a glass of Anisette.

But Brad was just so exhausted and had dozens of voice mails to answer and he needed to pack for his trip in the morning. He said "Silvi,

I just can't even think about food or running around the city tonight. But I promise I'll call tomorrow, and we'll have a serious catch up."

She blew him a kiss through the phone and said "Fine, good night."

Neither one said, "I love you."

Silvi was a little put off, as she thought after being apart for two weeks, Brad might have planned better to spend one night with her before he took off again. But she also understood what pressure he was under and didn't want to add to that by complaining. Her thoughts went to MeadowBrook, her grandpa and her new friend Luke. She was suddenly embarrassed by that. Luke was so attentive to her; he made her feel important, and it felt good. It had been such a long time since Brad looked at her the way Luke had. But she was engaged, and she loved Brad, and they had so much history, although it felt as if their life had really drifted apart. After the election, they would be together. And they would start making plans for their married life. After a long wait, it was just a few more months. It was October and the campaign would wind down the first week of January, win or lose. They had waited this long, a few more months wouldn't make a tad bit of difference.

Silvi started to unpack and crawled into bed early with a bowl of popcorn. She wanted to know more about the chestnuts, but it would be on the back burner for now because there was so much work waiting on her desk and a full calendar of commitments and events coming up this week. After a couple of hours of catching up on paperwork, Silvi fell asleep, only to wake again at 10:00 pm. The light was still on, and her files were strewn all over the bed. She got up to brush her teeth and when she got back into bed, she felt badly about how she got off the phone with Brad, so she called to say goodnight.

The phone rang and rang. Finally, a woman answered, "Brad Spalding's Phone," the voice said. There was silence. Silvi was stunned and did not know what to say.

"Um, may I speak to Brad, please?" Silvi murmured, confused.

The woman on the other end of the line declared in a Southern drawl, "Oh, he's in the shower, may I take a message?"

"Umm...yes, tell him his former fiancée called!"

Silvi got off the phone. She took a deep breath. She could not move. She didn't cry. She wasn't even angry. Shock better described her feeling. Disbelief. She wondered how long this had been going on. She felt betrayed and for a moment lost. Then, she felt something unknown to her, relief, and freedom.

Everyone just expected her and Brad to get married, but the truth is for an exceedingly long time, she felt that Brad was more like a brother than a romantic life partner. It had become simply comfortable.

When she and Brad first moved to New York City, they were a rising power couple. She thought, how lucky she was to have her best friend as her husband and looked forward to the active high-profile life, hobnobbing in Manhattan. It was always edgy. The sum of them together was more than each of them alone. They were powerful agents of change, and their intensity out in the world had peaked. The privilege of it was quite enchanting, almost addicting.

Being involved in law or politics is like a drug. But soon there is nothing but the drug, and you always need more of it. Once one campaign starts, you're looking for the next gig. It's the same with high profile legal cases, especially around environmental law, because they are always representing 'David fighting Goliath'. Which made the wins that much sweeter. But it is exhausting, with never an end in sight.

Silvi sat on the edge of her bed, her head dropped to her chest, her long silky chestnut hair fell about her face, one big alligator tear ran down her cheek and fell on her lap. She stared at it and took what might have been the deepest breath she had taken in years. She removed the engagement ring from her finger and put it in its velvet shrouded box and snapped it shut. She crawled into bed. The phone rang seven times. She closed the light and didn't set her alarm.

The next morning, she woke with the sun as she had become accustomed during the past two weeks on the farm. She missed the sound of the rooster and thought how different the buzz of life was here in the hub of America, the pulse of finance, law, art, and everything that was her life in Manhattan. New York City made her feel alive, invigorated and a part of the heartbeat of America. You experience the evening news firsthand, as it unfolds. It all happens on the streets, the offices, the restaurants, and the cultural centers of this city.

Yet, there is a fierce and unrelenting energy. A drive that sweeps you up like a wave into a ruthless and unflinching urgency for more. And more. And more. A hunger to be at the top of the heap, to be the best. And it never ends. Each success is a momentary lift and then the circus begins again. New York is like that. When you are in its clutches there is no moderation. It consumes your every thought, your every action, it engulfs you until you lose yourself to the contraption you created.

The next morning Silvi never bothered to listen to the messages that Brad had left. She didn't want to be distracted. She dressed in her favorite St. John, navy colored, knit business suit, with her matching high heels. She wore her sexiest black lace lingerie under the suit. The epitome of a take-charge, professional woman. She grabbed her leather briefcase, deadbolted her apartment door and stepped onto the elevator. Not saying a word, she nodded to the man staring at the numbers above her head in the elevator. Outside, the early morning air snapped at her cheeks. She hopped into a Yellow Cab and numbly watched the Big Apple come alive.

Silvi got her day started with cases she had left unfinished and with new files other lawyers needed her to review. The ringing phones, the buzz of assistants chattering incessantly, and the bubble of a water cooler all distracted her. She closed her corner office door. She turned in her chair to look at the busy scene below, overlooking Central Park, wishing she were back in MeadowBrook.

The next two weeks she put her nose to the grindstone and got caught up on everything that was pending on her docket. She tried a small case. It was a brainless win, but it didn't give her the thrill she normally felt after a successful day in court. She was going through the motions but felt nothing. She was numb. At night she went home and worked until the wee hours. She slept just enough to get her by, and up again to the office for yet another long day.

She finally talked to Brad. Strangely, she felt no animosity and they said they would stay friends, but she knew they would not. He had moved on and she felt relief at being able to pursue her dreams and goals unencumbered. Whatever they would be.

Silvi felt less and less attached to the high-powered New York priviledged life that she had created for herself.

CHAPTER SIXTEEN

New York City Bustle

Before dawn he moved about their lighted bathroom, eyes still half closed. Coffee pot on timer already percolated a full day's brew. The wife handed him a muffin as he headed to the elevator and straightened his tie. His raincoat thrown over his arm. The door slid open, and he stepped on. The car was packed like sardines, but no one said a word, they just stared up at the numbers...32, 31, 29, 24, ding, a bleary-eyed, coiffed woman in patent leather high heels, navy suit and silk scarf stepped on and squeezed in the front corner with a simple nod, yet not a word was spoken. Nobody took their eyes off the numbers above the door, but they recognized her perfume, Chanel No. 5. The elevator descended again 23, 21, 19, 10, 2, ding ding, the doors slid open and each silently stepped into the lobby, and out the revolving door to the drizzly streets of New York City. I tell ya', there is no place on Earth quite like the hum of "The City." The doorman is in his fancy suit and overcoat, a top hat covered in plastic against the rain. He hails a cab for the man, who gets in and mumbles 11 Wall Street. The cabbie's silver cross dangling from his rear-view mirror and the picture of his girl taped on his well-worn dashboard.

"Hey Mack, FDR drive has a F'in' accident, I'm gonna head

through Chinatown." The man's face buried in the morning Journal pretends not to hear him, but exhales a deep annoyed sigh.

For the well healed, the fast-paced life of The City is sensory overload. There is no traffic etiquette, cabs make the rules, darting in and out of side roads. The plethora of cabbies honking, flipping the bird and loudly yelling choice words to anyone in their way. The City's vibrant culture is on full display at every hour of the day and night. It is the pulse of America, and some say the world. From politics to business, to the arts, and sciences, the constant buzz of activity in New York City envelops you.

The people are vibrant and alive in New York; bustling pedestrians are blind to the steam from subways pluming through grates on the sidewalks as the chatter of street vendors fills the air. There is a dissonance that is the Big Apple. Throughout the soaring concrete towers, the city is besieged with smells of food from all over the world; freshly baked bread, sizzling meat, seductive pastries, fragrant Mid-Eastern spices, pizza, pizza, pizza. Nowhere in America is pizza more cherished than New York. "Eh, it's the water," they say. The crisp crust with a slightly chewy dough, the perfect Italian red sauce, rich with sweet oregano, garlic, and the mozzarella that stretches an arm's length with every bite. Mouthwatering doesn't begin to describe the smell, taste, texture, to the last finger licking morsel. And during autumn, vendor carts are pushed by old ethnic men in worn grey pea coats, and tattered, fraying-fingered wool gloves. On every street corner, these men hunch over baskets of red-hot coals. These carts define the breath of The City, from Washington Heights to the Battery, brimming with the scent of slightly smoky, roasted chestnuts. That is the essence and elixir of New York.

The depth and complexity of NYC is unmatched in energy and experience. Lincoln Center, the Met, the Museum of Natural History, and Carnegie Hall, where bright lights and the roar of a crowd are nonstop. The City is home to world-renowned museums, theaters, and art galleries, offering a wealth of cultural and historical experiences.

The hub of competitive business and finance attracts people from around the world, who have their finger on the pulse of opportunity, power, and wealth.

No place is more fast paced or bustling than the New York Stock Exchange, in the heart of Wall Street; "I got 500 shares of PFE", I'll take it, execute the trade. 10,000 JNJ at market price. Done." Hundreds of people rushing around, shouting, and gesturing as they try to buy and sell securities. The atmosphere is electric, intense, and chaotic. Just like outside those walls.

Anything you could ever want, or need is within these few square miles called Manhattan. It's easy to get caught up in the passion and power. Native New Yorkers love the pace and the droning beat. It's easy to get lost in the competition and greed. There's no choice if you're climbing the corporate ladder. Being seen at the best parties is mandatory. A weekend at the Hamptons, lunch on top of Central Park, dinner parties at mansions, hobnobbing with the rich, powerful, and famous. Risk and speculation are the adventure, and it's addicting: the promotion, the court win, the coveted invitation. To step away, for even a moment, is suicide to your career. Cut-throat and backstabbing define the backdrop. You need to be on your game, always, or you are obsolete and insignificant. But the win is sweet! And worth the effort. The City life, there is nothing grander.

The man wakes on a Thursday morning before daybreak, moves in the dim light of the bathroom, steps out of the shower, eyes half closed and with a start, his breath, sharp against his lungs, the crushing heaviness, he grasps his chest, winces, and collapses onto the cold, polished Italian marble floor. His cheeks turn white as alabaster, his lips blue and his eyes roll back in his head. His wife hears the thud, "Robert?" she calls from bed. She gasps, runs, calls 911 and in moments sirens blare as they screech up to the lobby and lift to the 32nd floor. On the gurney he comes to. The paramedics are asking him simple questions about the day; "Who's the president? Do you know your name?" His wife, she weeps and holds his hand. Her name could be Dianna, Cynthia, Katherine ... "This was our wakeup call Robert. Oh God, this was our wake-up call."

This time he survived. But things will change.

"We need to overhaul our life! Be intentional about what we put in our mouths. We know the benefits of a plant-based diet, 8 hours of sleep, getting more exercise. How did this happen? Swept up in this crazy, exhilarating, demanding, exhausting, exciting life. Busy, busy, busy."

Robert mumbled "No more muffins and donuts for breakfast. And we need regular exercise, we can do it together."

"Agreed, we can do this together, it's long overdue," said his wife.

And the vision grew in that moment, her face illuminated from within. She declared "We are done with this rat race. There is more to life than this. We are making a break. We were blinded by power and money. We lost reality for what is valuable; family, comfortably surrounded by nature and a real home. What good is all the money in the world if you aren't here to share it, to make memories. No discussion. Life changes today. And we must be so grateful to have a second chance."

Robert started to say, "But...."

She cut him off. "No! Now, not tomorrow, now. We are going to find a place in the country," she cried through tears. "We are going to get back to our roots. The pressure, the strain is too much, it's not worth it. I love you, Robert. And, the kids and I want to have you around for a long time. No discussion."

"But now's not the time. I have so many projects, obligations on my calendar."

She ignored him, moved within an inch of his face, her eyes lit up and she spoke in a low voice "Darling, let's move back to the country. Do you remember the warm embrace of the sun on our cheeks when we sat in the big wooden rockers in Upstate New York? Do you remember the gentle breeze rustling through the corn in the fields. Picking fresh summer berries and the smell of fruit pies baking, the rich smells wafting out the front window. Simple pleasures we haven't had in so long."

"Hmm, yeah, I remember, those are wonderful memories," Robert responded wearily.

In his dazed state Robert envisioned it too. "We'll get our own little farmhouse that we can fix up. And have our own vegetable garden, grow potatoes, and carrots, beets, and a whole variety of tomatoes fresh from the vine. Getting our hands in the earthy, rich soil and the smell of freshly cut grass, and sweetness of wildflowers in the meadows. I'm at home, I love being in nature, always have," he said groggily.

"Yes, back to nature, a community and simple pleasures and experiences that somehow got replaced by "*Things*," too many things, material things. And burdens, obligations, urgency," fantasized Robert out loud.

They knew life on a farm was not just about the beauty and bounty of the land. It would also be hard work and the determination that is required to tend the fields, caring for animals, and maintaining the gardens. But it's about the sense of community and family built among the people who live and work there, bonded together by a shared love of the land, and a common goal of sustainability.

In the end, life in the country is a rich and rewarding experience, filled with the joys of nature and the satisfaction of a job well done.

"Life will be different, priorities, priorities, priorities. What really is important in this brief lifetime?" the wife is decisive, and he does not argue.

CHAPTER SEVENTEEN

Grandpa Tucker's Birthday

MeadowBrook, Virginia

October 15, 1987

SEVERAL WEEKS HAD GONE BY SINCE THE BREAKUP. GRANDPA Tucker's birthday was coming up on Saturday. Silvi decided to fly down to Virginia to celebrate with him. And to surprise him with the little beagle puppy that the Burnham's dog had delivered. She was so excited to see her grandpa light up when he laid eyes on his new little buddy. He was very lonely since his faithful dog passed away. He talked about finding another one, but he just couldn't imagine loving one as much as his old friend, Pal. Her grandpa was a champion procrastinator, so Silvi knew he would not have found a new best friend yet. But, he would be thrilled to have the companionship, and a beagle would be the perfect fit for him.

Silvi left New York early on Friday and made her return ticket for Monday morning. She arrived at the farm at four o'clock. Her mom and dad were already there. She hadn't seen them since they left MeadowBrook in July. They didn't usually go that long between visits, but she had been so busy at work, and with the breakup with Brad, she wasn't much in the mood for a five-hour drive or a visit home. These weeks had been stressful, and she was excited to get out of the city and mostly to see her family.

Plus, Silvi was looking forward to talking with her dad about his memories growing up with the chestnut trees, and what life was like for him then. She also wanted to know what it was like when the trees fell ill. Ben was always happy to talk about his childhood. It was warm, loving and always filled with joy. What was difficult for Ben was the period after his mom died. The chestnut trees started to die in the same year, and nothing was the same after that. Silvi knew it would be a hard conversation for her dad, but she just had to know.

Ben was about 12 years old, and he always said that it was the hardest time of his life.

But, through hardship he grew up. And he embraced that. It was a period that shaped and defined his becoming a man. Everything about life was hard then. Ben swore that when he did grow up, he would get out of there. He wanted to have a career, put a roof over his head, and have a family that he would raise away from poverty. He would be sure they got educated. And not in a one room schoolhouse with a bunch of country bumpkins.

Out of respect for his dad though, he never spoke those words, but his actions were loud enough, for anyone that knew him. They would've known that the minute he was old enough, he would be as far from rural Virginia as his hasty little feet would take him.

Ben had good memories, but also demons, that he never wanted to discuss. But it wouldn't stop Silvi from asking.

It was a wonderful birthday reunion and Grandpa was sure surprised to see his favorite girl. He didn't think she'd be back until Thanksgiving, at the earliest, or maybe Christmas. They sat in front of the big old fireplace listening to the logs crackling and popping the way they did with freshly chopped timber. It smelled so good. Being around the people she loved the most gave her great comfort. Silvi was glad she decided to hop down for the weekend. After a hearty dinner of chicken, baked potatoes and the last of the summer asparagus, they all sat outside on the porch and watched the fireflies dance around the pumpkin patch.

They got caught up on MeadowBrook's gossip, the obituaries

and all of Grandpa's troublemaking. Everyone hit the sack early that evening in anticipation for the big birthday which would start with Silvi making her famous, homemade, breakfast sticky buns. The old familiar smells of home. Things she did not have in New York. The smell of yeasty dough rising and baking in their old farmstead oven.

Silvi was up early the next morning and had the sticky buns in the oven and the coffee brewing before anyone else was awake. She loved her quiet mornings alone, before the sun rose. She took her coffee outside on the old creaky, wrap-around deck. The screen door squeaked as she opened it and thwack, thwack, thwack as it slammed closed behind her. The color of autumn had crept in, and the mornings were brisk. She could see her breath as she sat wrapped in a fluffy bathrobe on the old white peeling-paint Adirondack chair, sipping her coffee, black. This was the same chair she and her grandpa shared when she was a child growing up during her summer vacations. Silvi would climb up in her grandpa's lap and lay her head on his warm chest. She remembered how she would always listen to the beating of his heart ,and the sounds of his voice, as he told her stories and taught her about life in Appalachia.

It was colder than usual for this time of year, and she wrapped herself in an old quilt and tucked her legs underneath, like a pretzel. She had on no makeup, her hair pulled back in a ponytail, and if you didn't know better, she could have passed for a 20-year-old. Silvi thought about the forest and this land. How it nourished her family for generations. She always loved autumn best and couldn't even imagine how much more she would have loved it with the chestnut trees this time of year. With their veritable free feast of nuts for the taking.

Her gaze swept up onto the forest above, just as her dad popped out, with a hot sticky bun and a cup of coffee. He sat on the chair next to her and tousled her hair.

"Silvi, it's so good to see you," Ben said.

"How are you managing in your new life of freedom?"

"Oh, Dad, my only regret is that I spent so much time, wasted so much time, waiting and thinking Brad was the love of my life, like Grandpa and Bessie. And you and Mom."

"I guess more than anything, I'm grateful that we didn't marry young and have children. It would have changed our lives and there is no way I could be where I am today had we taken that path," Silvi conjectured.

"The universe works in mysterious ways, my child, but it's always perfect. It unfolds just as it is supposed to," said Ben.

"Dad, I know that you and Mom have sacrificed a lot to give me a good life. You've given me a wonderful education. I've always wanted to make you proud. I've got a passion to preserve and protect nature and our natural resources, like you have. You've been an amazing role model, an example for my life. I feel the work I do is important. I've repaid all my student loans, and I know I can always find a job in environmental law because there is always something or someone to fight for. But right now, I feel as if I need a break from the rat race. I don't feel that spending my life in a Manhattan law firm, cooped inside concrete walls, fighting big corporations is the best use of my time. Don't get me wrong, I know it's important, for sure, but I don't feel a passion for the fight. I don't feel that it's fulfilling my purpose."

"I see. Law is a very noble career, sweetheart, making a difference to not only your clients, but to the greater good of the environment seems like a bold lifelong goal. If it is not this, then what do you think your passion or purpose might be?" asked Ben.

"That's a great question Dad. I am not sure, but I feel that taking a step back from my fast-paced life in New York feels right. I know it must seem crazy to you, at the top of my game, in demand across the country for environmental protection lawsuits, and patent infringement cases. I'm confident that those could keep me busy for decades and make me very rich. But the fire is gone. Maybe it's a phase that will pass, but I dread going into the office. I go through the motions but feel completely numb."

She sat quietly for a moment and continued, "I know you have worked so hard to give me a path out of the poverty you grew up in. A life away from Appalachia and the people who are stuck in this life for generation after generation. I am so grateful for that. I'm just..." Silvi paused. "I don't know, confused."

"Silvi, you know that your mom and I will always support whatever path you feel is right for you. But, you are good at what you do. You're a successful lawyer. And being a woman in a man's world has taken a huge effort, twice the work, for half the recognition. Look Honey, I grew up in poverty. I was uneducated and promised myself ,and Rebecca, that our child would never go hungry, never know what it's like to go to bed at night not knowing where her next meal would come from. We made it our goal to give you the opportunity of education and to create a life you love. Mom and I are very proud of you, but what we want more than anything is for you to be happy."

"We have provided the tools, and direction, and now it's your life path. We will always be here to support whatever you want to do."

She felt so relieved, "Thank you, Dad."

He kissed her on the head and went inside for a second sticky bun. By then, Grandpa was up, and so was Mom. Ben poured coffee for them, kissed his wife, and wished his dad a great big happy birthday. With a bear hug and a smooch on the cheek, "Happy birthday Pa. You are looking pretty darn spry for an old codger," as he kissed his dad on the head.

The sun rose and Silvi came inside and joined in the first rendition of the "happy birthday" singing for the day. She kissed her grandpa and giggled while she told him that she was off to pick up his birthday present, as she gave him a little wink and a gleeful snicker.

"Oh, that one, that one has some secret up her sleeve, I can just tell by the glint in her big blue eyes," declared Tucker.

She had that whimsical laugh that she sported since childhood when she was plotting something clandestine.

Silvi finished her coffee and took a long hot shower. Life was different in this little homestead cabin; from the time her dad grew up here.

Now they had indoor plumbing, hot running water, a real refrigerator, and electric lights. Still there was something very primitive about the home, not much changed on the decor since Bessie died, and Tucker liked it that way.

Silvi had told the Burnhams that she'd be by in the early afternoon to pick out the first of the litter. She could hardly wait. Before she left, she called that Dr. Woodbury to see if he wanted to join them for tonight's celebration.

"Hey Luke, this is Silvi Hayes, I'm back in MeadowBrook and its Grandpa's birthday. We are having a little celebration tonight. I was wondering if you might be available to join us?"

He was delighted to hear from Silvi and didn't hesitate one second ,responding that he'd love to join the festivities. She knew his drive was about an hour and a half so she had already talked to his aunt and uncle to be sure they were home and would be coming to the party. That way she knew he could stay late and not worry about driving back home in the middle of the night. Plus, she was anxious to hear more about his work with the *Hypovirus* on the chestnut blight, and the advances they were making at the lab. Silvi had questions, and wanted to ask him if there was really any way to bring back the chestnut to Appalachia and its native range.

Silvi arrived at the Burnham's at 1:00 to see the bundle of long puppy ears on the litter of beagle babies. She was bubbling with excitement as Mrs. Burnham opened the door. Silvi got down on the ground and those tiny 8-week-old pups tumbled right on top of her. There is nothing quite as cute as a beagle puppy. With their big brown eyes, and their long, soft ears, dragging on the floor as they climbed over each other. They still smelled of momma's milk. That oatsy sweet puppy breath is like nothing else in the world. She rolled around with them and tossed a ball and kissed each one on their little whiskered faces.

She didn't realize that she had been sitting on the floor for over an hour, just talking to them and rolling on the ground. There were six pups, four girls and two boys. One of the boys kept nuzzling under her right leg. She picked him up and looked him right in the eye and said "Ok, little buddy, you're gonna have a new home with the greatest man on Earth. He's gonna be your new best friend, you will be exceedingly loved. And you will be his companion and you will be his incentive to get up every day to face another sunrise, no longer alone."

Mrs. Burnham said, "Oh, you've chosen little Phil. He is a lovebug, he only wants to snuggle close and give "Pup kisses."

They both laughed.

"I think he will be a perfect companion for Tucker." Silvi had brought a wide powder blue grosgrain ribbon to tie a big bow around the pup's neck, and she brought a beautiful extra-large picnic basket with a fluffy, soft, light blue blanket inside. She asked the Burnhams to bring "Phil" along to the party tonight. She thanked them, gave them each a big hug and bounced out.

"See you at 7 o'clock," she called back.

Grandpa Tucker had a wonderful birthday. Thirty family, friends and neighbors came bundled up for a night under the stars. There was too much food and lots of laughter. He made his way around to each guest, talking and reminiscing about all the good times and fond memories together over the years.

Silvi spent most of her evening talking to Dr. Luke Woodbury.

She had to admit, she was curious about this man and wondered what motivated him. She was particularly interested in his work with the chestnut trees. Luke was clearly intelligent. She knew that fact, all the way back to when she was 8 years old. He had kind eyes with long dark eyelashes that naturally curled up on the ends, the kind that women are always jealous of. He also had a warm smile and perfectly white teeth.

Silvi found out that although their grandparents had been lifelong friends, his mom and dad raised him near Charlottesville. Luke attended the University of Virginia and got degrees in agriculture and environmental sciences. And then, he got his PhD from University of Pennsylvania in their department of ecosystem science and management.

"So, Luke, did you always want to work in research?" Silvi inquired.

"Yeah, Silvi, I have to say, nature and the mysteries of the forest always fascinated me. I loved the laboratories and the never-ending experiments, they felt like real life puzzles to me. And I enjoyed school, which is why I went on to become a professor in forest biology at the University of Virginia. Plus, the longer I stayed at school, the longer I avoided getting a real job." They both laughed at his absurd joke.

"So, tell me Luke, what projects have you worked on?"

"My work has primarily focused on sustainable environmental ethics, conservation, and the politics of nature. Yeah, yeah, you could say I'm a nature nut," he chuckled. "But, I feel a deep sense of peace being in nature, I love the sounds, the smells, the playfulness of all the animals in the forests and the natural world around us."

"I completely know what you mean. Having grown up with a forester and spending summers with a farmer on this rural land in Virginia, I too love the innate connection, for people like us, to preserve and protect the beauty that surrounds us. It's really magical, don't you think?" affirmed Silvi.

What struck Silvi the most about Luke was his thirst for knowledge that seemed to be insatiable. She remembered that from when they had met so many years ago as children.

Now, Luke was working in conjunction with a laboratory in Blacksburg, on the campus of Virginia Tech College of Natural Resources and Environment. He was lead researcher in their lab in forestry and wildlife management. That is where they were working on the development of a virus that could possibly neutralize the fungus that caused the death of the American chestnut.

Being Sunday, he knew he could check on some experiments without having to chitchat with any of the other professors or researchers on the weekend.

"Silvi, if you want to see firsthand some of the work that is being done on the chestnut, we could take a drive in the morning, and I'd be happy to share with you what I know, and what is being done on this front. You know, to see firsthand how difficult this journey will be, if it is even possible."

Silvi did not hesitate, "Sure, that sounds like fun. I'd love to learn more about what you are working on, and pick your brain about what happened to the chestnut forests. Yeah, definitely let's do it. I want to understand how new trees are sprouting up out of the roots. And if they can survive or will they die from the blight too?"

Silvi paused, "I will bring along a picnic. I just need to be back before dinner so I can spend the evening with the birthday boy before I head back to the rat race in Manhattan on Monday morning," she said as she rolled her eyes.

So, they planned to meet in the morning. Luke would swing by at 9:30 for a little road trip. And he would give her a one-hour course in chestnut blight 101 on their drive up to the college.

She and Dr. Woodbury said good night. Silvi watched Luke get in his car and drive off. Her eyes lingered in the yard until the taillights were out of sight. Silvi then went inside to join her family.

Grandpa was like a little boy, playing on the floor with his new puppy. When he first laid eyes on that beagle, his eyes lit up and sparkled like a firefly in a total eclipse. He liked the name "Phil" and it stuck. The little guy seemed to already know his name and responded to it when Grandpa called him. It was so cute to watch him smile and to see joy in his heart again. He missed his old hound dog, but this puppy was filling that great big void quickly.

Silvi slept with the window open and in the morning, at first light, she woke to a symphony; cicadas chirping, the birds singing their myriad songs, the wind blowing gently over the short white curtains that her grandma Bessie had crocheted, so long ago.

This was the bed her dad slept in when he was a boy. There was something cozy and comforting about that. She slept like a swaddled baby, better than she had in a very long time.

Luke pulled up at 9:30 sharp and Silvi offered him a fresh cup of coffee. And after a bit of small talk with the family, she kissed Grandpa goodbye and told him she'd be home in time to prepare dinner, and spend the evening with him, mom, and dad. He said, "You kids have fun. Be safe."

Luke and Silvi drove in his truck through back roads with beautiful scenery. Leaves were turning color; orange, yellow, red and that stage where they are still green but their veins pop yellow and just starting to curl at the tips. It would be a couple of more weeks before the oaks, and beeches would be in full regalia, and the aspens would be shimmering and quaking like they were on fire.

The two gabbed and gabbed as they drove through the Virginia countryside. Luke asked about Silvi's schooling, and she asked about his. He was surprised to know that she had a science background as well as law.

"No wonder you have an intense interest in the forest, I thought you were just interested in ME!" he said.

They both chuckled nervously. They arrived at the college, walked into the lab and he showed her the experiments they were working on.

"Researchers collect nuts and sprout them," he explained. "The nuts are stored carefully, in temperature-controlled environments and in certain mediums to prevent them from getting moldy."

Luke explained to Silvi about the *Hypovirus*, and how many different strains there were.

Silvi smiled up and him, "This is all so fascinating."

He talked of the history and the mechanism around the functional death of the chestnut forests.

"Please stop me if this gets too technical, but here, come closer... look at this sample. The purpose of fungus is to decompose organic matter. Trees are organic. The fungus attacks the chestnut and the first symptom we usually see is an orange area on the bark. It's called a canker. The fungus produces an acid, called Oxalic acid."

Silvi was enjoying her time with Luke. Her mind was racing in four different directions. She was interested in what he was saying but, she was distinctly distracted by him. There was something about being this close to him that made her feel, hmmm? Happy. She liked the way he smelled and how he gently touched her back when he was showing her something that he was excited about.

He was still talking, "The canker starts to sink and then the bark sloughs off. When the rain comes the fungus spawns orange oozing tendrils. Like this one over here," he touched her back and showed her a sample.

"The fungal spores on these tendrils are carried by wind or insects or birds. That is why it spreads so fast. The spores then germinate and infect a new tree, and if cankers continue to form and move around the bark of a tree, it will literally strangle the plant from getting its flow of needed nutrients and water. And this is when the whole tree above the canker starts to die," Luke told her.

Silvi did find all this interesting and thought, "What a noble cause it is to do this kind of work every day. If it were not for dedicated researchers learning about the natural world around us, we would not have advanced technology, nor most of the medical breakthroughs we have today." And Silvi wondered if she made the right decision leaving Dr. Baldwin's lab so many years ago.

Luke went on, "But, amazingly what is left are the roots, untouched by this process. The fact that the fungus doesn't kill the roots of the American chestnut is why we see small chestnut trees in the mountains sprouting frequently. But as soon as they are a few years old, the fungus strikes them too. And eventually the roots simply die. So, time is very much of the essence."

Silvi really tried to listen intently, "So what do viruses have to do with saving the chestnut trees?"

"The method I am working on combines the virus with the fungus. The *Hypovirus* will naturally neutralize the acid that's toxic to the tree and theoretically, it could make the infected tree survive the blight!"

Luke took a breath, "You see that would be a huge step in our quest to bring back the American chestnut."

"Wow, that is very exciting Luke, has there been any success with the virus stopping the blight?"

"A few years ago, I saw a mature chestnut tree with the typical orange fungus still growing in an old orchard in Tennessee. When I looked at it under a microscope it looked different than anything I'd ever seen before. It turned out there was a virus enmeshed around the fungus. It appeared to weaken it enough that the tree had a chance to heal itself. It was like a miracle!"

The wheels in Silvi's mind were turning. Science was so fascinating to her.

"For the first time I wondered if we could replicate that virus, and infect other American chestnuts that had the blight, and maybe it would spread throughout the forest. So far, we have been able to infect individual blight-stricken trees with consistent success, but this mechanism we see with the *Hypovirus* does not naturally pass on to future generations of chestnut trees. So far, the only blighted trees we can save, are ones we physically infect with the virus."

"Oh, that's too bad," thought Silvi.

"There is still much to learn and so much work to be done. But it has given us great hope. It's very complex and complicated."

Silvi had so many questions. She peppered Luke with a barrage of them.

"Woah, woah, slow down Silvi. These are all great questions. You need to realize this is an exceedingly long project. We need answers, and we need lots of volunteers, who are willing to do manual labor. A real labor of love," said Doc Woodbury.

"So, what are you doing now? Is there a plan?" asked Silvi.

"Well, right now, we are experimenting. Out in the field, research teams go into the forest and collect dozens of canker samples. Back at the lab, they scrape the bark samples and spread the tiny spores from the chestnut blight fungus on scientific Petri dishes filled with gelatin. As this culture grows, we'll be able to see if the *Hypovirus* is in any of the samples. Eventually we will understand not only the blueprints of any helpful *Hypovirus* that exists, but also how they can help more chestnuts survive," Luke said as he walked to a lab desk.

"Come here and take a look." Silvi moved close to Luke, and he put his arm around her waist and moved his hand down to the small of her back as he moved her closer to the desk in front of him. She felt the warmth of his well-toned body leaning over her shoulder. She stiffened and inhaled sharply.

Was she imagining something or was he flirting with her? Or had it been so long since she felt the rush of sexual excitement that she was simply hoping it so.

Luke went on unaware of Silvi's monkey-mind ramblings, "We are taking bark samples with a core of the fungus in it. Then we carefully label the samples and photograph the site before searching for the next tree. See, this is a tray of samples," he showed her where the researchers sit and do their experiments.

Silvi slowly turned to face Luke, their bodies just inches apart. She felt her face flush and her heart pound. Her palms were sweaty, and her breathing quickened. Embarrassed, she turned away and gazed at the floor.

Luke, hesitant, instinctively stepped back and continued,

"The bottom line Silvi, is that the chestnut blight isn't going away, it doesn't appear, yet, that *Hypoviruses* can effectively control the disease. Year after year, however, *Hypovirus* research will continue. Along with some other methods of crossbreeding and genetic studies to understand more about the genetic makeup of the American chestnut."

Silvi realized that these sudden feelings were all in her head. The breakup with Brad, being at a crossroad in her life, not knowing why she felt unfulfilled, it was making her emotional. She imagined it, that was all.

Luke was still excitedly sharing his work with Silvi, "What we need is a dedicated nonprofit foundation that will help us plan a future for American chestnut trees."

Silvi snapped out of the deep recesses of her thoughts and was once again wide eyed and focused.

"OK, I think I get the gist." The truth is she didn't hear what he said for the past five minutes. But she summed it up, "Basically, if I understood you, there is a fungus that the American chestnut has no immunity to, so when it was brought here unwittingly through Asian chestnut imports, it infected the entirety of the American chestnut forests and an acid attacked its vascular system which was toxic to these trees and it eventually killed off four billion trees in less than one generation."

Luke laughed out loud. And said, "Precisely." She laughed too.

He was really enjoying being with Silvi. And he loved that she understood the importance of this work. He had never met anyone so excitedly fascinated by his projects. And she was beautiful, smart, and looked extremely sexy in her snug jeans that hugged her thighs and round, firm bottom. He loved the way she smelled; it was a distinctive fresh scent, like newly cut grass.

He tried to stay focused on the science, and not be so distracted by her.

"Silvi, there are some American chestnuts that have survived the blight. But not many, for all intents and purposes, it is ecologically and functionally extinct."

"Is it possible to propagate the American chestnuts that did survive, I'd imagine for some reason those must have immunity to the fungus?" asked Silvi.

"Ha Ha, Yeah, that's right, Silvi. That is exactly how it works. In fact, there is a cooperative of people who are actively breeding those trees. There is such a comparatively small number of those trees that they alone will never repopulate the chestnut range. But it certainly can't hurt. Keep in mind that although American chestnut is a fast-growing tree, it still takes several years before it flowers and matures to where you can breed new trees from it. So, although it appears to pass on its immunity, it would take a thousand years of active breeding to repopulate a forest with that method alone. That is why we are exploring other methods," explained Luke.

Silvi quickly picked up, "You said other methods, like multiple paths? What are the other methods? Is anyone working on those?"

"Well, I'm not sure if I mentioned that the Chinese chestnut trees have strong immunity to the fungus. So, there is talk that if you cross-breed Chinese chestnuts with American chestnuts that you might be able to transfer or pass the gene that confers immunity through crossbreeding. It's been tried, but not very successfully," said Luke.

"Oh, I'm very interested in the cross breeding to create a chestnut that is immune to the fungus. I'd love to work on a project like that," said Silvi.

"I'm very interested too, and hopeful in this method, but again it will take a coordinated effort and money to find the right location to be able to grow thousands of these crossbred trees and someone willing to do it," said Luke.

"A project like this would take the dedication of someone with the land and the foresight to launch this project," said Luke, as he stared right into Silvi's magnificent azure blue eyes."

"That seems like a hopeful and very worthwhile project," said Silvi.

"Indeed, it is, I would love to see someone work on that. It will be a long road. But, hey we are talking about trying to recreate the most prolific and valued tree in all of American History," said Luke. They both laughed.

"Is there anything else, Luke?"

"Well, there is other work being done to create immunity in the American chestnut by genetically modifying the DNA, but there is of course a huge anti GMO push in the United States that makes that method seem highly unlikely."

"Oh, actually I am familiar with this method and with the backlash of GMOs," said Silvi.

She told him about her years of anti-GMO rallies and activism. She shared her work with Dr. Baldwin, during her years at the College of Environmental Science and Forestry, in Syracuse, in what seems like a lifetime ago.

"Really?" said Luke.

Somehow, he was not surprised. It made him chuckle.

"It would be interesting to see if they are working on this, I'd be curious to know what the Environmental and Forestry college researchers had going on."

Silvi told Luke, that she and Nita had spoken briefly by phone but, that she'd give her a call when she got back to New York City.

"That would be great. I'm not up on the progress they have made. In any case Silvi, you can see why it is a real uphill battle to even dream about the rebirth of the American chestnut forest in its natural range," suggested Luke.

Silvi's brain was in overdrive. Her eyes were as large as a deer's in a headlight and she had a thousand questions. For the first time in a long, long time she was feeling moved. Silvi tried to envision what it would be like to live in the bountiful banquet of the chestnut forest. She also wondered what the chances would be to bring back the beauty of those trees with their huge canopies, and the abundance of free food. Not to mention the lumber, and lifestyle and even the environmental improvements like the oxygen that a canopy of that magnitude would bring to the Eastern Seaboard.

That was enough science for one day, and they grabbed their picnic lunch and went outside. It was a beautiful sunny day and they walked around the campus and talked about their families and their childhoods. They reminisced about the time they were young, and their two families took a nature walk in the forest behind MeadowBrook farm.

They found a big oak tree and spread out a blanket underneath it. The canopy of the tree was cozy, but it was chilly. They bundled up and moved closer together.

Silvi and Luke laughed and had an extraordinarily perfect picnic. Luke asked questions about her life, and she asked about his. He had a longtime high school girlfriend that he expected to marry. By junior year of college, she had met and fallen in love with a medical student. Luke threw himself into his work and didn't have a serious girlfriend since. He shared stories about several short-term relationships but nothing that took him away from his dedication to his studies and his lab work.

Silvi told Luke about Brad, and how they evolved into more like best friends or a brother and sister relationship. She explained how their lives just drifted apart. She did not feel it necessary to make him out to be the bad guy who cheated on her and ran off with a campaign worker. But he got the spirit of what happened.

Silvi was easy to talk to and quite easy on the eyes. Luke found himself intently focused on her full lips, as she spoke, wondering what it would be like to kiss them.

They got home about four o'clock and set to making dinner for the family. Luke stayed and his aunt and uncle joined them.

Silvi's heart was fluttering. She felt like a schoolgirl. It was fun cooking with Luke in the kitchen. They laughed and teased each other. She did most of the cooking. He lit a fire and sat on the floor playing with Phil, Grandpa's new beagle.

"Got to love a guy who loves dogs," she winked at her grandpa. During dinner, Luke's hand brushed up against Silvi's leg, very innocently, but it sent electricity up her spine and all her hairs stood on end. She caught his eye with a lingering look, then she gazed down and even in the glow of firelight, he could see she blushed.

After all the family goodbyes, Silvi walked Luke to his car. He took her hand, and Silvi propped herself against the driver's door. It was impossible to say who leaned in first but, she slid her arms up on his shoulders, and he kissed her good night. Under the scarlet blossom of moonlight, she had butterflies in her stomach for the first time in a decade.

CHAPTER EIGHTEEN

Syracuse Labs, New York
Silvi Hayes
Autumn, 1987

Silvi got up early the next morning. Her flight was at eleven o'clock and she wanted to spend some time alone with Grandpa before she drove to the airport. She put on coffee and took Phil out for a walk. The air was cool, and the leaves were flushing their autumn spectrum of warm, comforting hues.

"I love this time of year the best," she said to the new puppy.

It felt peaceful, the smells of the season started to permeate the air. She spoke out loud to herself, "I feel alive." The air in MeadowBrook was clean, and crisp. "Why did Dad want to protect me from this life? It seems idyllic."

She reflected, "He worked so hard to take me away from this. But then again, I guess the times were very different. He was so adamant about leaving this 'hell hole', I believe were his words. I feel guilty about having such a different view of MeadowBrook. But then, because of Mom and Dad, I'm a successful, educated, financially secure woman of the world. I suppose I just have gratitude for all the gifts that I have in my life."

She was pulled out of her reflection with the thwack, thwack, thwack of the screen door.

"Come on Phil, let's go see Grandpa." They ran back to the house, and he was sitting in his old rocker with coffee in hand. He waved as he saw them approaching down the long, packed dirt drive. Silvi bounded up the old wooden steps to the creaky landing and kissed him on the cheek. She grabbed her coffee and came out to her Adirondack chair.

"Another birthday under our belt," he said.

"Yup, it wasn't so bad, was it?" she quipped.

"Thank you for coming, Silvi. You are my best girl."

"Aww Grandpa, I wouldn't have missed this for the world."

He told her that she was the most important woman in his life. In fact, aside from Ben, and now his pup Phil, "Wink, wink." She was the most precious gift in his life.

"Grandpa, you know I feel the same way about you. You've taught me a love of nature, a love of life and compassion and to be the champion to all who need a voice."

Grandpa suddenly got a bit wistful. "Silvi, I don't know how long I will be here. You are the next generation; you are my legacy."

She listened.

"Did I ever tell you how much you look like your Grandmother Bessie? Your eyes and your hair, your build. You are the spitting image of Bessie when she was a young mom." She hugged him and he pulled her close.

"I want you to have something that has meant a lot to me over the years. I have kept it among my most precious possessions."

He took out a well-worn, brown bag that looked as if it had been fondled by intention and folded over, several hundred times. It evidently had been in there for years. And he handed Silvi the bag. She carefully unrolled it. It was a cotton apron. It had strawberries on it and little white jonquil flowers along the eyelet trim.

"Every time I think of your grandma, I see her wearing this apron. She would wear it in the kitchen cooking dinner, in the garden picking our veggies, whistling as she collected chestnuts right at this time of year and it always reminds me of her. She made it with some fabric

I brought home one year from selling chestnuts in Abingdon. I want you to have it."

She unfolded the apron and placed its red straps over her head and turned around so Grandpa could tie it. When she turned back around, for the first time in her life, she saw Tucker Hayes cry.

Silvi hugged him tightly and said, "I recognize this apron, Grandpa. Grandma is wearing it in the photo on the fireplace mantel. Of course, that photo is black and white, so I never knew it was such a beautiful bright red. Thank you, Grandpa. I will treasure this my whole life."

"Silvi, I also want you to have something else. I want you to have MeadowBrook farm when I go. Your dad has no interest in this land, he couldn't wait to leave. His and Rebecca's life is in Upstate New York. You have always loved the land and this place and its people. It has been in the Hayes family for generations. My dad homesteaded this place, built the cabin with his own hands. It belongs in this family, and it would be my dying wish to see you be the steward of this beautiful mountain and these beautiful valleys."

"Oh, Grandpa, you are not going anywhere for a very long time," she said with a tear in her eye.

"I'm just saying, Silvi that is my wish. I know you love MeadowBrook Farm and I want it to go to you. Promise me you will care for our slice of nature's grandeur. I want you to have it."

"Ok Grandpa, I promise," Silvi said as her mind raced refusing to believe her grandpa would ever leave this Earth.

She got up and kissed him gently on his cheek. Silvi was not ready to lose him. He was her anchor. He grounded her to terra firma and gave her wings upon which to fly. He could easily live another ten years. They hugged. And he kissed her again.

By now, her mom and dad were up and getting ready for their day. They were all planning on going for a hike down to the creek to show Phil the lay of the land.

Silvi took off the apron and carefully packed it in her suitcase. She would treasure this for the rest of her life.

She kissed everyone, said her goodbyes, and headed home. On the plane back to Kennedy airport, she drifted in and out. She thought about everything that happened over the weekend. Her grandpa was getting older, she knew this, but he was the foundation of their family. She could not imagine life without him. He was strong and would probably live for another decade. Watching him so joyful with his new puppy Phil brought a smile to her face.

Then, her mind jumped to what was going on with Luke. She felt like a young girl around him. He was the kind of person she could be herself with. He was in some ways like Grandpa, the strong, handsome, silent type. But when he had something to say, people would stop to listen. His life was such a far cry from her competitive, industrious, kinetic New York City professional life. Luke had a calling, a passion and he was living it, following it. He had purpose.

Silvi realized in that moment what was missing in her life. She needed to follow her dream. Up until now she did not even know what her dream was. She couldn't wait to call Nita and tell her everything she had learned. And to get caught up with the work going on at the Environmental labs in Syracuse.

The plane landed. She grabbed her bag from the overhead bin and walked outside into the brisk autumn night and hailed a cab. Passing Central Park made her realize this was a sorry substitute, an inkling of a life in nature. And that she needed to be back firmly planted in her roots. She needed to be in the forest.

The next morning, Silvi had to get to the office to catch up on work that had piled on her desk while she was gone. She grabbed a power bar and a cup of coffee and started plowing through enough paper to reconstruct an entire chestnut tree. By the time she came up for air, it was 2:15 in the afternoon. She had worked right through an all-office lunch meeting at noon. Silvi's assistant, Laura, was the most organized woman she had ever known. She had a warm smile for everyone, and you couldn't help but like her. She had one of those Irish mane's of naturally bright red hair and a face full of freckles.

Silvi trusted her implicitly. On this day, Laura was instructed to only bother her if the building was on fire. Laura held all her calls and now Silvi had a stack of those to return. Those would keep her busy for the remainder of the day.

One of the notes was from Brad. The message said, "Please call back, must talk." She found that odd as she hadn't heard from him since the breakup. Well, that would have to wait until later.

She finally finished up work, it was well after seven-thirty, and it was already inky, dark outside. The office had an afterhours aura. Custodial crews were cleaning. The low hum of vacuums and the clatter of trash bins were tumbling in the background. Silvi gathered up her stuff, grabbed her heels and headed home. She had the cab stop at Sung Ming Chinese to grab a quick take out, that she had called in.

When she finally got home, she stripped off her clothes, put on comfortable sweatpants, grabbed a glass of wine and plopped down on the couch. There were three messages on her machine. One was from Dad, just checking that she had gotten home okay, one from Laura, with a reminder that she needed to be at a meeting at seven am and one from Brad, that simply said again, "Please call me, we need to talk."

Silvi was exhausted, it was already eight-thirty and the only person she really wanted to talk to was Nita. But it was too late to call her. So, she finished her Szechuan chicken and turned on the news. She never heard one word. She woke up on the couch at 1:30 in the morning, turned off the TV, and crawled into bed.

The next morning, Silvi was at the office at six-thirty and was in a frenzy, like a subway platform at rush hour. The whole day was a blur. She darted from meeting to meeting, answered calls, met with clients, ran to another meeting, and went to lunch with her business partner over a big patent infringement case. The firm had just taken on another large agribusiness suit, that she would be asked to lead. And then she had a dinner meeting with a judge that was courting her to help with an New York University law review competition. All Silvi could think of when she finally got home, just before ten o'clock was, "It's a good thing I don't have a dog."

It was now Thursday. Silvi called Nita in the morning and scheduled a time to chat at seven-thirty that evening. Nita was thrilled to hear from her and could not wait to catch up. She had been thinking about their last brief conversation, and wondered how so much time had gone by, again.

There was another note from Brad asking her to call back. She left work early, if you consider six-fifteen early. The walk home in the brisk air was just what Silvi needed to unwind. Last night's leftovers were all she could muster, along with a call to Brad. As the phone line rang, she hoped he wouldn't answer. His voicemail clicked in, and she left a message that she'd been out of town, and was swamped when she got back and apologized for taking so long to get back to him.

In truth, he was lucky that Silvi returned his call at all. She had no interest, whatsoever, in talking to him. But he was so persistent that she wondered if someone had died, or if he had gotten married and didn't want her to hear about it through the grapevine. Her message was brief, "I'm returning your call. If it's urgent you can reach me tomorrow after lunch in my office."

Then Silvi sat down. It was seven-thirty, she got comfortable with a nice glass of wine and called Nita.

They were like two schoolgirls at a pajama party. They caught up on what was happening in their lives, how work was, what was new at the Environmental College and of course gossip on some of their old colleagues' love lives.

Then, Silvi told her all about what she learned at MeadowBrook, and about meeting Luke. Amazingly, Nita knew of his work, although she was not involved with the biocontrol pathways at all. She knew of some of his groundbreaking studies that had been published. They talked about all the advances in her lab since Silvi had left. She delved particularly into the transgenic work, mapping the genome of the American chestnut, exploring ways to confer resistance by understanding what causes the blight and discovering and implanting genes that can neutralize the toxic acids that are produced by the fungus.

Nita suggested that getting together would be so much more valuable. And wondered if there was a time that Silvi could drive up to Syracuse and spend a couple of days at the lab, at the Environmental Science and Forestry College.

Silvi was so inundated with work and events, "I just can't imagine how I would get away," she said.

It was a four hour drive from the City and she didn't want to stay at her mom and dad's because they were too far away from campus.

Nita offered for Silvi to stay on campus with her. She lived in a cute little garden cottage with a darling guest bedroom and bath.

She said, "You've never been to my place. It would be fun and productive to get together in person."

Silvi knew she was right, and the break from the city would do her good. They set a week from Friday to get together. It would be a beautiful drive and if she were lucky, she might even see some flurries along the way.

"The only obligation I have that weekend, is my mom's birthday on Saturday. We have a tradition that every year I cook mom's favorite lasagne dinner. So, if you are okay with joining my family for that, we would go over on Saturday evening and hang out with mom and dad and my sister Lily for a couple hours."

"Sure, that sounds like fun," Silvi said.

So, they hung up with a plan to rendezvous the week after next. Silvi was actually really excited to get back to Syracuse and have a girl's weekend. But she was particularly eager to learn all about what Nita was doing on the genetic side of the Chestnut challenge. She could hardly wait.

CHAPTER NINETEEN

Silvi and Nita Rendezvous in Syracuse

There was so much to do in this next week but at least she had something fun to set her sights on.

To say the next week was hectic would be a colossal understatement. Fridays were typically the busiest day of her week, and Silvi regretted leaving Brad that message to call after lunch. She certainly did not expect to return from a business lunch to find him sitting waiting in her office.

Shocked, she said, "Brad! What are you doing here?"

He had come all the way across town from Wall Street and he was already inside her office sitting on the couch. She flashed a perturbed look at Laura, who just grimaced and shrugged.

He got up, closed the door, and looked at Silvi for a full, painfully long, minute without saying a word.

Finally, he said, "Silvi, I'm sorry to barge in unannounced, but I needed to see you face to face."

Her brain was whirling a hundred miles an hour. Did he have cancer? Had someone died? Was he embroiled in a political scandal? She was glad she looked good that day. Frequently, Fridays are dress down, no meeting days. But what was he doing here? He must have traveled over an hour during lunch hour to get across town.

"Silvi, I made a huge mistake. I have missed you so much. I can't bear my life without you," declared Brad.

Her mouth gaped open. Yet, no words would come.

"Silvi if you have any room for my repentance in your heart, I would like to earn your trust back. Can we get together for dinner and talk?"

She just stood there dumbfounded and in shock. She never saw that coming. Silvi had a two-thirty meeting that she needed to prepare for, and a four o'clock after that. Her head was spinning. She didn't have any words; she closed her mouth and just shook her head. She couldn't get into it right now. It would throw her in a tailspin for the rest of the day.

All Silvi could get out was, "You got me at a bad time. Could we talk about it later?"

She walked to the door and held it open for him. He started to walk through, turned back, and kissed her right on the lips. She watched him say goodbye to Laura and walk out the main double glass doors to the elevator. He pumped his fist, and his feet lifted off the ground, like he scored a win at the Superbowl.

Silvi looked at Laura, shook her head, and closed her door.

She sat at her desk and was bewildered. He looked good, it had been six months since she had seen him or even talked to him. She thought out loud, "What am I feeling? I dont know." A maelstrom of emotion flooded over her. She had to focus on work. People were counting on her; it was Friday and she had so much to do before the week was out.

Silvi finally went home after a long day and Brad called her later that night. She let it go to voicemail. He asked if he could pick her up at seven o'clock tomorrow, Saturday. He had made a reservation at Mama Marchi's, their favorite Italian restaurant, where they got engaged.

Silvi called him back and told him that she had plans for the weekend and a very packed week and needed to go Upstate next Friday so dinner would need to wait until she got back. She hung up feeling relief. Or was it terror?

The next week passed quickly, and Silvi was able to avoid talking to Brad. On Friday she left work at three o'clock to get on the road before rush hour. She turned onto Central Park West and took Amsterdam Avenue onto Broadway. Traffic was still light, so she decided to go through Albany. It was a little longer, but that way she could drop off some government filings she needed couriered to the Capitol for a case they were working on with the Governor's office. Kill two birds with one stone. And that way, when she reached Syracuse at rush hour she'd come in from the east and hopefully avoid going through downtown. Silvi pulled up to Nita's Lab at 7:15. Perfect timing, she was just finishing up for the day.

Nita let her in, and gave her a big hug. Nita showed Silvi around. Not much had changed in the years since she was Nita's assistant, but there were definitely some large pieces of equipment that she'd never seen.

"Oh, Silvi, look at you. It has been too long. I'm so glad youre here," blurted Nita.

"Nita, it seems like another lifetime that I worked here with you. I was just a kid!"

"Indeed, time flies when you are conquering the world."

They hugged and laughed. And after some superficial catching up Nita said, "Let me give you a quick tour of our work on the chestnut gene mapping project and our accomplishments on the genetics side. Then we have all day tomorrow to get into the nitty gritty, if you are interested. Unless you are starving?"

"Oh no, I'm so anxious to learn everything. I can't wait to hear what is happening with the research on the chestnut blight, so let's get a foundation and then dinner is my treat tonight," Silvi said.

"So, we now have two separate labs working on trying to identify what the blight is, what causes the death of the tree, and how genetically we might overcome the certain death from the fungus. So far, the mapping project is going well, but controlling the blight has been a lot of brick walls," said Nita.

"First, come over here. This is our genome sequencing lab. Here, we are mapping all the genes in a chestnut. It's a daunting job, and tedious, but we are making great progress. The reason we need to do this is eventually we will want to find a gene to insert into this sequence of genes that will give the chestnut immunity to this dreaded, destructive disease. With the increasing knowledge of molecular biology, the possibility of transferring specific genes that may confer blight resistance is a captivating promise. We don't know much yet about the characteristics of the American chestnut chromosomes. But that's what's happening in this lab."

"The goal is to map the entire genetic sequence of the American and Chinese chestnut genomes so we might find the precise gene or genes that confer the immunity to the blight. The American chestnut's genome is hard to study. It has 780 million base pairs of genetic material, DNA. Knowing how the genome is organized into chromosomes is a crucial step towards developing blight-resistance. But then, we need to identify the exact chromosomal location of important genes. This information will greatly increase our chances of creating blight resistant American chestnut trees."

"I'm following you, that makes sense," mumbled Silvi.

Nita continued "That brings us to the other lab. Walk over here with me. Do you have any questions?"

"No, not so far, it's very interesting. Let's keep going, then we can talk over dinner," said Silvi.

"This other lab.... Hey Richard, you are here late. Richard, this is Silvi, she used to work here when she was a student at the college a hundred years ago."

"Ha ha, thanks Nita, let's see you are about 15 years older than me, right?" joked Silvi. They all chuckled.

"So, in this laboratory we are bringing field samples of the fungus to study and grow under controlled conditions. We look at trees that are infected with the blight and we experiment different possible explanations of what kills the plant tissue."

"You know Nita, being here feels like coming home. I spent so many days, years in this lab. It's fun coming back again. I've often wondered whether I made a mistake leaving and not sticking with research. This kind of work gets my heart racing, it's really embedded deeply in my gut."

Nita smiled and said, "It's great to have you back. Really, it's been too long."

"Listen, we can get into this in more detail tomorrow, but you already know some basic things. When they found the fungus at the Bronx Zoo, so many years ago, they didn't know what to do. These poor trees died a tragic and horrible death. Thousands of years of growth were destroyed in the blink of an eye. It was a devastatingly sad story. As you are learning, an entire way of life vanished for millions of families, especially mountain people like your family."

"Yes, I had the opportunity to talk to some of the ladies that saw the whole thing happen. But they are getting old now and, these stories will die with them. It's so heart wrenching. It defined the rest of their lives," Silvi interjected.

Nita went on, "This is an unparalleled catastrophe, the likes of which, we have not seen in the world's forests since the Ice Age. Many attempts to stop the spread and cure the fungus have failed. It is unlikely that we will ever eradicate the fungus. It lives underground and in other hosts, like oak trees. But we believe we do have the ability to find ways to control the spread by creating trees that have immunity to the deathly effects of the fungus and maybe if we are smart enough, and if we have enough resources, we might be able to bring back or at least pull the American chestnut out of functional extinction."

Silvi said, "But I heard that one good thing about the blight is that it does not kill the roots of the tree. So far, they have survived. Isn't that, right?"

"Yeah, Silvi, that's right, but we just don't know how long we have before they exhaust their lifespan, reduce diversity, and potentially die off too. That is why this research is so critical right now. There are millions of saplings that are potentially waiting to blossom into full grown American chestnut trees. If we can develop an American chestnut that is resistant to the blight, they can cross pollinate with the saplings and their offspring theoretically could be immune too."

"Has no one ever succeeded at saving a chestnut tree from the blight?" asked Silvi.

"For decades, there have been many who have tried to bring back the tree to its rightful place in the range. But so far no one single method has been able to claim success. Perhaps it will take a combination of several methods to bring back a thriving American chestnut forest. Only time will tell."

Nita could see that Silvi was tired. She said, "Our goal here at the Environmental Science and Forestry College is to develop a transgenic blight-resistant American chestnut that is capable of surviving this infection."

Nita stopped to see if Silvi was glazing over.

"Nita, this is fascinating. I can't wait to come back and get our hands dirty tomorrow," said Silvi.

"It's really great to see you again Silvi. Let's hop over to Danzers, I've been dreaming about one of their Big Reuben's, some old-fashioned German potato pancakes and a frosty mug. Do you remember where it is?"

"On Ainsley?" Silvi recalled.

"Yup. My mouth is watering already. See you there. Then we can go straight to my place."

The girls got all caught up and had a great evening. The next morning, Silvi got up early. She scrounged around Nita's kitchen and made them a hearty mountain breakfast. She brought along her grandma's apron because she knew they were cooking lasagne for Nita's mom's birthday. She loved wearing it, as it reminded her of her grandpa. It also connected her to her grandma that she never got to meet, but felt close to through endless stories and a few pictures.

After a brisk morning hike, they headed over to the lab.

"Silvi, do you have any questions from yesterday?" said Nita.

"Not yet, Nita."

"Dr. Woodbury went over a lot of this with me when I spent a day at his lab in Virginia. The basics, I mean," Silvi reminded her.

"He is more focused on biocontrol methods with viruses. But I really want to be open minded about the benefits of gene therapy. As you know, I have been a community organizer, an activist, really fighting against genetically modified organisms since I was a teen. My whole legal career has been a slugfest with big agribusinesses who are mostly interested in corporate profits, in this genetically modifying business. So, this is a huge internal conflict for me to span the chasm from fighting GMOs to embracing genetic modification as a potentially productive, useful, valuable, and safe tool for good," said Silvi.

Nita quickly retorted "Yet, you are a scientist, and a damn good one. You know that knowledge is the bridge over that chasm, and understanding the facts is the key. It is absolutely essential to recognize the vigorous testing that we will need to go through to be approved by the US Department of Agriculture, the Environmental Protection Agency and the Food and Drug Administration, for use of GMOs in the wild. It will be an arduous and precipitous climb to prove it is practical, yet a judicious, cautious, and a prudent journey.

And to demonstrate that, it will entail the least tampering with nature. This is why you will be very excited about the specifics of how we go about developing a blight-resistant, transgenic American chestnut that is capable of surviving this parasite," explained Nita.

"Nita, I am keeping an open mind inspired by my abiding intention to recreate the iconic chestnut forest that was stolen from my ancestors."

"Silvi, what we know right now about the fungus is that it produces a destructive acid."

"Yes, Luke taught me about this, too."

"Did he also tell you that this acid attacks the living tissue of the tree, which moves nutrients up and down the tree?"

"Yes, that is what he said."

"This oxalic acid can be neutralized by an enzyme that is found in everyday food. Like strawberries, bananas, oats, barley, and wheat. It is called oxalate oxidase. Or "oxo", as we call it. Oxalate oxidase breaks down the acid that kills the plant, so with it, we can theoretically save the tree! We have found that if we can surgically remove this gene from wheat and implant it into an American chestnut embryo, VOILA! We could theoretically have a mature American chestnut to repopulate the forests."

Silvi listened intently. And Nita went on.

"So, that's why we are mapping the genes. And then, we must find just the right spot to implant this oxo gene. The other thing we are hoping for is that this blight resistance is passed to the next generation of trees. If that is true, we might finally break the code to naturally repopulate future generations of chestnut trees in the wild, without any further human intervention," said Nita excitedly.

"So, what you are saying is, if it were possible, and we could get approval from the government oversight agencies, these trees could be the first genetically modified forest trees released in the wild in North America, with the potential to self-populate the entire range of American chestnut trees, once again?"

"Yes, that is exactly what we are hoping for Silvi," affirmed Nita!

CHAPTER TWENTY

The Accidental Discovery

Silvi and Nita spent the entire day at the lab at the College of Environmental Science and Forestry. After a few hours in the decoding lab, working on the genome of the American chestnut, Silvi had a lot of questions, and Nita had lots of answers. Nita was a brilliant scientist and researcher and Silvi remembered why she looked up to Nita so, all those years ago.

Nita said, "Once mapping the genome is complete, we will insert at the exact location in the chestnut, the spliced oxo gene, to hopefully confer immunity to the chestnut. It's very encouraging. It's like a puzzle, but this is a puzzle of real life," she smiled.

The afternoon was spent on the field work. Although it was cold at the research farm, they examined the trees in different stages of growth. Being pretty close to winter, everything was bright yellow or had lost leaves and stood bare naked and vulnerable against an azure sky. It was quite beautiful, yet eerie at the same time.

Back in the lab, they discussed which plants would work to best neutralize the acid and methods to extract that gene for insertion into the American chestnut plants.

"Once we have success at the transfer, the real work begins of testing it in the field. It will be necessary to craft safety and corollary testing, as well as certify the repeatability of the experiment in real life terms and conditions," mentioned Nita.

It was a full day and the girls worked closely. Nita answered lots of Silvi's questions. But, Silvi wondered what it would take to accomplish this monumental task and if it were really possible to create a viable rebirth of the American chestnut forests across the natural range. It excited her, she felt passionate about the idea of doing something meaningful in life and leaving a legacy that mattered when her physical body was gone from this lifetime.

Silvi speculated, "Aside from the anti GMO activists, who else might oppose the work of bringing back the American chestnut? What obstacles would someone likely run into with the rebirth of these stately trees?" Silvi's mind was spinning in overdrive.

"Yeah, that's a great question Silvi. There are some strong advocates and detractors. The commercial nut companies are strong advocates. Chestnuts that were once abundant are now rare and very expensive. Lumber mills and the construction industry are very interested and supportive as the American chestnut is a unique, one-of-a-kind lumber. It grows fast, and straight for 50 feet, before branches start to sprout. It is a beautiful hardwood and can be used for anything from split log fence rails, wood plank for flooring to carving a piano. Also, it is high in tannins, and the reason why leather companies are big supporters of a comeback. Some environmentalists support the American chestnut resurrection from the edge of extinction. Thousands of Appalachians and mountain dwelling families are in favor of restoration because of its history and its culture. And certainly, nature-based education organizations are supportive. We would need to find national, regional and local partners," Nita rattled off the top of her head.

"Is there any kind of coordinated organization that is currently focused on restoring the American chestnut to its natural range?" Silvi wanted to know.

"That is a great question. Most of the funding so far has come from universities on the East Coast. And some has come from the government, but that is long gone."

"Hmmm," grimaced Silvi.

"There is a desperate need for a dedicated foundation with a passionate advocate. It would need someone with a vision to run it. Perhaps a few scientific researchers, and geneticists on staff. Oh, and an incredibly strong volunteer community that consisted of legal scholars familiar with the government process and belief in the rebirth of the American chestnut forests," said Nita

Silvi heard Nita, but the fire was already burning, and the wheels were already turning in her head. She did not have a plan yet, but the movements were meshing like a finely precisioned Swiss watch. She was so excited at the prospect of being involved with this project that she was giddy. The girls had a very productive day, and Silvi learned a lot. She realized she had more questions at the end than she did at the start of the day.

They left the lab about four o'clock and headed home to Nita's place to pick up the ingredients that they needed to make the family dinner. Nita again thanked Silvi for agreeing to help her cook her mom's birthday dinner.

"Oh, Nita, truly, this is a treat for me. I don't get to cook very often with my lifestyle in New York City, and living alone and all. Plus, in Manhattan it is so easy to grab a bite to eat or takeout on the way home from the office that I barely food shop, let alone cook for myself. No, this is fun for me. And I'm so happy to be part of your family dinner. In all these years, I really don't know that much about you outside the college labs.

Nita gave Silvi a rundown of who would be there.

"In addition to my mom Sara, the birthday girl, my dad George, and my sister Lily will be there."

They gathered up their groceries and changed into nicer clothes and headed over to her mom's place. She knew they would have a couple of hours before anyone would get home, which would be enough time to get dinner prepped and in the oven. "Mom is spending the day with friends and should be home by six o'clock. Everybody else will be there by 6:30 for the celebration."

It was only a fifteen-minute drive from Nita's place. Her mom and dad's home was quaint. It was in an old, quiet little neighborhood. The street was lined on both sides with big beech trees. The leaves had already turned bright yellow and orange, and they touched in the middle of the street, forming a kind of tunnel to drive through. It was as if Monet had painted an autumnal fairytale. They pulled up the packed gravel driveway at 17 Shadow Lane and unloaded the groceries into the kitchen. They were laughing and gabbing and started making the marinara sauce to go into the lasagne. Nita put on an apron, and she handed one to Silvi.

"Oh, that's ok, I've got my grandma's with me. It's in my bag, I'll be right back."

Silvi came back in wearing the apron Grandpa Tucker had given her. She pulled her hair back into a ponytail, washed her hands, and started chopping onions.

They poured themselves a nice glass of Cabernet Sauvignon as the sautéing onions started sizzling. As they drank in the sweet smell of onions and garlic caramelizing, they talked about their personal lives, and gossiped about how life had changed in Syracuse.

A couple of hours passed, and the lasagne was in the oven. They sat in the kitchen laughing and drinking their wine, and right about six o'clock, Nita saw her mom drive up. She ran out to give her a kiss and wished her a happy birthday. The two of them walked back into the kitchen as Sara was prattling about how the ladies had made a lovely birthday party for her.

"Oh, Nita we had so much fun working on that quilt this afternoon, and the girls made me a cake and ..."

Sara stopped dead in her tracks. She stared at Silvi. She had chills run up her spine, and she was breathless. Nita started saying "Mom, this is my friend, Silvi..."

Sara couldn't speak. She couldn't believe her eyes. Her mouth gaped open.

"Mom, are you okay? Nita said concerned.

"Oh sorry, yes, it's nice to meet you Silvi." Chills ran down her arms and she could not take her eyes off Silvi.

"I apologize. You just look like someone I used to know. There is an uncanny resemblance. But she died many years ago."

As Sara stared, her head tilted and her eyes focused. Sara slowly uttered almost under her breath, "she had an apron just like that too."

She half chuckled as a tear came to her eye. This friend of Nita's was the spitting image of her mother at that age. She knew it would sound ridiculous to even say that out loud.

Sara didn't know what to say and thought back to the last time she was with her own mom. It was the day Lily was born. The day her mom died in her arms. In a breath, she snapped back in time to a sixteen-year-old lithe, sweaty body on a beastly hot and sticky day. She felt her face flush.

Sara excused herself and went to her bedroom to change clothes and compose herself. But her thoughts were of her childhood, the times with her mom, Bessie. Simple moments like picking corn together out in the garden or singing in the kitchen while shelling summer peas, and when her mom taught her at a very young age to sew. Sara had experienced flashbacks at an old familiar smell that would elicit an intense reaction back to another place or time, but this was different. She literally couldn't speak, and she could barely breathe. This girl was the reflection of her childhood, a throwback to a simple time with her best friend. It was eerie and fantastic all at once. Sara finally collected herself when she heard her husband's voice, and she went back to the living room. George had come in, and then Lily showed up. There were introductions all around. Sara looked at George, when he was introduced to Silvi to see if there was any degree of recognition or perception. But he didn't seem to flinch or skip a beat. Dinner was just about ready, so everyone moved to the dining table.

Sara didn't say another word, but she kept looking at Silvi the entire evening. The resemblance was uncanny.

She wanted to wrap her arms around this stranger and embrace the memory of her mom. But that would have been inexplicable.

The dinner was a great success, and Sara was so grateful to the girls for preparing such a lovely evening. Lily brought a beautiful cake, and everyone retired to the living room. Silvi and Nita cleaned up the dinner dishes. Lily lit the candles on the birthday cake. She made her mom's favorite, a yellow layer cake with raspberries in the center and a coconut icing. They brought the cake with lighted candles into the living room where everyone was sitting with coffee. Sara was cozy in a chair, in front of the big stone fireplace. Lily bent down and was holding the cake for her mom to blow out the candles. Silvi and Nita stood behind her. They all clapped. As Silvi looked up above the fireplace, a black and white photograph on the mantel caught her eye. She walked closer and lifted the framed photo. She turned around and looked at Sara.

"Why do you have a picture of my dad and my grandpa on your fireplace?" She was completely confused. But she absolutely knew the people in that picture. She had seen one just like it her whole life. She knelt in front of Sara. She looked her in the eyes. Then she looked up at Nita. There was silence.

Sara gasped, and then teared up. She couldn't speak. At that moment George said to Silvi, "Please excuse my wife, but who are you? You look so much like Sara's mom when she was your age." George was never one to scatter the dust of hints and suggestions. For once Sara was relieved at his bluntness.

Silvi, photo in hand, looked directly at Sara again, and said, "My grandpa has a very similar picture to this one on his mantel in MeadowBrook, Virginia."

Sara started to cry alligator tears now. She wept uncontrollably. She got up and hugged Silvi. She did not let her go. Sara was visibly shaking. She knew this girl must be her brother Ben's daughter. She had not seen or talked to Ben since the day she left MeadowBrook. Lily, with an inquisitive stare, was trying to figure out what the hell was going on.

Silvi said to the family, while looking directly at Nita. "This boy in the photo is my father, Ben Hayes. This gentleman is Tucker Hayes, my grandpa."

Sara who could not speak until this moment said, "Silvi, please sit down."

Sara continued, "All of you. This concerns you all."

"George!" He came by the side of his wife, and he held her hand. George knew exactly what was happening, but Nita, Lily and Silvi were utterly confused.

"Silvi, I apologize for staring at you all night. But you looked so familiar when I first walked in and saw you. Now it's evident why. Your dad, Ben, is my younger brother."

She burst into tears again and could hardly catch her breath. With tears streaming down her cheeks, she went on.

"The woman in the picture is my mother, Elizabeth Hayes." She could barely go on. George hugged her and whispered something in her ear. Sara again took a deep breath.

All Lily and Nita ever knew was that Sara had lost her parents many years ago, well before they were born. She never wanted to talk about it.

"We lost her in childbirth in July 1938. I was there holding her hand when her baby was born. My momma died that day, and nothing was ever the same. Tucker Hayes is my father. I haven't seen him for almost forty years."

Silence saturated every fiber of the room. Lily and Nita were completely confused. The blank page of Sara's life was about to be written. It would be a lonely abyss, or it would be magical.

Sara finally spoke. She knew the biggest trauma would be explaining to Lily. She took a deep breath and turned right to Lily and said, "Darling, come sit by me."

Lily moved next to her mom and held her hand. "Mom, what is going on here? Is Silvi related to us?"

Sara ignored Lily's questions. She looked Lily in the eye. Only George knew what was about to come.

"Lily, I know this is going to come as a life altering surprise, no, a life altering shock, to you. I hope you will hear me out and listen to this whole story."

Lily was baffled. How was this going to be a shock to her? Why is her mom concerned about her instead of Silvi? Sara looked to George for support. George nodded his head and Sara began. "Nita? Lily? Dad and I must tell you a story that goes back to 1938. We, our family, lived in MeadowBrook, Virginia."

Nita piped up and said, "Wait, I thought you lived in North Carolina?"

"No darling, Dad and I grew up in MeadowBrook, Virginia. We were best friends, and we loved each other since we were old enough to walk. When I was sixteen, I got pregnant. Back then, I would have been sent away to a girl's home to have my baby and then it would have been put up for adoption to a good Christian family. George, your dad, and I were in love, and we decided to run away and get married. We got a job at Grandma Charity's place. Dad was the chauffeur and I helped in the house. That is where we raised you girls."

"Wait, who were you pregnant with?" Nita's brain was moving faster than Sara's tongue.

"I was pregnant with you Sweetheart," said Sara.

She looked right into Lily's beautiful blue eyes, and she said "Lily, you are not actually my daughter." She paused for a moment and didn't know how to say it.

"Mom, what are you saying," said Lily. "Was I adopted?"

Again, silence filled the room as thick as honey. A tear rolled down Lily's cheek.

Sara mustered every bit of strength she could, "Lily, you were born the night Mom died. You are my baby sister. My mom, the woman in the picture, is also your mom."

Nita lost her balance. Her face grimaced with disbelief, she practically collapsed, and a flush rushed up her chest and face. She had to sit down. She felt her knees buckle beneath her.

Lily had a bewildered look on her face. Every bit of blood drained from her cheeks. "But, but, then who is my dad?"

"Your dad is my dad, Tucker Hayes. Silvi's grandfather," Sara paused for a moment.

"Life was extremely complicated and difficult in Appalachia at that time. Our mom, my best friend, had just died. All the chestnut trees were dying, which meant we would have no farm, no food, it was the beginning of the depression. Mom's last words to me were, 'Sara, take care of this new baby, Lily. Promise me.' I promised her I would."

"We did what we had to do to keep our baby, Nita, and to care for and raise you."

Silvi did not see this coming. She also realized that Nita, her friend, her mentor for all these years, was actually not just a friend. Nita was her first cousin. And Sara and Lily were her aunts. Silvi, who was not prone to emotional breakdowns, just started to weep. These were tears of joy.

Silvi never knew she had extended family. She always just thought she was an only child. She always wanted siblings and a big family. She had a family now. She was the cousin to the woman who had been her mentor since she was a teenager.

It took a while for all this to sink in for everyone in the room.

All from their own life's perspective.

Lily naturally was the most shocked. At first, she felt betrayed, and lied to all these years. She needed some time to process it. Her life had been a lie, a complete lie. Everything she believed to be true was a complete fabrication. She didn't know who she was, or anything about her real mother or father. She couldn't process this all. She was angry and scared. Her brain was tinctured by a creeping shadow. A bewildered daze settled upon her. Lily felt faint.

The crackling of the fireplace logs filled Sara's ears. It was a welcome distraction, anything to drown out the emotional whirlwind that followed. Many more tears were shed. All that was left to say was, "I'm deeply sorry I hurt you."

Humility and resignation permeated the air. The room was heavy with the dark web that she and George had spun for the entirety of the girls' lives.

There was a lot of processing of how this could have happened, and how it was never shared. Most of the questions were targeted at Sara. George stood by her side, as he always had done.

The questions ranged from Sara and George's life as children in Virginia, to questions about making the decision to leave, starting a new life, questions about their indiscretions, honesty and how in the hell they never got around telling the girls the truth, at some point during their growing up.

"How did I get to be well into four decades of life, and not know that you were my sister?" Lily implored. The truth clung to Sara like the perfume of a skunk, as every pair of eyes in the room hovered above her head. Her answer was thin, but it was honest.

"Darling Lily, I never meant to hurt you. I was a scared teenager; Dad and I did what we thought was best for all of us at the time. We were afraid that if someone found out that we basically kidnapped you, they would take you away from us and make me give Nita up for adoption. As the years went on, you **were**, our child. It seemed hurtful to craft another narrative at that point. What would have been the purpose? Would knowing have changed anything? Dad and I made the decision that it was better this way. We were all the same family, and whether I was your big sister or your mom, we felt it didn't matter. We loved you the same."

Lily tried to understand but, it took her breath away. It did matter, she grew up not knowing her own father. And living a lie.

Within the stillness, she felt adrift. She mostly sat in silence. It would take her some time. Lily excused herself and left to go home.

A ferocious wind blew through the slit in her open car window. Her thoughts crowded the car with a suffocating fog.

This was the worst moment of Sara's life.

Days passed. Eventually Lily went to Sara to ask questions. She needed answers and she needed time. Sara gave her the space but was there for her. When the shock wore off, she realized that Sara and George did what they thought was right. It was the best they could, given their circumstances. And they did it out of sheer devotion and love.

Lily realized it was probably what she would have done faced with the same difficult set of circumstances. She found her way to gratitude. In part because she came to understand that she would have had a very different life had she grown up without a mother, in some hillbilly shack in rural Appalachia. Sara would always be her mother and George her father. But she wanted to know her real father. She wanted to know more. She wanted to know what happened that fateful night she was born. She wanted to know every detail. She wanted to know her roots. She needed to know all about her mother; where she was born, what she was like. She needed to know who she was, and she wanted to go to MeadowBrook and meet her father.

It had been almost 40 years since Sara and George left. They couldn't explain why they never went back or kept in touch. They just took on a new life. And perhaps out of fear of losing their truth, they created a new truth. Never, ever thinking they would face the certainly of fundamental fact.

Now they were embarrassed, and in some ways horrified at how they handled this whole situation. But a part of Sara and George were relieved.

And Sara, too, desperately wanted to go home to see her Poppa. If he would agree to see her.

CHAPTER TWENTY-ONE

Farewell City Life and Welcome Forest and Farm

Silvi connected to Nita differently now. She always felt close to her, but now, now they were family, first cousins. Silvi's Dad and Nita's Mom were brother and sister. She just couldn't get over it. Somehow everything shifted.

Silvi saw her life through a different lens. She saw herself as a part of something bigger. She now had a pedigree that connected the small world of her mom and dad and grandpa to one of the tribe. Daughters, cousins, aunts, and uncles. She couldn't imagine how her precious grandpa would process this after all these years.

She was excited and hoped he would be too. They say, in an instant your life can change, and for Silvi, this was a defining moment. Her life would never be the same.

Silvi went back to New York, and she told her partners that she would be taking an extended leave of absence at the end of the year. That she needed time to reorganize her life and figure out what this all meant.

She needed to explore what her legacy would be. She was getting older, and she felt lost. She felt like her direction had changed and she needed to not just go through the motions of life but step up and live life.

She was motivated to create a life she loved. Up until now she felt that she was doing something that resembled that. Her work in environmental law was important and made a difference, not just economically and environmentally for individuals she represented, but to the health of the Earth.

But now, it seemed like she had a bigger calling. She was not yet sure what her role would be, but it was becoming clear to her that she had a role in saving the wild American chestnut and bringing it back to its pre-blight glory, as one of the most dominant and important trees in the Eastern Forests of America.

Silvi spent the next month clearing off her calendar. She tied up loose ends. She passed all new cases on to her partners. Silvi still had two lawsuits that she was in the middle of. But they would both resolve by the middle of next year. She would finish those and then move on to the next phase of her life.

She couldn't wait to call her grandpa. Her dad, she knew, would not be happy about any of this. Silvi's remaining days at the law firm sped by like a Japanese bullet train. She was there physically going through the motions, but her mind was already elsewhere.

Silvi settled her affairs in New York City. She finally reached back out to Brad and agreed to set up the meeting he was waiting for, so patiently. They decided on dinner on a Thursday night in early November. Brad was distinctly excited at the thought of their reunion and was counting the days to see her again.

That night, Silvi showed up at Mama Marchi's just before eight o'clock. Brad had been waiting at the bar. He stood when she walked in. His fingers hovered over her cheeks, and he gave her a kiss. They sat and had a cocktail. They reminisced about old times. It was warm and comforting, but she had made up her mind. This was not the life she wanted. Not now.

After they got caught up on the niceties, Silvi turned pensive, "Brad, we have gone through a lot of years together. We have really grown up together, and I can see the vision of this life we would have together."

Brad interrupted, "Yes Silvi, we were always meant to be together, and I am truly sorry I hurt you. We are so much better people together. We are the couple that everyone in New York envies. The campaign is over in just a few weeks. Our guy is looking like he is going to win in a landslide. Then I'm thinking we could get a place together in January when our leases come due. We can start looking for a place near your office. I'll likely have a job with the new president and can go between New York City, and D.C. Then we can set a date for our..."

Silvi cut him off, "Brad, I'm moving to Virginia. I've taken a hiatus from law and I'm going to live on the farm with my grandpa."

There was a moment of silence.

"What? What are you talking about Silvi? You're giving up your law career? For what? To do what?" Brad said astonishedly.

"Brad, This, isn't the life I want. I won't deny it's been a thrill, and I've loved our busy, high-power careers, up until now. But it feels empty. It is not who I am. You know when you met me, I was a community activist. It started in high school and in college I rallied the grassroots for conservation and the organic edible movement. That is where my fire burns. It's what excites me. I need to get back to my roots. I believe it is where my legacy awaits me."

He sat with his mouth gaping open. He thought at first that she was joking. He could understand if she needed time to forgive him. He certainly owed her that, but an upheaval of their careers seemed irrational.

Silvi assured him that she was as serious as a mouse in a snake pit. She didn't get into details, but she told him that she had made up her mind.

Sliding from her perch on the bar stool, she signaled the bartender that she needed to go. Brad paid the check, and they grabbed their coats. They stood outside the restaurant, facing each other. Brad was not expecting this. He was speechless. She looked into his puppy dog eyes, kissed him goodnight on the cheek and wished him well in D.C. And knew she would likely never see Brad again.

Friday after work, Silvi came home to continue packing. Her apartment was chock full of memories from her life in the Big Apple; theater tickets, museum openings, programs from concerts, Broadway plays, fundraisers, and law conferences and newspaper clippings. There were so many photographs, most as a couple with Brad. Each image held recollections, flashbacks of a prominent, provocative, and prosperous ultra-urban life in the asphalt metropolis that is Manhattan. She took a deep breath and carefully crammed them all in the incinerator.

Silvi called her grandpa and told him that she missed him and couldn't wait to see him in a few weeks for Thanksgiving. She did not say a word about finding the family. She felt it wasn't her place or her story to tell. But she did tell him about her decision to take a hiatus from law, and that she would like to move down to the farm.

Tucker was beside himself with joy.

"Silvi, Darling, are you sure you want to walk away from everything you have worked for? You are at the height of your career. You are the consummate voice in the country for environmental law and patent infringement. Why would you do this?"

He obviously wanted what was best for her, and wanted to make sure she knew what she was doing.

"Grandpa, last summer with you and the ladies in the quilting group. I felt like I belonged there. It felt like home. I want to get my hands in the dirt. As I learned more and more about the work being done on the chestnut blight, I felt a connection to this movement. It may go nowhere but I feel drawn to find out. May I come home and stay with you for a while to figure it out?"

Tucker told her in no uncertain terms that this was her home. He reminded her of their conversation at the end of the summer when he told her of his plan to endow and trust her with the family farm. That this land, that her great-grandparents homesteaded, was hers. He reiterated that he had already made up his mind that this farm at MeadowBrook was her legacy now.

Tucker could not believe it. He was beside himself with joy and anticipation. He thought his granddaughter leaned on the thin side of crazy, but he would make her feel at home in MeadowBrook.

Tucker knew she would love her own space. A place where she could work and create and plan. He had about 26 days until she arrived, and he set about fixing up the little one bedroom, log cabin on the east side of the farm for her.

Tucker and Bessie had built that cottage for his mother Ruth to live in after his dad, Emery died. Ruth insisted that he and Bessie and the kids move into the larger homestead house. They raised Sara, Ben, Shirl and Berti there and through thick and thin times, Tucker had never left. After Ruth passed away, the cottage sat empty.

Tucker asked a few friends to help him clean it up for Silvi and make it a cozy cottage for her to live in when she arrived. The floor was made completely of flagstone. There was a large hand loomed rug on it. The fireplace, dark limestone with little flecks of mica, feldspar and granite that they had dragged up from the creek bed on the property. The windows needed new curtains, but the house had good bones and a beautiful view of the sunrise. It had its own little garden that he knew Silvi would love to putter in come spring, just like her Grandma Bessie did, growing beautiful flowers and vegetables. And it had a lovely front porch with a hanging porch swing for two. She would love it here; he would see to it.

Autumn Transitions 1987

Over the next month in New York, it turned unseasonably cold. People were already wearing scarves against the brisk autumn wind and now winter coats were being pulled out. Her lease was up on December first, but she would be moving out, lock, stock and barrel in time to be in Virginia for Thanksgiving.

Silvi nervously reached out to Luke, to tell him of her plan. She had an idea that although, the science of biological control and laboratory researchers were critical to the comeback of the American chestnut, she felt that there needed to be a full-time concerted effort in the field to crossbreed American and Chinese chestnuts for a true American chestnut with blight resistance.

She wanted to spend the next several years totally focused on that. She had done very well in her law practice and had a nice nest egg tucked away, and she still had a decent residual income coming in as a partner in the firm. She was sure that she could raise the consciousness of this plight and recruit volunteers to join her effort.

"Silvi, breeding chestnuts, this is a very ambitious project, and this has already been tried and it has not had much success," said Luke.

She said, "I know, but I've been thinking that there just hasn't been the right science yet. We understand so much more now than they did 50 years ago. I have an idea, a different way of succeeding in creating a backcrossed tree that would confer resistance. It will take patience, but I want to go deeper into back-crossing for resistance. And perhaps cross and select, and cross and select for several generations of seeds. There has got to be an answer."

Luke didn't interrupt her as she was on a roll.

"I have some ideas and feel like it's worth the effort. But I need your help, and the help of others who are committed to the cause. I love the science and understand enough to be dangerous. I'm a critical thinker, it has served me well in my years in scientific research and in law, but what I do best Luke, is organize. I'm a community organizer. We need to identify the community. I'd like to create a foundation whose sole purpose is the rebirth of the American chestnut forests across the natural range of the Eastern Seaboard. I envision a group of scientists and naturalists, environmental experts, forestry hot shots, an education brain trust, an advisory board, a cabinet, a council. And a lot of volunteers. Lovers of the land, people with a passion to bring back the American chestnut forests all up and down this side of the country."

Luke was taken under her spell. He couldn't wait to see her. He had never met anyone with the depth of passion that she had.

She had a ravenous pull to be a voice for these lost veterans, these ancient forebearers of another life, another time, a life that after thriving for thousands of years on Earth, were snuffed out almost to extinction in one generation. She was someone who recognized the extraordinary value in these trees and wanted to raise the consciousness of their story, so other visionaries could too.

She said, "They deserve their life back. Our callous, careless, incompetent mismanagement of nature wiped out a giant among the forests. It's our duty to do what we can to right our misconduct, as unintended as it may have been. It is time to raise the collective consciousness and make people aware of what happened and attempt to bring back the American chestnut to the forests of America.

"Yes, unequivocally yes," Luke shouted. He was inspired by her passion. His heart was pounding, and he knew Silvi, this crazy, brown haired, crystal blue eyed, natural beauty was ***the*** person who could do it.

CHAPTER TWENTY-TWO

Sara Reconnects with Ben

Sara, George, and the two girls were planning a trip back home to Virginia. Sara hadn't talked to her dad yet, but she did call her brother, Ben.

Ben recognized his sisters voice immediately. It had been 43 years since they spoke, and he was only 12 years old when Sara left. But he knew the moment she uttered his name, that it was her. He harbored some anger in the beginning for being left behind when the chestnuts had died, Mom had died, and he was alone with Dad. He felt abandoned by Sara, and it took many years to let it go.

In retrospect, he did create a beautiful, full life that he loved. But he would never understand how after losing their beloved mom, Sara could just up and abandon him too. He held a grudge for many years. When he heard Sara's voice all the resentment flooded back in an instant. He listened. His heart raced as she explained. He wanted to keep an open mind. Yet, hearing Sara's voice ripped the bandage of the old wound right off, and it bled profusely.

Processing thoughts from his now mature mind altered his reality when he heard she was pregnant. He felt for what she must have been going through when she left. Ben could sympathize with how she feared being sent away. He understood her desperation. He knew she was right. And her words were true. He finally understood all these years later why she left. Why she had to leave.

"What happened to the baby?" he wanted to know.

"Well, that is a remarkable story, Ben. And it's how I've found you after all these years."

She took a deep breath and explained an abridged version of the story to her brother.

"George and I went to live on an estate in North Carolina, where George's Uncle Joe was working. We had our baby that year and we raised the two girls as sisters. They grew into lovely young women and they each pursued a life they loved. Baby Lily, our sister, loved cooking and became a wonderful chef and has her own bakery in Upstate New York. And, our daughter Nita became a doctor and has been working for years in environmental science with this lovely young woman at the college in Syracuse.

Ben said, "That's funny my daughter went there, and was in science too."

There was silence for a second and he said,

"Wait, what? Your daughter, Nita, is Silvi's mentor, the one that she has talked about all these years? That is a freaking incredible story."

Ben got chills and tears welled up in his eyes.

"We know of Nita over the years. Silvi has always looked up to her. She has been a dear friend and mentor to Silvi," Ben burst out laughing.

"Well, what are the chances of those two crossing paths in life? About 100 million to one!" He burst out laughing again.

In an instant, his perspective shifted. He was thrilled to hear his sisters voice, and all the anger and resentment melted away.

He asked, "Have you called Dad?"

"No, Ben, I haven't. I don't know how he is going feel. I'm so scared he will reject us, and I wouldn't blame him. I kidnapped, stole, his baby daughter and raised her as my own. There were so many times I wanted to come home, or at least let him know where we were and hear his comforting, familiar voice. But I was so afraid he would have taken Lily and forced me to give up Nita. I just couldn't take the chance," cried Sara.

"As the girls got older, I wanted to call him. I picked up the phone so many times. And each time, out of fear, I just couldn't do it. I know now it was wrong. I would have died if anyone had tried to steal my child. But at the time, I had promised Mom that I would always take care of her new baby, and being pregnant at sixteen, I couldn't stand the idea that Dad would have sent me away to have the baby, and she would be adopted out to another family, and I'd never see her again," she rambled on through sobbing tears.

"I was so young and afraid, and I had George and he loved me, and I knew he would care for us. Oh, please Ben forgive me. I'm so sorry for hurting you. I'm so sorry I wasn't there for you all these years. But I never stopped loving you. Or dad. Never one day were you not on my mind."

Ben was speechless. His head wasn't processing as fast as his brain had questions. And he felt a range of emotions he didn't know he had. But most of all, he felt joy to be reconnected to his sister after all these years.

"Sara, you need to tell Dad in your own way. That is your story to resolve. I believe Dad will be very happy to see you. He kept your note that you left in his tackle box. It's still in there to my knowledge. He tried and tried to find you and George, but obviously to no avail. One day he accepted you were gone, and he said it would be up to you if you ever returned."

Sara cried at all the lost time. She cried at how old her dad would be now, and how much she had missed the old homestead.

"I love you, Sis. It will be good to see you again."

CHAPTER TWENTY-THREE

Silvi, Home

MeadowBrook Farm

Thanksgiving, Tuesday, November 25th, 1987

Silvi said goodbye to all her friends and coworkers. She stood at her office door and looked around the room for the last time. It was bitter-sweet. Everything that defined her time in New York was packed and removed. The shelves and walls were empty. Her designer silk dress and black pumps seemed oddly out of place. She walked around the large desk and gazed out the window, down to the bustling city. Sunlight streaming from the East created a dust beam that she had never noticed before. Under her breath, she prayed that she was making the right decision. Intellectually it made no sense, and she knew it. But the universal tug was undeniable, and she had to seize her truth.

Laura, her assistant, took her to lunch and wished her well. They had a tearful goodbye, but promised to stay in touch. Laura would miss Silvi at the firm. Laura admired and respected her as a woman and a kindly boss, in a large ego'd, white collared, white men's world. Silvi was the epitome of an independent, professional woman. She shined like a dime amongst a bowlful of pennies. She donated everything she didn't need. Lots of high-heeled shoes and expensive St. John knit suits went to her law intern who was about her size.

The next morning, Silvi woke while it was still dark. She bundled up the last of her belongings that were coming to Virginia. She was finally, completely packed, and her car was loaded. She did a final sweep, and was prepared to leave her city life memories, at least for now. She took a deep breath, and one last look around her now empty rent-controlled apartment overlooking Central Park.

Her thoughts drifted to Thanksgiving morning where she would be enveloped in a real forest of trees. Amber grass, and shrubs would embrace her, and a clear, crisp November breeze would blow through her long chestnut hair, calling to her, and welcoming her back home.

This was the first decision that Silvi ever made in her life that wasn't planned out and organized in great detail. The first time that she flew by the seat of her pants. One that was carefree and illogical. She had always been focused, had an agenda, and followed the path everyone expected of her.

Silvi was beyond excited, but a bit of jitters fluttered where confidence usually perched. She walked down to her car. The sun was now spilling down on her like beams of forsythia, with just one crenulated white cloud in the sky. It was rare to see an autumn day on the East Coast with almost no clouds. Usually, the sky would be filled with a wispy haze that would obscure the sun and paint a grey complexion on everything it touched; which was everything in Manhattan.

She jumped in her car and although at only forty-two degrees, she opened all the windows. It was brisk, and she tucked a scarf around her neck. Her long brown ponytail had flecks of red when the sun glinted off it. As she drove, her hair flipped around in the wind. For the first time in a long time, she felt vibrant and alive.

It wasn't that long of a drive from Manhattan to MeadowBrook, Virginia, but she decided to stop overnight in D.C. to spend an evening with some old law school friends on the way down. She also wanted to meet with an old colleague who was working at the Department of Agriculture, to see if they were familiar with any work being done on the restoration of the chestnut forests.

It turned out that minimally, they knew of some work being done at the environmental college in Syracuse, on the regulatory requirements for transgenic trees. Which of course she already knew about. The intern explained that being the day before Thanksgiving, the Department of Agriculture had only a skeleton staff on and those were only there for half a day. Silvi got phone numbers and decided to circle back at a later point.

When she got to MeadowBrook farm that afternoon, she took a deep breath of fresh autumn air. Silvi intentionally came a day early to cook and help Grandpa Tuck get ready for the holiday. The best she could decipher, nobody had told him the big news yet; the fact that Sara, George, Lily, and Nita were showing up. They all felt it was better to do this face to face.

She pulled up in the bladed and newly wood chipped drive. She started to walk to the front door and take her bags to her bedroom. Just then, Grandpa came out and said, "Hello my love, I have a surprise for you." Grandpa Tuck's new beagle puppy, Phil, bounded right by his feet. His long ears, clearly too big for his little body, flipped around as he ran. You could see they were already the best of friends. Tucker gave her a big hug and kiss and grabbed one bag under each arm.

"Happy Thanksgiving Grandpa. You are looking terrific," she said.

And he was; Tucker Hayes was still a strapping, handsome mountain man. She looked at him with amazement at how at 87 years old, he was still working the farm and living on his own. That, she concluded, was due to what she called 'clean livin'; fresh healthy home grown food, lots of exercise and being surrounded by people who loved him.

Silvi started to walk into the farmhouse, but Grandpa reiterated, "I have a surprise for you. Come follow me." With her bags under his arms, he led her to the cottage. He walked up on the front deck. And motioned her to come inside.

"Grandpa, what is this?"

"Sweetheart, come on into your new humble abode!" Tucker said with a grin as wide as a honey mushroom.

The entire neighborhood must have helped him because he had this old, musty cabin cleaned and fixed up like a country chalet. It was absolutely cozy and charming.

He had a blaze nesting on the grate in the old stone fireplace. As Tucker opened the door, the smell of the crackling wood wafted to her nostrils, and a sweet woodsy scent filled the room. The bed was made up with a fluffy down quilt and big goose down pillows. The small hand loomed rug by the side of the bed was like an invitation to hop up and into the fluffy featherbed, and curl up with the cool autumn breeze and a captivating novel. There was an old chestnut wood trestle table that Grandpa and her dad, Ben had built for great-grandmother Ruth. The table had a glass vase sitting on it. It was filled with autumn flowers. There were six quilted powder blue placemats around the table, along with an old pewter water pitcher. The windows had beautiful white crocheted window covers, and the deck had a white painted porch swing next to two old, white Adirondack chairs graced with soft sheepskin pillows hanging from each. One chair was a rocker and had a cozy, powder blue checkered blanket folded over the arm. The floor of the cottage was polished flagstone that had a spectacular blue and white loomed cotton rug on it. Silvi recognized the rug as one hanging from a special hand knotting loom that her quilting ladies had worked on last summer. The whole place was like a dollhouse, and she was stunned.

Adjacent to the cottage was a spacious drive through barn; on one side it had an old, well-worn plank chestnut wood floor that could serve as a perfect office space and the rest was packed earth where the hogs were raised, and machinery at one time was stored.

"Oh, Grandpa!" Silvi jumped in his arms and hugged his neck and kissed him on the cheek.

"This is perfect!"

"Silvi, if you are going to be staying for a while, I just wanted you to be comfortable. Besides, it was high time I got this place fixed up."

She sat on the bed and the nervousness in her belly vanished. It felt right. The universe pulled her here, for what reason, she still did not know, but it just felt that this was where she belonged.

As soon as Grandpa left, Silvi went back into her cottage and called Luke. She told him all about the trip and the information she had gotten in D.C., and contacts she made at the USDA. They talked for an hour and then she strolled up to the old homestead. She and Grandpa had dinner and turned in early. He kissed her goodnight, "Silvi, I can't tell you how happy I am to have you back home."

Tomorrow would be a big day…and she felt a twinge of guilt for not telling him this big 'Hayes Family Secret'. It took all her will power to not share the big news and excitement about this reunion, but she didn't dare say a word. What if he didn't find it exciting or joyful and he was still feeling betrayed by Aunt Sara at being abandoned at the lowest point in his life? She went to bed knowing that he didn't even have a clue of what was in store. But she said a prayer that he would accept his daughter; well, daughters, back into his life.

The next morning Silvi got up early, came over to the big cabin and made biscuits and gravy for her grandpa. Phil came out to greet her and she lifted him and was surprised at how big he had gotten in just a month. Grandpa rose with the smell of coffee. She was already wrapped up in her soft, warm blanket sitting in their old Adirondack chair on his porch, watching the sun rise toward her little cottage. She felt excited about the future, yet anxious that she may be getting in way, way over her head. She was so grateful that Luke seemed to be as excited as she was. There were lots of plans to make, but first, a Hayes family Thanksgiving.

As she sat listening to the rooster crow, she thought, "I need to call Nita right after the holiday and let her know I have arrived in Virginia ,and tell her about stopping in Washington, D.C. at the department of Agriculture."

Then, she laughed out loud when she realized that Nita would be ***here*** in just a few hours.

Grandpa and Phil joined her on the porch. He had on his flannel pajamas, and he looked so cute. He was a real mountain man but with his fluffy slippers and the flannels that Silvi had bought him last year for Christmas, he just looked like a little boy. They ate a relaxing breakfast together and then she slipped inside to get the turkey going. It had been basting overnight and it was ready for stuffing and cooking.

Silvi said, "Grandpa, I love what you've done to the old cottage. Thank you for doing that for me. It's perfect."

Tucker smiled. It warmed his heart that he could do something special for his best girl.

Grandpa said, "When I was a youngster, we kids would go out on Thanksgiving morning and bring our moms back a whole bushel of chestnuts that would go into her special Thanksgiving chestnut pie and the dressing for the turkey. I sure miss those days. They are memories that last a lifetime." He looked wistful.

Silvi smiled. She loved to hear him talk about the memories of living on this farm and what life was like at the turn of the century. She told her grandpa about her thoughts on helping to bring back the American chestnut. She was visibly animated as she told him about her research, the genetics, the virus work, and how she wanted to focus on breeding the American chestnut with the Chinese chestnut, to see if there was a way to confer immunity from the blight onto the American chestnut trees.

He cocked his head and said, "And this is what you gave up your thriving law business for?"

"Grandpa, I want to not only restore the American chestnut tree to Virginia, and our Eastern forests, but from here at MeadowBrook farm, I want to build an expansive volunteer network of state chapters all over the East Coast that will ensure diversity and regional adaptability. It will be essential to the long-term survival of the American chestnut. We need a breeding program that renders American chestnuts immune from the blight. We need to plant these hybrid trees, and we need to locate and inventory wild American chestnuts that might have survived the blight. And I can envision having outreach events and getting local communities active in the project. It is the only way to be successful. We will need money; I'll apply for grants and do fundraising. I want to start a nationwide million-chestnut challenge." She demonstrated with her outstretched arms, as she took a deep breath.

"Whoa, whoa sweet girl. You've got some big plans there. Maybe you should just start with a vision to cross an American chestnut with the Chinese chestnut and see if you can get it to be resistant to the blight. Ya Know, many have tried this and so far, failed. You'll need all your smarts and all your smart friends to overcome that first. Then we can talk about branch offices and volunteers in every state."

Tucker chuckled, as he shook his head, muttering to himself and shuffling in his fleecy slippers into the kitchen for another coffee and biscuit with that delicious gravy.

He worried that his granddaughter had lost her mind.

Silvi did get a tad carried away, but she was determined. And she was excited. Grandpa went to get dressed and chop some wood for the Thanksgiving gathering. Silvi set about making the turkey along with an apple lattice pie and a homegrown pumpkin pie. Other neighbors would be bringing their specialty side dishes. And lots more desserts.

Round about noon, she saw her mom and dad arrive. She ran out with her apron on and gave them a big hug.

Ben whispered, "Does he know anything? About Sara and her family?"

"I have not said a word, heavens, no. I did not want to get in the middle of that one. When are they arriving?" Silvina asked.

"They expect to be here about two o'clock. Sara is so nervous," Rebecca told her.

"Good,"said Silvi,

"The neighbors; the Burnhams, the Winslows and the Pinchots will be here about five-thirty, so that will give us plenty of time to get over the reunion shock before they all arrive. Gosh, I hope this goes well."

Silvi and her mom, Rebecca, got back to work in the kitchen. Setting the long tables to accommodate everyone. Ben and Grandpa went out to chop more wood together and to get caught up on Upstate New York forestry challenges. Phil followed them, spirited, and frisky as a duck in a puddle.

When they arrived back a couple hours later, all was set, and the girls must have appeared antsy.

"What is up with you girls? You seem like you're waiting for John Wayne to come back from the dead?"

Silvi and Rebecca glared at each other, waiting for the other to say something.

"Oh, it's me Grandpa, I invited Luke Woodbury, that smart doctoral, environmental researcher, you know the one that is Bill and Clara Pinchot's grandnephew. Remember him? I like him. It will be nice to see him again," chirped Silvi as she shot a glance at her mom.

Grandpa Tucker flashed her a look, and then cocked his head at the table settings and wondered who else was coming, as there seem to be too many places set.

"Who else did you invite, the Abingdon choir?" said Grandpa.

And just then their car pulled up. Grandpa was facing Silvi and by the look on her face, he knew something was churning. He knew Silvi too well. She would be a terrible poker partner.

Tucker turned around and started walking onto the wood deck. He didn't recognize this group of folks that were getting out of the car. But his eye caught Lily. She looked a lot like Silvi, and of course, the dear love of his life, Bessie. He was fixated on Lily.

He had not seen her since she was 5 days old.

Sara was shaking. She was so nervous the entire drive to Meadow-Brook. The journey meandered across the entirety of the Earth that she knew, back to the roots where she was born. She didn't know what she would say. How he would react, and if he would even talk to her. She took a deep breath, and she stepped out of the car. She lingered silently in the stillness of that November afternoon.

Tucker's eyes were still riveted on Lily, but he had no clue who she was. He walked down the steps toward the car, and in an instant, he saw Sara. He squinted. She froze and chills ran down her arms. Tucker's brain was trying to figure it all out. He cocked his head as he looked at this carload of people.

Sara stepped forward and spoke, "Poppa?"

He slowly walked right up to her, then stood in disbelief. His brain was trying to process... He was paralyzed for what seemed to be an eternity. It was the longest 10 seconds of Sara's life.

Then his mouth dropped open. She was all grown up, a woman, but unmistakable. Panic briefly overcame Sara, she wanted to run. Tucker grabbed Sara and lifted her off the ground. He set her down but didn't let go. He looked at her face and he shook his head. And he started to cry. He couldn't utter a word. She buried her face in his chest and she sobbed. It had been forty years, but he never gave up hope. Not one day. He prayed that he would once again have his beautiful daughter in his arms and this time he would never, never let her go.

CHAPTER TWENTY-FOUR

Hayes Family Reunion

Luke and Silvi

2:15 p.m., Thanksgiving Day, 1987

Tucker was without words. His brain was still trying to comprehend what his eyes were seeing. He stood in his front yard with his holiday red and black checkered flannel shirt, his holiday denim pants, with his arms around his daughter that he never thought he would see again. And there was George. Much older, he'd become a man, an older man. He chuckled at the thought. He slightly let go of Sara and he spoke, "What? How? Where have you been all these years?" And before she could answer, he hugged her again so tightly that she was lost in his arms and couldn't speak if she wanted to. Which she did not.

Finally, George stepped up with an outreached hand and said, "Mr. Hayes, It's George Baldwin." Tucker kept hold of Sara and brought George into the hug. He took a deep breath and then stepped back, now holding Sara's shoulder.

Sara didn't know the right way to do this, so she just blurted it out, "Poppa, this is Nita, she is your granddaughter. The night George and I left; I was pregnant. I was so scared to tell you. But this is our baby girl.

"He looked at Nita, his eyes were wide and wet as a country pot-hole in spring, and he smiled. And said, "Aww, you are a beauty Nita, Welcome. Welcome to you all."

Sara went on, "And Dad, this is Lily. "There was silence. It was as if someone "Muted" the moment. He looked at Lily and walked toward her. He knew the moment he saw her from the window she was somehow related to Bessie. Lily had a tear run down her cheek. She stared into Tucker's eyes, and he stared at hers. Lily's eyes looked like sapphires. He gently took her delicate alabaster hands in his rough, calloused, coal-stained paws.

"Poppa," Sara said, "This is Lily, your daughter." He gasped and felt lightheaded. She was magnificent. She looked very much like Silvi only older, and she too was the spitting image, but an older version of his beloved wife, Bessie. The baby Lily that was birthed the night his wife passed away. She lost her life, giving birth to this child. He ran his hands through her long chestnut hair, and he couldn't take his eyes off her. Tucker was speechless. The moment was intense, and 20 seconds felt boundless, he finally grabbed her into a bear hug and they both sobbed tears of joy.

Ben and Sara embraced like they hadn't seen each other in 40 years. In fact, everyone hugged and eventually made it inside to reconstruct the story of Sara and George.

Then the incredible story of how Silvi and Nita connected in Syracuse and how they had this chance encounter on Sara's birthday. What shock and wonder it was to find out that this Nita Baldwin, Ben's daughter, was the Nita that Silvi had talked about all these years. She had been her research mentor since college. It was a miracle that they never knew, never suspected they were cousins.

Silvi took a deep breath and said a little prayer to the universe that things didn't crumble from past hurts and betrayals, and abandonments and anger that might have happened in another family. She was raised in gratitude. And that ran deeply today.

By five o'clock Luke arrived with a homemade batch of au gratin potatoes. And a tray of home-grown asparagus that he picked in spring and froze especially for Thanksgiving dinner. The au gratin potatoes were his specialty. Uncle Bill asked for them every year.

Silvi introduced him around to her family, as she held his shoulder. Grandpa broke out his famous fermented apple cider and as the family continued with toast after toast, they started to break into more intimate, deeper, one on one conversations.

Luke whispered, "How did the reunion go?"

Silvi said, "I want to show you something." She grabbed his arm, and they walked out front.

"Oh, Luke it was beautiful. It was an autumn day like so many others, but it stood alone as the end of a very long journey, and the start of that very same journey. The skies were bright and the affections and spirits brighter. There was not a dry eye. Grandpa was like a boy again. Aunt Sara was like a young girl who looked up to her daddy with awe, as if he were God himself."

"Silvi, that is great news. What a relief, what a wonderful homecoming," said Luke.

"And Luke, Grandpa was awestruck meeting Lily. There was no regret, only gratitude that his baby daughter was raised to be a beautiful woman. Monet couldn't have painted a better reunion. Grandpa melted into the moment, something you don't ever see in an old mountain man like him."

Silvi walked the handsome doctor over toward the cottage and the barn. She briefly showed him her cottage and then the large adjacent space for an office and garage.

Luke saw the vision too. It could be crafted into a perfect office and laboratory. It would need some modifications, but an easy construction project.

"Wow, you are really serious, arent you?" said Luke.

They stepped up on the porch. Silvi leaned back against the outside of the cottage and Luke had his arm leaning above her on the logs.

"I'm not sure how, but I see a vision," said Silvi.

She chastely looked up at him and their eyes met. He slowly touched her cheek and leaned down and gently kissed her. His hands were shaking, and his heart was pounding. Silvi moved in closer. She raised her arms around his shoulders while he put his arms around her thin waist, gently pulling her into him. She inched her hands up on his neck, to his dark, thick hair. And she grabbed tightly as he perceptibly moaned, he kissed her neck.

He moved his hands from around her waist onto the small of her back. Her shapely breasts pressed against his chest, and it pulled open the front of her soft sweater. Luke's heart was beating so hard he thought it might fill her ears. He was full of passion and sexual desire for this incredible woman.

Silvi had never felt anything like this before. Never with Brad. Her heart pounded harder, and she felt lightheaded.

He lightly fondled her long, thick, dark hair with one hand, and kept the other firmly on the small of her back, pulling her deeper into him. Silvi arched her back. He groaned again and gently repositioned her between his legs. She moved her hands down his chest and caressed his back and buttocks. Their bodies were flush with heat as they continued to kiss passionately.

Silvi's eyes were fixed on Luke's, and then she closed them. Her heart jumping out of her chest. He was breathing heavily on her face, and she savored the smell of him. Her knees felt weak, and she fell into his arms. Luke lifted her up to his lips again, and she completely surrendered. Silvi's only thought was, "So this is what falling in love feels like."

As the neighbors were starting to arrive, Luke half-heartedly suggested they get back to the group. The sky turned to twilight as the horizon went from cornflower blue to orange to grey. They hadn't noticed.

Luke and Silvi giggled and walked hand in hand back to the party. It was a wonderful Thanksgiving. The sun started to set, and Ben lit the fireplace. There were introductions. There were reunions for Sara and George after all these years and there was entwining of new family into old. A reunion of old friends with new. There were many toasts made and there was a lot of fermented cider and hootch consumed. So much chatter, so much good home cooking, so many stories.

There was a retelling of memories of the old days, when the canopy of chestnuts hung as a haven, as a shelter to all who lived under them, and the rich, sweet delicacy of that nut was taken for granted. When that beautiful smooth seed of the chestnut was not simply a symbol of Thanksgiving, but a symbol of life itself. Its mahogany blush, its bowed side and flat side, and its pointy little furry tip was just a part of the everyday landscape.

Later that night, after all the neighbors bid their goodbyes, and only the family remained, Grandpa changed into his work boots, and they all walked out to the forest. He and Ben built a campfire. Something they had done thousands of times before. Normally, they'd toast marshmallows on sticks, but the whole group of them were stuffed from dinner and dessert. The wind whipped up and everyone pulled their sweaters and jackets closed, and they all scooched closer to the fire. Grandpa sat on a log, surrounded by his three children: Sara, Ben and the youngest daughter, Lily. For the first time since he wore a young man's clothes, they were all together. Silvi was flanked by Grandpa on one side and Luke on the other. She snuggled close to Luke, and they inhaled the comforting spirit of the kindled wood and listened to the popping of sap from the not quite dry branches. All eyes were fixed on Grandpa, as they listened to stories that Silvi had heard all her life. And Ben had lived through.

Tucker Hayes, this elderly old soul, still a lumbering man in his red and black hunting coat and his flannel shirt, told the tale of growing up in this forest. He told about a way of life that thrived in these parts for a millennium. With deep passion in his voice, he painted a color word picture for his whole family, so they would remember why the wood from the American chestnut was used for everything, from "cradle to coffin." What it was like, right at this time of year, when the mast of nuts was so deep on the forest floor that you needed nothing more than a bucket or burlap sheet to collect a year's worth of food without moving your feet.

Then he paused, in reflection; his voice cracked...."I want my children, all of you, and the ones yet to come, to know the richness of our past here in Appalachia. When the chestnuts bloomed in abundance, the earth thrived with life. These trees were not simply a forest, but they represented our culture, a sacred bond to the land that sustained us and bound together our community."

He told of the year he lost his precious Bessie. And how almost overnight, all the chestnut trees on their land were infected with a strange disease, a blight, and had died. He wanted his family to know, he wanted them to carry on the stories, the memories and the culture that were so much a part of his heart and the foundation of many generations before him.

In that moment, a tear ran down his weathered cheek. They were all haunted by his words, as he spoke of the underpinnings of life crumbling right before his eyes. And being helpless to do anything to change the course of history, and the course of his very own family's life. The truth, the beliefs, the sureness of life; crippled and collapsed right before his eyes.

Through choked words Tucker said, "The loss of the heart of this forest is a tragedy. It's a poverty we imposed on all the children yet to come, that they are deprived of the magnificence of nature; the nature that I knew growing up. It stirs a fire in my soul, to somehow restore people's bond with this beautiful land."

It was in this instant, as her face flushed with campfire light, watching that tear roll down her grandpa's cheek, that Silvi knew what her life path would be. The truth clung to all their hearts. Panic flashed between she and Luke knowing the enormity of their thoughts. She'd heard chestnut stories all her life, but it hit her... this tree wasn't just the heart of an amazing ecosystem stretching from Canada to Georgia. It was the architecture and fabric of a culture, a way of life. Now, seemingly gone forever. The loss of the chestnut was an American tragedy, the worst environmental disaster this country had ever seen. All she could think about was, how do so few people know about this incomprehensible slice of American history?

Grandpa's stories inspired Silvi, right then and there, to her life's work. She knew in that moment that she had to do everything in her power to create a vision, a living legacy, a vigorous, hardy, blight resistant forest; A forest of chestnuts restored to its former splendor. She needed a plan to return the iconic American chestnut to its natural range.

Silvi's mom and dad, out of an abundance of love, tried to protect her from the harsh life of rural Appalachia, but she realized that the modern urban lifestyles that have evolved, have stripped us of our connection to the land.

Silvi always loved nature and forests, but she realized that she'd never *known* the forest. Not like Grandpa Tucker. She never had the relationship with nature that was reciprocal, that was symbiotic, like Grandpa had. It was a moment of certainty for Silvi. She wanted that deep connection to nature. In a way, she had been preparing for this "David vs. Goliath" crossroad her whole career. She needed to tell the story that should have been told so long ago; the story of why the American chestnut is worth saving. And how for the first time in American history; science and technology had evolved to a point where the tools existed that would make that possible.

Silvi was so glad Nita and Luke were sitting there with Grandpa on that night. She knew she would need them.

His memories painted firsthand pictures that they could only imagine. It was hard not to be moved by his words. Silvi was moved. For the first time, her head and heart seemed to join hands. The journey wasn't perfectly refined yet, but she had a direction, and that direction felt like her "True North."

Silvi knew that she was teetering on a precipice, with nothing but a leap of faith. She knew this endeavor must be far grander than one girl's vision. It had so many implications and would need a lot of work. Yet, someone needed to initiate it. And then the world needed to be educated and the word needed to be spread, and people needed to embrace the importance of this undertaking.

They all lingered silently, reflecting on Grandpa's words. Silvi was projecting into a future that quite resembled the past… the functionally extinct American chestnut forest needed an advocate; it needed a champion.

And then, in front of her whole family, on that brisk November night, she spoke softly, but more surely than any words she had ever uttered,

"This American chestnut is the tree that called us home. We must save them before they, and the memories are truly lost forever."

CHAPTER TWENTY-FIVE

When Fireflies Danced

They were the jewels of the darkness, the glitter of the night, that brought joy and magic with their soft, golden light.

Fireflies were some of the most spectacular creatures you'd ever lay eyes on. They were not much bigger than an ant but had this amazing ability to light up the night sky with their glowing bums. Young and old alike have always been fascinated by fireflies. They were universally adored. Has anybody ever seen a firefly for the first time and not stood in awe and curiosity? They were fascinating, secretive, and mystifying. "How do they do that?" children would cry.

There's just something enchanting in watching them play and flutter about, their little lights twinkling and glowing like a field of stars on a canvas of darkness.

Summer nights brought out the magic and mystery of fireflies. The fascination permeated all children of forests and marshes, those lucky enough to have lived where the fireflies danced. Nothing was as extraordinary, enchanting, or bewitching as sitting on a log watching the waltz unfold. A glimmer here, a twinkle there, and then darkness again. The flicker was life itself. The murmurations fascinated all that sat amongst them.

Summer nights brought out the mystery of a bug we cherished.

Curious and inexplicable they would sparkle in the darkness. Fairies of the night, thriving in their natural habitat.

Until something changed.

Most bugs were considered pests. Something to exterminate from life but, fireflies, they were spellbinding, and you wanted to hold them close to have them for yourself. But sometimes, we find ourselves obliterating that which we love. Fireflies aren't the only thing we've loved almost to death, but these were a slice of whimsy and delight that we thought would always be our muse. They were mysterious pixies of darkness, thriving in a world that embraced them. Embracing them a little too much; we've loved these bugs almost to death.

We didn't mean to hurt them. We wanted to collect them, put them in jars and take them to our bed to watch their magical glow, under the covers as we fell asleep.

Out of curiosity and entertainment we coveted them. But our love for fireflies became a destructive force throughout their habitats. And as we grew up and began to realize the mistakes we had made; it was too late. The damage had already been done. It was a harsh lesson learned, one that taught us the importance of preserving and protecting the beauty and magic of nature.

The fireflies may have been small and seemingly insignificant, but their loss was a reminder of the larger impact that our actions can have on the world around us. We didn't know how the simple pleasure of fireflies in a jar would change the world.

It wasn't just our greed and unintentional actions that ravaged their population. These little guys also faced some significant threats from habitat loss, pollution, and the use of bug spray for other pests. It's a real shame too, because not only are fireflies beautiful and magical creatures, but they played an important role in the environment around us.

It turned out that it wasn't just their twinkling magic that was so darn special. These critters had a design and purpose which we never knew. It darned well never crossed our minds that they used their light to talk to each other. Different species had their own unique pattern of flashing, which they used to attract mates and send messages to one another. Like their own little Morse code of secret stories. Many species of fireflies were busy pollinating and helping to fertilize flowers and plants as they went about their business. They were also an important food source for other living things, like bats, birds, and spiders. Not just a spectacle for us to behold.

But maybe all is not lost! There are plenty of folks out there that love fireflies and are working hard to protect and preserve them and bring back their habitats. Working hard to raise awareness about the importance of these insects is imperative. By supporting efforts, lending a helping hand to create conducive surroundings, and to protect their natural range, will ensure their survival. We can bring back these amazing wild natives of the summer night. But for the firefly to make a comeback, we need to continue to support their environment and wellbeing. It will take an intention, an effort from humans to see these beauties, once again light up the night sky for generations to come. We need to raise the consciousness of folks across America.

To relive the fascination of past generation's youth, and share that enchantment with generations to come, we must become aware. To once again share special nights that remind us of a simpler time, an age of abundance, and the beauty of bygone times, we must educate people and curtail our detrimental actions in nature.

As we aspire to find an old wood log and watch the fireflies dance on a summer night, we hope that their numbers will continue to grow and that their magic and mystery will never fade.

We may have loved them to the brink of death, but maybe, just maybe, it's not too late to restore the balance and protect the creatures that bring such joy and wonder to our lives. So, the next time you see a firefly dancing about in the evening twilight, take a moment to just watch and admire, and appreciate the gift of hope, joy, and happiness that these tiny creatures bring.

CHAPTER TWENTY-SIX

American Chestnut Restoration Plan

MeadowBrook Farms

1987

Nineteen eighty-seven turned out to be the best Thanksgiving Silvi could ever remember. She slept deeply, and woke in her cozy, little dollhouse cottage to the sound of a rooster, and the sun peeking through her east facing window, casting an amber light across her bed. She laid tucked up under her thick down comforter with a smile plastered across her face. She felt light as a feather, and knocked for a loop. But for the weight of the bedding, she felt she would float to the ceiling. Silvi replayed her evening with Luke in her head and could hardly wait to see him again.

The morning was cold, but she slid out of bed and stoked the logs in the fireplace. And then got dressed.

She was in a unique position, everything Silvi knew, that mattered, balanced on the pinnacle between the boondocks and Broadway.

She went over to Grandpa's place to put on coffee and start a hearty breakfast. She knew he would love to wake to the smells of the kitchen. His puppy, Phil, came bounding out from the bedroom and she took him on the front porch while she drank her coffee, bundled in her favorite blanket, on her favorite Adirondack chair.

Silvi's mind was racing between her feelings for Luke and her plans to save the chestnut forest.

When Grandpa woke for breakfast, they moved inside the old farmhouse. They sat at the handcrafted chestnut table in the middle of the cabin. Her great-grandfather, Emery, had built it. And it was still in the same spot it had been for 3 generations. Grandpa ate and listened to her intently, as Phil sat on his lap, nudging Grandpa to scratch his ear. Silvi was sipping her third cup of coffee.

"Grandpa, so this is what I know for sure. Based on all the research done to date, it is not likely that we will eradicate the fungus, so we need to discover ways to render the fungus nonlethal to the trees. And that is not my area of expertise, so I will need help. And that is where Luke and Nita come in. Luke is knowledgeable about using a virus to render the fungus less toxic, and Nita has worked her lifetime in genetics to identify the exact DNA sequencing in plants, like the chestnut. She already knows that there are genes that are responsible for promoting natural immunity in the Chinese chestnuts.

But what I'm most excited about is breeding hybrid chestnuts by cross pollinating the American and Chinese chestnuts until we have an almost pure American chestnut with the immunity gene from the Chinese variety. Scientists and farmers have tried this, but they haven't been successful yet. But I have a new idea that I believe will work. It should, in theory, at least."

"Silvi, didn't you spend your school years as an outspoken opponent of this genetic modification stuff?" asked Grandpa.

"I remember you going to Washington, D.C. and lobbying the Congress at a young age. Remember that article about you in the newspaper? You were so proud!"

"Yeah, it is pretty comical, or disturbing," she chuckled. "That I'm even considering a genetic answer to the rebirth of the American chestnut. You're right. But Grandpa, I've always been fascinated with the science of it. It's the ultimate puzzle and we may have found the key to a miraculous cure."

"I see," Grandpa said, unimpressed.

"What I finally realized is that I have two problems with tampering with genes.

It's not the technology and the science of genetics, but it is the process of an entity, like a business, commandeering something that belongs to all the world. The idea that nature can be patented. That a corporation could own of a part of nature. And that ownership gives them the right to do anything at all they want with the varieties they own. Such as destroying the sale of heirloom varieties and organically diverse seed. All in exchange for holding hostage *"their"* seed and the profits that large corporations demand from farmers to grow a crop. Do you see what I mean?"

"Companies can *'own'* a particular seed?" Grandpa questioned unbelievably.

"Yes, if they develop a hybrid seed, they own it. They legally can say who uses it, how it's grown, how much it costs. And they can, and **do,** sue farmers if any of their patented seed blows onto a farmer's land! That's what I was fighting against in my last big case on Long Island."

Tucker trembled at the thought. He had no idea.

"The second issue is safety. A crop can be genetically modified to survive toxic pesticides being dumped all over a farm with the specific intent of killing everything growing but the crop, such as corn. The issue here is that everyday people then consume everyday staples like corn, wheat, soybeans and such, that have been doused with poison! That cannot be healthy," Silvi said.

"Gosh, that is insane," gasped Grandpa.

"Anyway, I can't do this myself. So, I'm going to set up lunch tomorrow while Nita and Luke are still here for the weekend and bounce some ideas off of them. I must get them to buy into my crazy, long shot idea!"

Silvi then spent the day with her family and prepared for her lunch on Saturday with Luke and Nita.

Saturday After Thanksgiving

Luke, Nita and Silvi agreed to meet in the barn on Saturday.

Luke had spent all day Friday with his family, so this was the first time that Silvi had seen him since they sat around the campfire on Thursday night holding hands. And then his lingering kiss goodnight. That evening she fell asleep with a full tummy and a full heart. She had never had such intense feelings for anyone before. It was fun.

Nita and Luke arrived at eleven-thirty. Silvi had made turkey salad sandwiches and warmed up some leftover potatoes au gratin. She also brought fresh pressed apple cider that Grandpa had pressed that morning.

After some superficial chitchat, Silvi began, "I asked you two to come together because I have a crazy idea that I need help with. And you two are just the brain trust to make it work. I need your knowledge and experience if a project of this magnitude would have a chance of succeeding."

The two of them stared quizzically; with cocked heads, raised eyebrows and pursed lips. She started by regurgitating what these two had taught her:

> *"As we know, the American chestnut is an historic and beloved part of this country's history. Its functional extinction has altered life for millions of families, and animals, that counted on its bounty for a millennium. Its total extinction, if the roots died, would be an immeasurable loss for all our planet. If there is a chance of saving the chestnut and restoring it to forests across its native range, it is incumbent upon us to try. Bringing back the American chestnut could salvage a way of life to millions of folks and also directly offset the effects of climate change and deforestation by increasing carbon dioxide consumption, as well as a release of large-scale oxygen into the air.*
>
> *Now, there have been attempts at controlling chestnut blight by crossing it with the Chinese chestnut, however, the results have been less than stellar. The hope was that some of these hybrids would show some*

resistance along with the desirable traits of the American chestnut, but so far, nothing."

They were impressed at how she captured the essence of what they taught her and honed it to a simple message.

They nodded. She went on,

> *"So, I believe the first focus must be to continue to cross the hybrids with more hybrids or maybe with pure Americans until we have an American tree with resistance and the characteristics of the native tree."*
>
> *"Here is our plan; we should set up right here at MeadowBrook farm with that purpose. It may take many generations of crossing but in my calculations, I believe it can be done."*

Nita interjected with a smirk on her face, "What do you mean ***our*** plan?"

Silvi ignored her and continued *"While I understand we have few answers today, I believe putting our skill sets together, will move our cause forward. It's unlikely a single intervention will eradicate chestnut blight. But together; between the evolving science of breeding, and Luke's biocontrol, and your biotechnology breakthroughs in genetics, I truly believe that we are poised to be in the best position we have ever been, to join forces in hopes of rescuing the American chestnut tree."*

There was silence. Luke and Nita looked at each other. Then they stared at Silvi. If they were excited, they didn't show it. Just deadpan poker faces.

She was so nervous, and for what seemed like a month of Sundays, they didn't say a word. She went on sharing her ideas of turning MeadowBrook into a research farm and an experimental field farm for preserving, studying, and breeding American chestnuts.

"I realize this is quite an endeavor," Silvi moderated, not wanting to seem like an utter clodpoll.

They looked at each other again, and finally Luke spoke.

"I love this idea. A nonprofit formed exclusively to bring back the iconic American chestnut."

Nita jumped in and hugged her and said, "Silvi, I always knew that we would work together on an important project. I am proud of you for being open to genetic biotechnology. You will see what good it can bring to the world."

So, it turned out, they were as excited as she was, just not as brave to suggest it.

Silvi went on, "I don't think this crazy idea could work without putting our heads together. We need to come up with a vision statement and a mission and we need a name."

The excitement level in the room was palpable. All three of them tossing around thoughts and ideas and stories they had accumulated over the years. Silvi broke out the lunch basket and they bantered about a vision and a name for their new foundation. They were playful and put everything they thought of on the table.

But in the end, they decided to call themselves:

WILD AMERICAN CHESTNUT RESCUE MISSION

And the mission statement; To Rescue and Breed the Historic American chestnut tree back to its Native Range.

And their long-range vision; To create a Vigorously Extant American Chestnut Forest restored to its Wild Resplendence.

There were no illusions. They all were seasoned enough to know that this would, no doubt, be a very long process. They understood that none of them would likely ever see a chestnut forest in their lifetime. But their actions today might well thrive that their grandchildren and generations of children to come, may walk in the footsteps of their great-great-great-grandpa's legacy. None of them were sure they could pull this off. But, IF they succeeded, it would be nothing short of extraordinary, to bring back the American chestnut.

They were confident that the research alone might even help with other threatened wild struggling species facing their own devastating blights.

They were all elated.

Silvi spent the month between Thanksgiving and Christmas paying a visit to everyone she could find that had lived during the heyday of the chestnut forest. Everyone had chestnut stories, like Grandpa's. Memories that were part of their heritage and family fabric. By and large, these stories were all retold by those of Grandpa's generation. Her dad had a chestnut tree fort in his youth, but he wasn't old enough when the blight came to be aware of the devastation to the forests across America.

She drove to Abingdon to search the library for archives and articles that were written at the time that the blight arrived in Virginia. There weren't a lot. However, staying in touch with Nita and Luke with daily updates was fun for her.

Silvi particularly wondered why something this devastating economically and culturally, and catastrophic, had slipped from the annals of history. Why were children never taught in school about the functional extinction of this most dominant and important tree in America; it's lumber, its wildlife sustenance, and the subsistence lifestyle on the Eastern Seaboard? Everyone knew of the demise of the Dodo Bird and the dinosaur. But millions of trees were lost and virtually no memorial, no dedication, save for the remnant small town street signs or park square names etched a hundred years ago.

What Silvi quickly realized had been lost besides the economic and the societal changes, was "*The Spirit*" of the chestnut tree. How day to day life changed for millions of Americans. She felt that it was incumbent upon her to bring that back. And to tell that story.

It didn't take long for all three of them to comprehend that this was an enormous and prodigious project that would require an accord, a kinship between science, and passion, law, and love.

They all agreed that as farfetched as it might seem, they must initiate a plan to bring it back to its former glory and motivate people to get involved.

Silvi coordinated the work, "We will need to captivate people.

Entangle them knee-deep in the lost culture, the promise of the simple past, projected into the future. We will engage them in something bigger than themselves. A movement back to camaraderie and community, and simple healthy food. It is not just about trees, or forests, but the foundation, the infrastructure, the underpinning of what connects us to all other Americans, across the range. And to find the folks excited enough to be part of the Million Chestnut Challenge; the summon to have a hand in growing the first million blight resistant American chestnut trees in a hundred years," she said to her partners.

They couldn't wait to get started.

CHAPTER TWENTY-SEVEN

Kitchen of Culinary Chestnuts

Chestnuts were an important food for a millennium before wheat and potatoes were grown commercially. The American chestnuts were abundant and the staple foundation of meals long before European settlers ever arrived on America's shores.

Every year without fail, large spiky burrs, as big as a man's fist, covered the trees and encased the smooth brown nuts within. In autumn, when the first chill of the season came, they would explode and drop the shiny brown nuts onto the forest floor. Wild animals of all kinds; squirrels, bears, wild turkey, hogs, and deer all thrived on the chestnut bounty. The ground was littered with an unlimited source of calories for all who lived amongst them.

Native Americans lived off the copious amounts of chestnuts they collected each year and used them to make everything from soups to well, nuts! When the Europeans began to settle these shores, the natives taught them how to roast, peel, and pound these nuts into flour for everyday use.

In the rolling countryside, chestnuts flourished for centuries, and they were an essential part of nearly every meal. Their earthy flavor intensified soups, and their addition to breads produced loaves with a soft, light texture and a nutty essence. American pioneers incorporated chestnuts into their meals because of their abundance and their ability to be stored once ground into flour. Unlike acorns, they could be eaten raw right from the tree, and their sweet taste was delectable. However, their abundance led people to take them for granted, and nobody could imagine their disappearance. The chestnuts were a staple that was rarely missing from a meal.

Chestnuts paired well with many savory dishes, such as pork and sweet potatoes, acorn squash roasted with caramelized onion, pasta with savory mushrooms, chicken breasts with whipped rutabagas, roasted Brussels sprouts with raisins, and of course, chestnut stuffing. In sweet desserts, they were excellent, such as chocolate truffles, sweet chestnut puree, chocolate chestnut torte, chestnut and hazelnut shortbread, raspberry chestnut scones, cheesecake with chestnut crust, and blueberry chestnut tart. In the cities across the United States, chestnuts became a coveted delicacy, especially during family celebrations and holidays. The aroma of roasting chestnuts on open fires created memories for many on chilly autumn nights and in snowbound, cozy winter scenes.

Chestnuts elicited warm feelings and festive family fare, like scenes out of the Saturday Evening Post. Chestnuts were unlike most other nuts in that they were low in calories and fat, with almost 80% carbohydrates. They had a low glycemic index value and were rich in vitamin C, gallic acid, and ellagic acid, which are strong antioxidants. They were high in magnesium and potassium, which help boost heart health. Their buttery, sweet essence and lightly nutty flavor were unique. When turned into flour, it could be used in many autumn-inspired recipes, and cooking with chestnut flour was simple, as it could be substituted for all purpose wheat flour in most recipes. Blending chestnut flour with other flours like wheat, rice or oatmeal delivered varying flavors and textures, and it gave a soft texture to most baked goods. Chestnuts complemented rich autumn comfort food flavors such as brandy, chocolate, caramel, fresh cheeses, cinnamon, figs, brown sugar, maple syrup and other nuts like pine, hazelnut, and walnut. Tarts, shortbread, and cookies were all elevated with chestnuts.

Before the turn of the century, chestnuts were an everyday staple, especially for the subsistence farmers of Appalachia who relied on this nut and this tree for their basic existence. But not today. What will it take to get this nut back in our pantry, our cookbooks, and our lives? Time will tell. And in the meantime, we can savor the memories and flavors of this once beloved and essential nut.

CHAPTER TWENTY-EIGHT

Becoming the Wild American Chestnut Rescue Mission

Silvina Hayes Woodbury

1990's

THE NEXT TWO YEARS BROUGHT FOCUSED RESEARCH, FOUNDATIONAL work, and the building of infrastructure at the newly expanded laboratory at the Wild American Chestnut Foundation on MeadowBrook farm.

And it brought a wedding, and a baby.

Luke and Silvi married in the spring of 1989. It was the toast of MeadowBrook. They grew a network of many friends since moving to the farm. Both Silvi and Luke were personable and welcoming. Their enthusiasm about their mission was contagious. They loved to share it with anyone that would sit still for 5 minutes. People were drawn to their passion, devotion, and warmth. They were also building an extensive network of volunteers that wanted to be in on the ground floor of this important work, to change the landscape of Virginia, and beyond. Everyone Silvi and Luke knew were invited to the wedding. It was a blending of more than just a man and a woman. It was the start of a partnership to transform life on Earth through diversity and innovation.

Their wedding initiated a dream, to redeem and rekindle a massively monumental lost piece of Americana.

The following year they had a son. They named him Sam. Samuel

Woodbury. He was a joyful baby, and Silvi didn't know she could love anything as much. It was a relatively easy and seamless birth. Sam seemed to harken a renewal of the farm. He was the first baby at MeadowBrook since Grandma Bessie gave birth to Lily fifty years earlier. Grandpa Tucker adored his great-grandson. Although Grandpa was slowing down, he would sit with Sam and tell him stories like he did when Ben and Sara were small. He would regale Sam with stories about the land and the farm, and what life was like with the hogs and the chestnut forests.

Sam's arrival also signaled the genesis of the rebirth of the American chestnut. Strides were being made at MeadowBrook. Silvi started crossing American chestnuts with blight resistant, high mountain Chinese varieties. By the time that Sam turned five years old, they had 2000 chestnuts planted on the farm. It was starting to look like a forest. It would take a few more years, but soon they would know if the fungus would attack these young trees, as they expected. If so, they would re-cross the most resistant hybrids again with another American chestnut seed to keep the traits of the pure American but produce a tree that would exhibit resistance to the blight. They always knew it would be a long and tedious journey. But they were making strides. Most importantly though, they were on that journey.

Grandpa, with his worn and weathered boots, would trudge through the tall grass on the path to the conservation fields every day, even on days when he felt fatigued, and his back nagged at him. His loyal companion, Phil, with his floppy ears, would bound alongside him. Their bond strengthened by countless hours spent exploring the natural beauty of their land. Grandpa Tucker beamed at the tiny trees he remembered from his youth. His rosy cheeks radiated joy as he walked amongst the rows. Some of the older trees had gotten taller than him. He was Silvi's greatest advocate. He would bend anyone's ear about how proud he was of her work. He was at peace at how life was starting to shine again at MeadowBrook farm. He said it often. Grandpas was the voice that Silvi could always trust on this slippery journey.

Life on the farm was full and happy. Luke and Silvi continued to make friends in the community. It seemed everyone was extremely interested in their project. As the years went by, they recruited more and more volunteers in and around that area of Virginia, and from places far and wide. Word spread even faster than the blight did in its heyday. Volunteers came from as far north as Canada, as well as folks from the Ohio River Valley, Alabama, New York, and Georgia. They built rustic little cottages to house volunteers that committed to their project. It was starting to feel like a little commune for common good.

Silvi spent a lot of time on the road spreading the word of the Wild American Chestnut Rescue Mission. She had more invitations to speak at nature collectives, forestry conferences and universities, than she had days in the month. It was essential for exposure to the rescue mission. She was such a popular speaker that membership to the foundation was growing by leaps and bounds. She spent most of her time helping influencers understand practical ways in which they could be part of the recovery effort.

On a nippy autumn day in October, Silvi was in Boston giving a keynote address at the Harvard Historical Society.

She took the podium and thanked the organizers:

"One day, a group of Harvard professors took a field trip to the far-reaching forests of New England to study the local flora. As they were hiking through the woods, they came across a bear. The bear stood up on its hind legs and said, 'Excuse me, do you have the time?'

The professors were stunned and one of them stammered, 'Uh, yes, it's 3 o'clock.'

The bear checked his watch and said, 'Thank you, I have a meeting at 3:30 at the Harvard Biology labs.' And with that the bear turned and walked away, leaving the professors standing there in shock.

The moral of this story: even in the deepest, darkest forest, you can't escape the Harvard alumni network."

A hearty chuckle swept across the room and Silvi went on....

"Thank you all for having me here today. As you know, the Wild

American Chestnut Rescue Mission is a nonprofit formed for the sole purpose of bringing the American chestnut forest back to its rightful place up and down the Eastern Seaboard. At MeadowBrook farm, we focus on backcrossing for resistance to the blight that wiped out the forests at the turn of the century."

She went on to describe the work being done on the farm and why this project was so critical. She shared the work being done with the *Hypovirus* and told of their successes and challenges. And she took them back to her days working in the labs at Syracuse and how genetics played a potential role in saving the chestnuts.

"We are learning a lot, and we are securing tremendous support from Americans like yourselves, that want to see the return of the cherished free banquet of chestnuts to the Eastern forests."

She went on, "Much support is coming from botanists, foresters, and geneticists that learn from our research on how to manage forests. And from the scientists that spend lifetimes teaching us the truth about the importance of all trees with which we share our planet. The fact is, that these magnificent trees are living and breathing organisms, just like we are. They teach us all about biodiverse ecosystems. We need healthy forests to cool our world. We need them to be home to birds, and wild animals and pollinator bees. These chestnut trees would once again play a role through photosynthesis in filtering our air and water to provide clean habitats and shade.

The statistics are staggering. We have lost 98 percent of the world's pristine old growth forests. It is up to us to do something to participate in reversing this life-destroying trend. Support from our project comes from some obvious places like the Forest Health Initiative, and the U.S. Forest Service, arboretums, and plant biotechnology researchers. But we are finding it is also coming from some not so obvious places like the Wild Turkey Federation, the Hardwood Lumber association, and Hog Farmers of America. There is so much good to come from turning back the hands of time to the heyday of chestnuts in America, before we unwittingly destroyed our gracious bounty."

She took a deep breath and finished her keynote, "But we must beware. Not everyone is supportive and on this bandwagon. We can see the handwriting on the wall. There will be those that will challenge us. And at one time I would have been at the front of the line with a megaphone marching with a banner against GMO research. There are those who worry about safety, and rightfully so. We will need to spend a lot of time proving, verifying, and confirming the safety and security of any transgenic or *Hypovirus* trees that could be released into the wild.

And finally, some ecologists worry that a return of the chestnut forest will disrupt a century old ecosystem that has developed without it.

This is a journey, an uphill and long journey. I know that I will not see the American chestnut forests to the likes of my grandpa's youth, but it is a responsibility that must be initiated for our future generations. Maybe for my son Sam, or maybe Sam's great-grandchildren. But we must start. We must undo the damage of our past to restore and rescue the glory of the nearly extinct *Castanea dentata*; The Wild American Chestnut Tree."

Silvi finished to a standing ovation....

"It is our legacy now in life, to hold a seed in our hand and see the vision of a million chestnut canopies."

CHAPTER TWENTY-NINE

Lily and Andy
SunnyCroft Dude Ranch

The Hayes family had a wonderful Thanksgiving on the farm in 1995. Ben and Rebecca, and Sara and George drove down to Virginia from Upstate New York. They took turns driving and did it in one 10 hour shot. They were exhausted when they arrived but planned to stay a week. Nita flew in, as she didn't have the time to make that drive and was not planning on staying as long as her mom and dad.

Lily drove down too, and brought her husband, Andy Colville. Theirs was a whirlwind romance. They met at SunnyCroft Dude ranch over the 4th of July weekend in 1990, up in the Catskill Mountains. She went up with some staff from her bakery, for a group retreat.

Andy and a group of his friends drove Upstate for the holiday weekend. He was joined by his best friend, Todd Baielli, Todd's wife, Liz, and Todd's younger sister, Evelyn. The dude ranch was well known for its beautiful horses in a rich, stunning setting just a couple of hours outside of New York City. The accommodations for singles were dormitory style with six to eight women or men per bunkhouse. There was a shared bathroom with four showers and four commode stalls and a wall of 10 sinks with a dappled, oxidizing, worn looking mirror plastered above the sinks, for the length of the wall. Most of the girls were young, in their late 20's to mid-30's. Lily felt like she was a house mom to them. So, she mostly kept to herself. She was there for riding. Fondly remembering her days growing up in North Carolina on the estate with horses. She was quite a proficient horsewoman.

On their second day at the ranch, she came into the dorm bathroom after a morning ride and saw a beautiful delicate silk scarf laying on the wet muddy floor. It had obviously been kicked under the bay of sinks by one of the younger girls. She picked it up and rinsed it out and hung it over a towel rack to dry.

Later that evening when all the girls had returned to the bunk, Evelyn said to the group, "Hey gals, whomever picked up my scarf and washed it, I wanted to thank you. I didn't realize I dropped it until I saw it hanging up in the bathroom this afternoon."

Lily piped up and said, "It was nothing. Really, I just saw it after a morning ride and gave it a quick rinse."

"Well, that was sweet of you. That scarf means a lot to me. It was a gift from my grandmother, who was a lifelong equestrian. She's passed on now, so I would have been heartbroken to have lost it," said Evelyn.

"I'm Lily, what's your name?" she extended a hand.

"Oh, I'm Evelyn. Everyone calls me Evie."

"Well, it's a pleasure to know you, Evie," said Lily.

"I live up in Barryville, where are you from?"

"I'm in the City and am up here with my brother and his friends for the holiday weekend," said Evie.

"Oh, that's great. Hey, I'm just going to meet my friends for dinner, but let's exchange numbers before we leave? Maybe we can reconnect to ride sometime?" Lily suggested.

Again, Evelyn wholeheartedly thanked her and gave her a hug.

The dude ranch had a warm, cozy feeling to it. As you walked into the lobby there was horse blanket plaid carpeting, well-worn leather furniture, and the living area was adorned with oil paintings of horses and western scenes. Wagon wheel chandeliers hung high in the rafters and knotty-pine paneled walls lassoed you back in time, to the turn of the century wild west. The activities ranged from horseshoes to archery to nightly campfire gatherings of s'mores, singing and scary ghost stories. It was a fun getaway for Lily, and a great way to deepen the connection with her staff. Lily loved being back in a saddle for some deep relaxation and playfulness.

On Sunday morning, Lily went to the lobby to pay her bill before her last ride of the weekend. Out of the corner of her eye she noticed a dapper, dark, curly haired man, wearing a pair of slippers that had a label on the instep that said, "Saks Fifth Ave." It barely registered for her, but didn't go unnoticed. The man came up to the counter asking for stamps for a letter he was writing and struck up a conversation with Lily.

"Hi, I noticed you at the campfire last night. You looked like you were having an enjoyable weekend."

Lily had grown into quite a stunning woman with her long chestnut color hair pulled back into a ponytail, her steel blue eyes, and in her form fitting, tan stretch pants with black leather chaps, knee high riding boots and her crisp black riding hat. At 51, she could easily have passed for 30-something.

She said, "I'm Lily Baldwin, it's nice to meet you."

He introduced himself as, Andy Colville. He told her that he, and a few friends had come up from the City for the holiday weekend. They talked for a few minutes, and clearly had an attraction. Lily said, "It's really nice to meet you Andy, and I hate that I need to run, but I've got a ride in just a few minutes."

He asked for her phone number and said he would like to continue the conversation. They exchanged numbers.

"It was such a pleasure to meet you, Andy. I do hope to hear from you," Lily said.

She skipped out the front door for her last ride. Andy couldn't take his eyes off of her as she walked out of the lobby through the set of double wood doors. She glanced back over her shoulder, smiling, and saw Andy was watching her. Lily giggled under her breath.

On the drive back to Manhattan at the end of the weekend, Todd, Liz, and Evelyn shared what a fun weekend they had. They all concurred that they really need to do getaways like this more often. Andy shared the story of meeting this charming woman in the lobby and how there was just something about her that really struck him. He also told his friends that they exchanged numbers. Everyone teased him with ooww's, and aahh's and cat whistles... and wished him good luck.

Evelyn told in detail about the lovely roommate she had for the weekend. She relayed the story about the silk scarf, and what a truly extraordinary gal she was for picking it up off the muddy floor and washing it. And that they too exchanged numbers and would stay in touch.

When she told the group the gal's name was Lily Baldwin, Andy spoke up and said, "Evie, are you kidding? That is crazy, that is the same woman I met!" he chuckled. "What are the chances? I had this odd feeling, like I had known her my whole life and yet, I know I had never met her before. I would have definitely remembered that one."

It wasn't long before Andy drove Upstate from the City to meet Lily. They have been inseparable since. If you believe in love at first sight, it was Lily and Andy. They had each been married before, and were hesitant to ever wed again, but they each felt it was different this time. They had a small May wedding the next year with just immediate family and friends. She catered it herself with Andy's favorites; double crust buttermilk chicken, garlic whipped potatoes and roasted quartered red onions. And dessert was her infamous secret Mereng-hata Cake, boasting melt-in-your-mouth amaretto semifreddo with a crispy lady finger meringue crust.

The day could not have been more perfect. Bright yellow Forsythia and cascading white Lady Banks roses spilled over the garden archway caressing the couple with the scent of spring, as they walked through to take their vows together.

Lily and Andy bought a place in Upstate New York, in a quaint but spirited town called Barryville, near her Gourmet Foods and Patisserie. Andy opened a branch office of his accounting firm in the Catskills and his partner continued to run the downtown Manhattan office. The new office was less than two hours from New York City and less than two hours from Lily's parents, Sara and George, near Syracuse. It was a perfect arrangement and Lily was profoundly happy.

CHAPTER THIRTY

Grandpa Tucker
MeadowBrook Farm
December 23, 1995

SILVI PLANNED A WONDERFUL HOLIDAY SEASON IN 1995, THE YEAR Sam turned 5 years old. The entire family came to MeadowBrook. Of course, the Pinchots, Burnhams, and Tom Winslow were all there too. They lost Tom's wife, Julia earlier that year. She was the first to go since Tucker lost Bessie so many years ago. Tom was hardly ever left alone, and he had enough casseroles to last until spring. There was also a large group of farm volunteers, who were now scattered around the farm, or living close by in MeadowBrook They all stayed for Thanksgiving and to join in the festivities. The food was simple but traditional, and the tables reflected a true Appalachian harvest with crisp, white linen tablecloths. Colorful leaves and autumn flowers were collected, and graced the tables. The smells of cooked turkey and roasted homegrown veggies wafted out of the old homestead. Logs were crackling in an open fire, and there was laughter, lots of laughter. And of course, children running around everywhere.

Everyone felt that they belonged there. Silvi saw to that. She stood before the fireplace and smiled warmly, looking around at her family and friends all gathered for the holiday. The cabin was filled with the delicious aroma of a home-cooked meal, and the sounds of joyful conversation filled the air. Candles were lit, casting a warm glow over the faces of everyone there. Luke caught Silvi's eye and smiled, and she felt contentment, gratitude and love spread from her gut, up to her heart.

The whole scene tumbled out of a Norman Rockwell painting. It was a perfect moment in time, a moment that would be forever etched in Silvi's memory.

Grandpa had a big day, and he quickly grew tired, as the last of the guests said their goodbyes. He went to bed with a big smile on his face.

The days quickly turned colder during the week that the family was there. The colorful autumn leaves desiccated brown, and dropped. All available hands spent chilly, sunny afternoons raking big piles and then burning them at night. You could smell the mulchy leaves in the golden glow of the blaze, and you could watch the crackling sparks dancing about like a constellation of fireflies. The gardens were wintered over, pulling the remainder of the autumn vegetables; winter squash, acorn and butternut too, carrots, beets, cabbage and cauliflower. And the last of the herbs. They set about covering frost sensitive plants.

Silvi and Luke could not have been happier. Ben and Rebecca, and Sara and George left on Wednesday. By the weekend, everyone on the Rescue Mission was back to work on the farm. And finally, there was idyllic silence.

After everyone left, there was a lot to prepare before years end. The family decided to all come back for Christmas given Grandpa's advancing age and his apparent slowing down. They didn't want to miss a holiday with him.

Silvi started sleeping at the homestead after Thanksgiving so she could be close by, to care for her grandpa if he needed anything in the middle of the night. Luke and Sam stayed in their Woodbury cottage. Silvi would come home to make breakfast for them, before they were awake, and readied for their daily chores.

On December twenty-third, 1995, with no fanfare or illness, Grandpa Tucker passed away in his sleep. Everyone knew he had been having a harder time doing everyday activities of living and he had trouble with simple tasks.

You never expect it, even when you prepare. Silvi knew it would happen one day. But she never really thought *that* day would be today. When Silvi arose on that Saturday morning, she found Grandpa sleeping in his rocking chair in the living room. He must have gotten up at some point during the night, maybe he couldn't sleep. When she walked over to him, he didn't move, she leaned over and kissed him on the head and realized that he was gone. He evidently peacefully drifted off sometime before morning. She wrapped her arms around him. And was grateful to be alone with him for a moment. Coming around the chair, she laid her hand on his shoulder and buried her face in his chest one last time. He was still warm. And he smelled like home.

Silvi softly sobbed, and she told him how much she loved him. She owed him everything. Life would never be the same without Grandpa Tucker on MeadowBrook farm. She was unable to move him herself, so she ran over to the cottage and woke Luke. She didn't need to say a word. One big alligator tear fell on her cheek, and he knew. He wrapped his arms around her, and they stayed there for what felt like an eternity. He let her cry her eyes out.

"It's alright Sweetheart," he kept saying to her. A big tear fell from Luke's face onto Silvi's thick head of hair. He rocked her in his arms, and she completely surrendered to him.

Eventually, they bundled up. Luke and Silvi walked back over to the homestead. Luke laid Tucker in his bed. They sat there holding hands and said a prayer. Grandpa Tucker was the patriarch of the Hayes Family. He was the sap that united the family, he was the trunk to all the branches of the tree. Like a ripe pomegranate, you couldn't be touched by Grandpa Hayes without carrying his rich color away with you.

The whole family was planning to gather for the holiday already, so there were no sudden arrangements to be made other than turning a Christmas celebration into a funeral.

A different kind of celebration of life.

CHAPTER THIRTY-ONE

The Fate of the Rescue Mission Falters

MeadowBrook, Virginia

Christmas, 1995

Everyone in the family arrived by the next day. People were in different stages of travel when Grandpa passed, so Luke and I decided it best to tell them when they arrived instead of frantically trying to reach them on the road somehow. By Christmas eve all of MeadowBrook was filing into and out of our home. Grandpa always told me that he didn't want us to be sad when he went. He'd had a long and wonderful life and he felt blessed to be the steward of this land for his entire lifetime.

Tucker Hayes was born on this homestead. He grew up in this cabin, fell in love and raised a family on this farm. He'd seen good times and desperately hard times. But it was home. It was his home. The Hayes Hog Farm and MeadowBrook meant everything to him. It was his soul. He wanted to be returned to the land here, and I intended to honor that in every way I could.

There were literally dozens of Grandpa's friends who visited us over the holiday week, from as far off as Abingdon. Tucker Hayes had touched a lot of people's hearts. And the stories his friends told about him really filled in some gaps that I had about his playful youth, and his finding the love of his life in Elizabeth Jenkins, his dear Bessie.

And there was food. Oh, my goodness, everyone brought food.

Like the stories of when Grandma died, and how Tucker was never left alone, and never without a casserole.

Finally, all the words were spoken, and all the neighbors had gone. Everything had been cleaned up by the quilting ladies. And we collapsed. Sam fell asleep on Grandpa's bed. There were no more tears to be shed that night. Tucker Hayes would be sorely missed, especially by me. I would miss seeing his bright eyes and sincere smile and his quick wit. I would miss his never-ending lessons about how to forge a life worth living and how to create a life you love. It wasn't so much the lessons he spoke as the ones he quietly lived that left me with the roadmap to finding a life of purpose. I would miss our times alone, surrounded by his big bear hugs as he told me, time and again, that I was his best girl.

I took out Grandpa's old underground hootch and passed it around for one last toast with Aunt Sara, Uncle George, Dad and Mom, Lily and Andy, Nita, me, and Luke. We each shared a brief toast to Grandpa, and told stories that touched our hearts and connected all of us together. In times like this you treasure family; it is the thread that weaves all of us into the same fabric.

Sara talked of her years being the oldest child at home with her mom and dad. How she and Bessie used to have summers alone when Tucker would take Ben fishing in the summer. She shared how her dad taught her to plant a garden and how to drive a truck. And how she missed him terribly when she left at sixteen years old to start a new life with George in North Carolina.

Ben talked about their summer fishing trips and how they laughed and slept under the celestial river of starlight in the wilderness. It's where he learned to live off the land and learned how to seamlessly blend duty with fun. He shared stories about the years he and his dad were alone in this cabin after mom died. He spoke of how they struggled for a couple of winters to stay alive on the little food they shared. And he recounted a few of the tales in the letters they had exchanged over the years when he moved to Upstate New York, and joined the Forest Service.

Nita and Lily listened. It was obvious that they realized what a gift these past few years had been. They grew into women without knowing they had a grandfather or an extended family. They said how grateful they were to have spent these years with Tucker. They cherished the time with him, as they got to learn about their roots.

We all shed tears and said our goodbyes, to a unique and loving man. I'm sure Grandpa Tucker was smiling from above, as he watched us unite and strengthen the bond of family between us.

And then as casually as discussing the weather Aunt Sara looked directly at Ben and Lily and said, "I'm guessing neither of you are interested in keeping the farm, as none of us rightful heirs live anywhere near here? Perhaps we should talk to a Realtor before we all head back to New York?"

Then she turned to me… "Of course, no rush, Silvi, whenever you and Luke and Sam can find another place to live."

The silence was deafening.

"I'm sure you didn't intend to stay in that little cottage all your life."

I was completely dumbfounded. I couldn't even form a sentence. I'm sure my jaw dropped open, as I sat there wondering if I heard her correctly. It completely came out of left field, and it never occurred to me that the three siblings of Grandpa would believe it was their responsibility to dispose of the land and the farm.

There was utter silence. Then, Lily chimed in and said,

"It never occurred to me but, do you think that is what Dad would have wanted?"

Sara proclaimed "Yes, of course, I don't imagine he would ever have thought any of us would move to Virginia and live out our lives on this farm."

"I guess the proceeds of selling the farm would help Andy and me remodel the old house in Barryville. And set us up for the expansion of the bakery that we were planning to do when we could afford it." Lily thought out loud.

Dad looked at me, "Honey, I guess the girls are right, we are the legal heirs to the property, and it would be a financial burden far beyond anything we could afford to maintain and manage it. I'm sure we can find you another place to work at a university, or college lab. But of course, there is no rush. We all need time to grieve and regroup. We can certainly talk about this at another time."

He shot a look at Sara, and we could all see the velocity of his virtual arrows grazing her shoulder.

I guess Dad felt it was inevitable, but certainly did not need to be brought up before his dad had even been buried a week.

Finally, the shock of this revelation diminished enough in my brain to squeak out a thought.

"But Grandpa wanted me to have the farm. He told me many times."

There was silence and all eyes were on me, "He told me he was proud of the work we were doing here, and he felt it was his legacy, a rescue mission, a foundation and research facility for the rebirth of the American chestnut forest. I do not think you all realize what we are doing here at MeadowBrook," I implored. "I don't think you know how much this land and this project meant to Grandpa."

"Or what it means to the world," I added.

Sara said, "Oh, I'm sure he was immensely proud of you, Silvi. But we are his children. And the property is worth hundreds of thousands of dollars, if not more. The mineral rights alone on almost 500 acres are worth a fortune. For you to stay here when we can sell it and all be pretty much set for life just does not make a lot of sense, now does it sweetheart?"

I didn't want to be rude and knew to hold my tongue, but at that moment, I wanted to remind her, and the rest of the family, that she left when she was a young teenager, and it wasn't even until a few years ago that Grandpa even knew what happened to her and to his baby daughter Lily. But I kept quiet.

If any of his children should inherit the farm it should be Ben. He worked the land and lived there when she abandoned him at the height of the blight and the depression. Ben was the only one there to pick up the pieces when Grandpa lost his precious wife, at his lowest point in life.

I knew there was nothing I could do to convince Aunt Sara, other than present a '*last will and testament*' which I was pretty confident did not exist.

We did everything on our word and a handshake here in Appalachia. I can't imagine that it would have ever crossed Grandpa's mind to hire a lawyer and draw up a *will* since he made it crystal clear on several occasions that he wanted me to inherit MeadowBrook and continue our work on the American chestnut reforestation.

I was devastated, and I could see in Luke's eyes, so was he. But there was no hope, no recourse. They were legally the next of kin and they had the right to do whatever they wanted with the property. I could see Mom and Dad were perplexed and frustrated, and Aunt Lily didn't say another word. I didn't know of a way, a shred of hope of saving MeadowBrook and the Wild American Chestnut Rescue Mission. It would take a miracle.

What I did know though was after six years of backbreaking, intensive, all in, dedication, we were just starting to see results in breeding a viable version of the American chestnut. The hard work of our small group of volunteers could not be replicated. There would be no starting over. And yet, no convincing Aunt Sara that Grandpa had told me how much he wanted me to carry on this work and to live out my life on this land. And that I promised him I would.

I bit my tongue. Luke grabbed my hand and a tear rolled down my cheek.

New Years Eve 1995

Luke and I were alone, at last. Aunt Sara tried to gather information about the land while she was here and had one real estate agent come out to see the property to get an idea of what they would list it for; what it was worth. It turns out that indeed it was very valuable acreage.

Luke and I were beside ourselves in grief. Grief from losing Grandpa and grief that everything we had dedicated our life to was facing a certain demise, not unlike the devastation of life that Grandpa experienced when everything that defined him changed in an instant.

What would we do? How could we save the foundation? It was just my word. And Aunt Sara would never understand.

Christmas came and went. We got back to work. We kept our schedule of speaking engagements. Luke kept working in the lab looking for virus solutions to the blight. An appraiser was sent out to value the property and determine if the land could be split up and sold off in sections to raise more money and get a higher price for the land. Other real estate agents dropped by, knowing the land might be up for sale soon. I must admit, I had little patience for chatting with them, and resented how the word travelled like they were birds of prey descending on carrion ripe for the picking.

It was determined that nothing would be done this winter as the property needed sprucing up and the trees and shrubbery were looking pretty bleak and desolate. In spring, when the place looked its best, renewed with life and flowers and greenery, they would sell it. Also giving us some time to get our life in order and figure out where we would go and what we would do. Luke suggested moving back to New York City. He suggested that I go back into patent law, and he try to get a lab position at New York University or Columbia. The thought of walking away from my passion, from my dream was crushing. But there didn't seem to be any other way. We did not have enough money to buy the property, even if Dad would agree to keep his share in the family.

Lily was silent on the matter. She felt more like a granddaughter than an equal share sibling. I know Dad and Mom would have done anything to keep my dream alive, but it was not financially plausible. It was impossible to consider without Aunt Sara agreeing, and she was hell bent on getting it sold and getting the money out of the land as soon as feasibly possible.

It was a long cold winter. We needed more heaters in the lab, but didn't want to invest money that would be a waste. In a matter of months the property would be sold. Our work continued; I kept lecturing. But I was getting more and more discouraged as each day went by knowing that it was just a matter of months before it would all abruptly vanish. Poof, like a slippery trout, slipping out of the hand of a small child on his first catch. It was like being in a story where the characters stood by helplessly as they watched life fade to black.

We were so close to answers, yet just out of our reach now.

Before we knew it, spring arrived. The first of the daffodils popped their bright yellow faces up through the frozen crusty ground. One Sunday in April, as I was packing boxes and getting the house clean, one of Sam's friends was over and Luke decided to take the boys fishing.

Sam said, "We need another rod, Daddy."

"You know Grandpa Tucker had several," I said, overhearing the conversation.

"Why don't you grab a couple, and take Grandpa's tackle box and bring that along with you? It should be in the bottom of the closet in his bedroom."

Sam and Ricky walked over to the old homestead and came back with all the fishing gear. The boys took out some of Grandpa's favorite lures and they all headed down to the river. They left the mess right on my kitchen table. When I went to move it, the smell of the box brought back a flood of memories. Summers spent fishing with Grandpa down by the river. We always had a big blanket with us, and his favorite peanut butter and banana sandwiches. It made me laugh. I haven't had one of those since I was a kid. Deep in memories, I lifted the pull-out drawer to see what was underneath and there were some papers. One letter was very old. It was from Sara, written the night she left MeadowBrook, pregnant with Nita. Ha, he kept it all these years.

And the other letter was newer. In an envelope sealed. I opened it. And it was in pen, in Grandpa's handwriting. It was dated eight years ago in November, the year when Grandpa remodeled the cottage and I moved to Virginia.

"To my dear Family. If you are reading this, I have gone to heaven to be with my beloved Bessie. I want you to know how much you all mean to me. You also know how much this land is the heart of who I am and the soul of everything I have lived for. My last wish is that the farm goes to the one person who I believe will carry on my legacy: Silvina Elizabeth Hayes. Further, I would like it to be put into trust so that it will live on forever as a place of solitude and beauty that this land represents to me and your dearly departed mother."

It was signed.

"Your loving Father Tucker B. Hayes 28 November 1987"

My jaw dropped and tears welled up. Then like big drops of rain they overflowed and streamed down my cheeks. I was paralyzed and in shock. I read it again. And then remembered to breathe. All I remember was running outside spinning in circles, running through the garden, laughing, and crying and then I fell onto the ground. Laying on my back on that verdant, rich land, I looked up at the clear blue sky, and spoke out loud to the universe.

"Thank you, Grandpa. I promise you that I will work tirelessly to fulfill your legacy and our dream of rebuilding the chestnut forest of your youth, all across its natural range."

"Luke!" I quickly hopped up and ran all the way to the river, singing and dancing. When Luke saw me running at top speed toward him, I'm sure he was suspect . He dropped his rod, and ran toward me. He lifted me up into his arms, and didn't know if I was laughing or crying. But I could not stop gasping and crying alligator tears. Finally, without a word, I just handed him the letter. He set me down and looked at it, then looked at me. Luke's mouth was agape, he was speechless too.

And I simply said, "Darling, lets order us some heaters!"

CHAPTER THIRTY-TWO

A Permanent Home: The Rescue Mission Comes to Life

MeadowBrook Farm

Spring, 1996

Silvi's first phone call was to Ben and Rebecca. She could hardly breathe. The phone rang, "Hi Sweetheart," said Rebecca.

"Mom, can you get Dad on the phone too?"

"Sure Silvi, is everything alright?"

"Yes, it's just something the two of you need to hear."

They were both on the phone now, a little nervous about what was so important.

"Mom, Dad, I have some extraordinary news." She was stumbling over her own words.

"I'm so shocked. I still can't believe it. I'm still trying to process it all, but it appears, Grandpa Tucker left a letter, in his own handwriting, bequeathing MeadowBrook Farm to a family Trust in perpetuity and designated me, as the custodial trustee."

There was silence and a long pregnant pause. And then Ben asked, "Silvi, are you sure? Where did you find it?"

"Yes, Dad. It was in his tackle box. It was dated the day I moved to the farm in 1987."

"Well, I'll be!" declared Rebecca.

Ben laughed out loud, "Hahaha, we could not be happier. Mom and I were praying. We were trying to figure out a way that we could keep the farm in the family. A way we could afford to buy out Lily and Sara. This is incredible news. The universe has crossed paths with fate."

Silvi began to cry.

"Luckily, Lily is in love, and has a nice life and was certainly not expecting to have a farm bequeathed to her. As for Sara, she and George have a nice, comfortable life in Upstate New York. And they have Nita and Lily close to them. I am confident that the girls will be very happy…After they get over the shock." Ben chuckled at the thought of breaking the news to his formerly absent sister Sara.

"Okay, young lady, seems you have work to do!"

Silvi, through choked back tears, expressed,

"Dad, Mom, thanks. You two have always been there for me. You have always been supportive, even when I had no clue what my direction in the world might be. You guided me, like Grandpa, every step of the way to find my purpose, to meet my hopes of making a difference in this life. I love you and I hope you're not too disappointed, but I promise, I will work every day to make you proud."

"Silvi, your mom and I could not be happier. We love MeadowBrook and to be honest, we were sick to think the farm and the community would no longer be part of the Hayes family."

Silvi sent Ben the letter, along with the letter in Grandpa's tackle box that Sara had written in 1938, the night she snuck away in the shroud of darkness, pregnant, young, and scared.

Ben sent Sara a copy of both, and she never said another word about it.

Back on the Farm

As the anesthetic of moving wore off, the spirit of the farm and the unconscious dormancy of the American chestnut Rescue Mission woke up to life, with renewed vigor.

Silvi and Luke started in earnest, organizing the technical side of the American Chestnut Rescue Mission. They established a formal structure and filed as a nonprofit organization in Virginia. She set about completing all the other legal and ministerial papers needed to initiate fundraising. She prepared a long-range plan to move forward with their American chestnut Rescue Mission.

After the legal constructs were in place, Silvi created a board of directors to chart a new course for restoration of the American chestnut forests. There was the immediate structure and the long range plan. She would allocate a few positions now and modify as they grew. Silvi started out as the president and chief executive, but hoped to find someone quickly with forest sciences, perhaps restoration and land management experience to take over as CEO. She would also need a CFO, someone with professional development, fundraising, grants and capital campaign experience.

She and Luke worked together to come up with a list of people they thought would be excellent partners and willing to serve as their board of directors. Luke would be director of science for the organization until they were able to find regional science directors that were versed as land conservation engineers, landscape architects, horticulturists, ecologists, and foresters.

Ultimately, they would need a media communications manager, a membership coordinator, certainly they will need a director of farm and field operations, and someone that works directly with Luke as a tree breeding coordinator. And of course, Silvi will move into the role of general counsel, director of restoration, and be the face of the organization. Her main role will continue to be spreading the word and educating people who are interested in helping to expand and promote the American chestnut Rescue Mission.

As for capital construction, they were so fortunate that they already had a surprisingly good lab set up, but there were things they would need so that the mission could seamlessly evolve into Silvi and Luke's vision.

"We will need to start recruiting more volunteers. This place will not run without dedicated and skilled advocates, benefactors, and endorsers of the project," Silvi claimed.

Luke mentioned, "There is already a list of a hundred folks from your lectures and speaking engagements who have indicated they want to be involved. You can start calling on that list, and see if we can find someone that wants to coordinate scheduling and training volunteers for the breeding fields. There will certainly be a learning curve for research, and educating the volunteers who will be working out in the fields."

"I know there are several professors and students at East Coast universities with a deep interest in being involved. We might also be able to set up an onsite mentorship program or a work study program with some of the universities," Luke continued.

"Additionally, we will need more equipment for the laboratory. The drive through garage is perfect but, we will eventually need more walk-in coolers for storing seed. The barn will need heaters if we want to work year-round. We'll also need a designated area to store machinery. And a greenhouse and some shade structures to grow seedlings and do our breeding."

Luke very quickly got wrapped up in Silvi's exciting vision. They both laughed. They were like two bemused kids with endless possibilities and no boundaries.

Silvi added to her fantasy, "Oh, and we will need to build an operations area with an indoor workspace, a real conference room and a private office with phones, computers, and filing cabinets… not my dining table!"

The thoughts floated around in their heads and swirled into a cyclone of words. She knew she was getting way ahead of herself. But she could not be more excited. Luke took her in his arms, and they stood in the middle of the barn kissing, with little Sam tugging on their pant legs. The family hugged.

"I feel like I am the luckiest girl in the world," whispered Silvi. Luke lifted Sam with one arm and brought him into their circle.

"I love my men, let's go on inside and celebrate," she said with a quick wink as she turned on her heels and literally skipped up the front porch into their cozy cottage.

Silvi twirled around and raised her arms to the sky and proclaimed, "Tucker Hayes, I promise I will make you proud!"

The very next day, Silvi got on the phone and started making calls to groups that she believed would be interested in partnering with the Rescue Mission; colleges, universities, state governments, federal government agencies; her contacts at the USDA, the U.S. Forestry service, Farm Bureau, conservation groups, even private industries like the American Nut Growers and U.S. Lumber Coalition. She even reached out to the National Home Builders Association. You never know where your friends might be lurking.

And you certainly never know where your detractors are either, so she also contacted her copious list of anti- GMO activists, conservationists, naturalists, and nature purists letting them know what her intent was, and why she felt it was important for them to have a seat at the table and a voice as they created policy on this restoration project.

There would still be some dissenters. She fully expected for either environmental or financial reasons, she would need to cross her T's and dot all I's. She would need to be meticulous in her work in building as many friends and supporters as possible.

She decided to wait until she presented a clear threat to some, like the maple and oak lumber growers. Perhaps importers of Chinese chestnut trees, farmers that have invested decades and dollars in growing fields of other varieties of chestnuts in America. There would probably be other industries that she couldn't even fathom at this point. She knew that if their little nonprofit ever got to the point of producing a viable, diverse, blight resistant, self-replicating American chestnut tree that passed safety, environmental and governmental regulatory scrutiny, she was sure they would find her.

CHAPTER THIRTY-THREE

Growth Brings Conflict

SOMETIME AFTER GRANDPA TUCKER PASSED AWAY, SILVI, LUKE and Sam relocated into the main homestead cabin. They remodeled with some modern amenities; another bedroom with ensuite bathroom and an upgrade to the plumbing in the kitchen. Otherwise, the old chestnut log cabin remained quite the same.

The work at MeadowBrook became known far and wide. Within a couple of years, the rebirth of the American chestnut caught the attention of mainstream media. Silvi had interviews on national network news regularly, as well as speaking engagements at major research universities across the country.

Silvi primarily talked about the backcross breeding program. But there was always interest in the biotechnology side, and what was happening with genetic advances at the Environmental College. The genetic biotechnology path that Nita Baldwin headed up was followed carefully by many who were involved with or supported its success.

And it was followed even more closely by those who vehemently opposed it. In the late 1990's as science progressed, and it became evident that a transgenic tree was a possibility, there were letters of complaint from some long-time members of the Rescue Mission. They lodged threats of pulling their support if the Mission didn't abandon involvement in genetic technology manipulation. These complaints led to several heated disputes, and lots of passionate arguments between 'breeding purists' versus those who believed in the enterprise of advanced science.

There were scientists: naturalists, ecologists and environmentalists that solely supported the long road of allowing wild American chestnuts to breed. There were those that also supported Silvi's backcross breeding program. They believed these methods were the safest and only feasible way to bring the American chestnut forests back to their former glory. They had seen how proprietary ownership of laboratory-created plants caused greed and could be driven by, and detrimental to nature.

The genetic scientists like Nita; biologists, geneticists and botanists who believed that if a safe American chestnut tree could be developed, it would move the timeline for reforestation up by decades, or even centuries. And that it was incumbent upon us to use the science of the day. They felt that this was the only way to reach the Mission's vision, before the chestnut roots were gone and the American chestnut became extinct forever. They understood diversity was essential to a reforestation project. And the only chance there was for success was to figure this out and get trees in the ground before the root stock died out. They believed backcrossing alone would not outpace the demise of the roots.

One thing became abundantly clear; this organization needed to take a formal position.

The board of directors were gathered at the farm in the spring of 1998. Word got out and they knew there would be a strong turnout for this meeting. But they were not prepared for what happened on that April day. The board invited public testimony. And they anticipated a hearty discussion and a vote to determine which direction the Wild American Chestnut Rescue Mission would move.

What they experienced however was sheer and utter chaos. The Pro and Anti-technology supporters were to send representatives to present facts and opinions to the board. But instead of getting 'representatives', entire groups showed up en masse that morning. They came in droves and were lined up darkening the approaching road for as far as you could see. By 7:30 trucks started descending upon MeadowBrook farm. By eight o'clock, Silvi realized that they could not accommodate all the people who wanted to speak in the Board meeting room. So, they moved the meeting out to the barn. Luckily, it was a lovely day, and no rain was in the forecast. They convened at ten o'clock and there were, what seemed to be, hundreds of people who wanted to voice their opinion. On both sides, passions ran high. There were folks from ecology projects, biofuel watches, environmentalists, geneticists, mathematicians, statisticians, mycologists, genetic engineers, farmers, lumber mill owners and university professors.

And Journalists showed up ! This event garnered news coverage from Virginia to all parts of the United States, and Canada. Silvi, Luke and the rest of the board had not prepared for this sort of turn out. As the meeting came to order, the board members all gathered at the far end of the barn. They pulled out as many chairs as they could rustle up. Lots of people had brought their own or threw down blankets. It would be a long day.

Luke called the meeting to order, and one by one people got up to share their thoughts on GMOs and how they believed it fit (or not) with the vision of the rescue mission. For the most part, it was orderly, and they wanted to hear what each person had to share. They gave each person time to express their opinions. At times, it got passionate and loud. Some stories were fiery and some heartwarming. Some people were opposed to the biotechnology because of genetic modification, itself. Some were opposed, claiming it was a trojan horse, and it would open the floodgates to other species using this as precedent for further forest tampering. Others argued that it wasn't safe to indigenous animals, and it would cause an imbalance in the ecosystem.

Some believed that the breeding program caused far more mutated trees than snipping one or two genes to implant in an otherwise pure

American chestnut. Some believed transgenic trees were simply unnecessary, as backcross bred trees alone would reforest the range and others said, this work needed to move forward immediately otherwise it would be impossible to recreate the iconic chestnut forests before the roots died out and they'd be extinct forever.

Little tussles occurred as people verbally jabbed at one another while they were presenting their viewpoint. Then some bigger outbursts. There were constant grumblings under people's breaths, on one side or the other. Luke had to gavel on numerous occasions for order and quiet. This went on until 4:15 that afternoon. With just one short 30 minute break for the board to use the bathroom and stretch.

When they returned from the break, a brawl broke out and a few big guys had to break it up and evict the offenders off the property. Emotions ran high as the day wore on.

The board decided it was best to not have any decision announced at that time and sent everyone on their way, with the promise that the board would reconvene for a vote by week's end.

By the time everyone was gone, it had gotten dark, and cold. They were all exhausted and realized that this rescue mission was a trigger for people across the country who had strong feelings about the blight, the American chestnut, and the future path of the American Chestnut Rescue Mission. Although chaotic and unexpected it was a great debate and it showed that passions ran very high for the chestnut tree.

Silvi softly chuckled, as she wished her younger self could see her now. To let her know that she had nothing to worry about all those years ago. That her purpose and passion in life would unfold in due time.

Just as the last of the chairs were put away and everyone headed inside for dinner, Luke spotted a bright light at the furthest end of the south research field. He walked past the barn and immediately could smell it. The orchard was on fire. He ran. It was burning with a heat and intensity never before seen on the farm .

Luke screamed to call the volunteer fire department and ran out to the field with as many hoses as he could carry. He felt helpless with irrigation water against a fire that was blazing 10 feet high already. Within minutes the flashing lights and sirens were in a frenzy. All the volunteers on the farm that evening lent a helping hand. It was precipitously close to the forest and there was a lot of dead wood that had not been cleared from the winter.

Silvi's heart was beating wildly in anguish, for all the work that was at stake in that moment. Her eyes were wide and her crystal blues reflected the reds and yellows of the blaze, as she dug firebreaks along the southern end of the field. She was running on sheer adrenalin as the firetrucks sprayed and extinguished the fierce flames. The smoke filled the air as they worked to save the farm. Silvi thought about Grandpa Tucker, and she said a prayer to him for guidance and strength.

It was sheer luck that Luke saw the blaze, smelled it, and caught it before they retired for the night. The police report said it was arson. Someone that came to the board meeting intended to send a blazing clear message that he didn't believe the Mission had the right to tamper with Mother Nature. Funny way of showing it?

Luke suggested it might have been the guy earlier in the day that had been physically thrown off the property. But nobody knew who he was. It just made Silvi furious. And she doubled down on her commitment to rebuild the American chestnut range and make good on her promise to Tucker, the Hayes family, and all the good people of MeadowBrook. And to do whatever was needed to see this vision through. She pledged to do it safely, prudently, skillfully and with great care for the environment and her people, who must coexist in it for all millennia.

It was nine-thirty, pitch dark with a brisk snap in the air, the fracas was over, and all was finally calm again. Silvi and Luke collapsed on the couch with a glass of wine and fell asleep in each other's arms.

The next day the police arrested a man who was drunk and bragging in a local bar in Abingdon about setting the fire out at the chestnut farm, "To teach them a lesson". Word travels fast in a small town. He was incarcerated and had to pay restitution for his release. Silvi didn't know him, had never heard his name before but she was grateful that he was a grandstanding criminal, so he could pay for his rebellious, dangerous actions.

The board reconvened privately that Friday to discuss this emotionally charged issue. After much debate, the question was put to a vote; *Does the Rescue Mission cooperate and coordinate with the transgenic program to assist in the development of transgenic trees to plant back into the wilds of the American chestnut range?* The vote was taken. There were two dissenters. Silvi recused herself because of her relationship with Nita Baldwin. The final vote was 10-2, with one abstention.

"Not only did we lose two votes today, but we also lost two dedicated directors that were adamantly opposed to the transgenic work. Dan and Peter resigned from the board," Silvi told Nita.

Silvi was deeply saddened by this. She greatly respected these two men and enjoyed working with them. But the board made its decision based on it's vision. She personally felt the research should continue to see if the work could pass the strict regulatory requirements by the government for distribution.

Every path should be explored and if lucky, maybe one will be the road paved in green and gold, and Chestnuts!

CHAPTER THIRTY-FOUR

Ecosystem of Hope— A Retrospective

MeadowBrook Farm, Virginia

December, 2020

THE NEXT 20 YEARS SAW EXPLOSIVE PROGRESS FOR THE FOUNDAtion. *The Wild American Chestnut Mission* grew by leaps and bounds. Their vision to save the American chestnut from the brink of extinction was well underway, with many successes. They had developed an experimental chestnut tree that exhibited resistance to the fungus.

The journey of Silvi Hayes and Luke Woodbury could not have been more exciting and yet, pillar to post. For over a hundred years, humans have sought to reverse the devastation left by the chestnut blight and find a way to manage it. It had been, for all intents and purposes, fruitless until Silvi moved to MeadowBrook farm and dedicated her life to the rebirth of the American chestnut forest in its native range.

After creating *The Wild American Chestnut Rescue Mission*; she, Luke, Nita, and their dedicated team, used their collective knowledge, to innovate and explore what had not yet been done. Or capable of being done, prior to the technology of plant science and genetics of the twenty-first century.

Every resource was tapped, every path experimented, and much was learned. A thriving organization was in full swing by the late 1990's. And with it, true breakthroughs in science. Silvi continued to support the biocontrol methods of Luke's hypovirulence research. She stayed fully involved with Nita, and her team on the biotechnology front too. By the time the Rescue Mission was formally and officially organized, Luke and his team had already discovered a *Hypovirus* that had the potential to mitigate the deathly effects of the fungus that devoured the lives of four billion souls as the 20th century opened. Throughout his life, Luke worked on a virus solution that would naturally pass the virus to next generations, so that the inevitable fungal blight might be stopped in its path. The challenge was to get the virus to spread on its own, from tree to tree, without man having to inoculate each one. So far without success.

The main breeding program at MeadowBrook farm, *"Breeding Hope"*, was central to the past two decades of research. Silvi was proud of the hybridization program's progress at the farm.

It took cues from the fathers of genetics; Charles Darwin and Gregor Mendel. They taught the world how genetics work and how those principles are basic to the rebirth of the American chestnut. Silvi just took it one step further.

The key to success, that eluded the generation before her was multiple back breeding of subsequent generations that exhibit the resistance to the blight....She bred the pure American chestnut with a Chinese chestnut that had immunity to the fungus. That tree was half American, half Chinese. Then that seed was crossed with another pure American chestnut. Two more generations had backcrossed seedlings with 1/8th Chinese genes and 7/8th American genes, and it produced a tree that visually looked like the American chestnut: tall and straight, but with some trees exhibiting immunity.

She then took the most immune saplings and crossed them two more times, she ended up with an American chestnut whose genes were 15/16th American and 1/16th Chinese. At this point she had a hybrid that was 94% American chestnut with immunity from the blight!

It was a long tedious process with many failures along the way, but she planted hope that one day these seeds would grow into seedlings that would naturally multiply and grow into American chestnut trees that are immune to the fungus. And be able to spread without any human intervention across the entire chestnut range.

This crossing, backcrossing, and intercrossing of successive generations was slowly proving successful. It would just take patience and time. And not something Luke or Silvi would ever likely see completed in their lifetimes.

But to have the vision to plant a seed today for the grace of forest nature hikes and chestnut picking parties of generations to come was indeed a legacy worth pursuing.

While Silvi focused into the 21st century on backcrossing at the farm, Nita was having breakthroughs in her lab, at the College of Environmental Science and Forestry, up in Syracuse. She and her team were decoding the genomes of the American chestnut and isolating the genes that neutralize the oxalic acid that strangled all the chestnut forests. Nita chose this gene because it is quite common. It is found naturally in all sorts of produce; including carrots, strawberries, oranges, avocado, olives, almonds, spinach, rhubarb, and wheat. By 2008 her team had been able to isolate this gene from the wheat plant and implant it into the American chestnut seed. This cutting-edge technology was starting to produce most extraordinary results.

Nita was very excited at their findings and early results were showing that a chestnut tree will grow with this gene and confer resistance to the American chestnut, without changing or harming the fungus at all. It simply oxidizes the acid and renders the acid neutral, thereby giving the tree the ability to grow to maturity and produce nuts. This research took decades worth of science, knowledge and work, and every discovery was monumental. And every knock was a boost.

In 2011 Nita and her team broke the code to the genome of the blight fungus and by 2014 her team had produced one hundred percent resistant American chestnut trees that pass its immunity trait onto the next generation.

"Decades of work are finally showing tremendous breakthroughs in the rescue of the American chestnut," gloated Nita.

But her work was far from done. Some of their biggest obstacles were still ahead. "It hasn't been an easy road. We are finally seeing productive results, but our next hurdle is to prove not only the efficacy of this gene therapy, but it's safety to humans, animals and to the environment."

This work still excited Nita after all these years. But she knew that genetically modifying any plant, but especially a long lived tree, would need a tremendous amount of data to prove that it was safe, and it would need to go through rigorous regulatory requirements for the Federal Government. And that work was just starting.

Nita moved down to Virginia to assist the field work that she needed before applying for authorization to release a blight-resistant chestnut into the wild.

It was long in coming but, finally in 2015 Nita officially left the College of Environmental Science and Forestry and moved to the labs and research fields at MeadowBrook farms. She moved into Silvi's old cottage. The two of them along with a dedicated team of scientists worked hand-in-hand delving deeply into every metric to prove the efficacy and safety of this transgenic tree.

Life was good and Luke and Silvi had created a life they loved. For them, there was no such thing as work, they couldn't wait to get out to the lab and fields every day, to continue to raise the consciousness and address the challenges facing the American chestnuts.

Sam was growing up and his parents were committed to ensuring a good education for him. He loved being on the farm, but by the time he was a teenager, he had his sights on something else. Silvi was thrilled when Sam was accepted to her alma mater, Georgetown University in Washington, D.C. Sam graduated high school and spent the summer working on the farm, like he had all his life but when autumn rolled around, he was off to Washington and very excited to start his own journey. Georgetown suited Sam, and he easily made friends. He was very affable, yet was a hard worker, like his mom. Being in a real city was thrilling for Sam, having grown up in a very small town in rural Virginia. He didn't miss a chance to take advantage of all that life offered there. His freshman year was eye opening, especially meeting kids from all over the country and all walks of life. Sam did not miss an event or party that year, and yet, with all his socializing his grades were still just shy of a 4.0. He came home that summer to work on the farm but couldn't wait to get back to D.C.

Sam's first week of his sophomore year on campus he met a freshman girl named Kim Thompson. She came from a long line of doctors, and she knew that she wanted to be a doctor too. She was one of those natural beauties that was also very mindful and had an old soul. Sam liked that about her. She was very mature for her age.

Sam took after his mom in his passion and intellect. He was dedicated and brilliant. But he had little interest in biology, botany, or any field of science. His interests were politics and the law. The legislative process fascinated him. He liked the fast-paced life in a metropolis where there was always something exciting going on. Having grown up on a farm in a very quiet community, he couldn't wait to dive headfirst into many urban activities. He loved the hubbub of a vibrant city life. He graduated in three years with honors with a Bachelor of Science in political science. After his junior year, Sam was accepted into the Georgetown law school following in Silvi's footsteps, all those years ago.

After Kim graduated from Georgetown, she was accepted to George Washington Medical college and got her MD, with a focus on pediatrics. She adored children.

The two were inseparable and were a great fit. Kim was beautiful and they quickly fell in love. They would come home to Virginia to visit the farm and Sam's parents, but they couldn't wait to get back to their active, all-consuming lives in the heartbeat of America's political world. Sam was very quick witted, and extremely outgoing. He thrived in the hustle and bustle of Washington. And yet, he always felt that

Kim kept him grounded and settled him down. It was really love at first sight. During his law school, and her medical school, they rented a lovely little flat in Alexandria and the two of them became known as hard working overachievers. He volunteered on many campaigns and when he graduated, he knew his career and future would be in politics.

It threw Silvi back to her years with Brad in New York City, hobnobbing with all the rich and famous politicians, all the parties in the Hamptons and the privileges she was privy to because of her status and place in the world of power.

Sam, in D.C., also thrived on the buzz, it made him tick. Yet, for Silvi, after the initial glamour wore off, she detested the superficiality of it all. She hated the vast divide between "*The rich and the poor.*" None more evident than in Washington, D.C. She did love the town, and the excitement of being on the pulse of news and policy. But she found the people shallow, self-serving, and greedy. And power hungry. She was always grateful to get back home to MeadowBrook and her life of passionate pursuit to restore the majestic chestnut forests.

As the years went by, Sam grew up and his life blossomed. He was fiercely loyal and believed character was everything. He believed that a handshake was as binding as a legal tender. His word was impeccable. This made Sam's dance quite unique in the Washington political shuffle.

He worked his way up the political ladder, having served on the Alexandria city council and several important non-profit boards. By 2010, after completing all their schooling, he and Kim were married. They had a lovely wedding on the farm in MeadowBrook. Their June nuptials found the mountains in full bloom with wildflowers. Many dignitaries, doctors, and elected officials attended this event. All of their urban friends were in awe of what was going on at the farm in MeadowBrook. It raised the consciousness of the American chestnut project with an elite group of movers and shakers from the D.C. area. That pleased Silvi and Luke.

They were really proud of Sam, and they felt blessed to have Kim join their family. Lily catered the whole affair and it could not have been more beautiful or delicious. They took their vows in the chestnut fields under an arbor completely adorned with white and green florals. The rows of white wooden chairs sat draped with white taffeta ribbons and clusters of tulips and baby's breath. The long wooden tables had lace table runners and glass votive candles surrounded by bouquets of white roses. The whole scene looked like it was out of a wedding magazine.

By 2013, when Sam graduated from law school, he ran for and was elected mayor of Alexandria. Sam was the youngest mayor ever elected in Alexandria. He was mature far beyond his years. By 2015 he and Kim were thrilled to welcome baby Tessa to their little world.

Tessa was named after her paternal great-great-grandfather, Tucker. That meant a lot to Silvi. Sam barely remembered his great grandfather who died when Sam was only 5 years old, but he felt he knew Grandpa Tucker through all the stories that his mom, Silvi and his grandpa Ben had told over all the years on the farm. Sam also knew that honoring her grandpa would make his mom very happy. Tradition meant a lot to her.

By 2025, at a mere 35 years old, Sam was elected as the youngest ever U.S. Senator from Virginia.

Silvi loved going to visit Sam, Kim and Tessa in D.C. It made her feel young again. It reminded her of her days as a carefree community organizer. She was so young and so unblemished by the world's harsh realities of selfishness and gluttony. She frequented D.C. because she was collaborating with the Department of Agriculture on the backcross program. So, it gave her the opportunity to see her kids, which was something Silvi always looked forward to.

Many times, she would also meet Nita in Washington, as the Rescue Mission coordinated with the transgenic program at the College of Environmental Sciences and Forestry Laboratories, and Nita had to make frequent speeches or presentations.

Silvi adored her granddaughter, and she made Kim and Sam promise that she could have Tessa for two weeks every summer at the farm. She wanted to teach her grandbaby all the wonders of nature and the natural world; like her Grandpa Tucker had taught her. These were the memories that stuck with Silvi into adulthood and would guide her legacy for her entire life.

As Tucker loved the land, so did Silvi. Her time spent on the Wild American Chestnut Rescue Mission was never work, it was a labor of love. One that she wanted her grandchild to embrace. Or at least understand, as one of the guardians of the future.

The Government Pitch

In 2020, Nita, the College of Environmental Science and Forestry, in conjunction with the Wild American Chestnut Rescue Mission, made application to the U.S. Dept of Agriculture, the Food and Drug administration and the Environmental Protection Agency for regulatory exemption to begin to integrate this iconic and functionally extinct giant back into its natural range. They had hopes of distributing it into the wild throughout the Eastern forests.

This request to the government was the culmination of decades of scientific work. It would give Nita, and the Rescue Mission, permission to plant genetically modified chestnuts out in the original chestnut range. This was one of the biggest days of Nita's life. She was as prepared as she possibly could be. Silvi was there representing the Wild American Rescue Mission, and to support her cousin. They had to pass muster with not one government organization but several. It all started with the top dog, the Unites States Department of Agriculture.

Silvi gave an impassioned testimony to the USDA.

"Good morning, I'm Silvina Hayes, the CEO of the Wild American Chestnut Rescue Mission, and I appreciate your time here today. In college, and law school, I was one of the loudest voices against GMOs. I was a professional environmental activist fighting against the destruction of our natural world by greedy corporations. I was labeled a top adversary by some of the biggest agribusinesses in the world. My deafening bull horn and big homemade signs sat in my living room, ready for marching, organizing, and fighting against genetic tampering of any kind. But especially to crops and plants that produce food. Food consumed by indigenous animals and humans.

I was passionately opposed to any tampering of our forests and our natural wonders with any kind of fancy science or newfangled technology, believing that Mother Nature knew best.

In many ways, I still believe that. But I'm here before you today to share a story: An American Tragedy. There is no precedent of a dominant forest tree destroyed so utterly and completely from its ecological place in the world. The loss of the chestnut tree ended the existence of American chestnuts, it destroyed a rich American tradition, and a way of life for millions of hardworking people.

The firsthand legacy of the American chestnut is dwindling day by day, because those that were fortunate to experience these towering giants become fewer and fewer with each passing year. We, by and large, are now relegated to stories and memories of this older generation. Soon, they too will become extinct."

Silvi took a pause, and a very deep breath.

"But this story can have a different ending, indebted to science, technology, and the passion of a community, that will not let her die. The story of this mass extinction, of this utter devastation, as unintentional as it may have been, was caused by Man.

Science with all our unimaginable advances, incredible depth of knowledge, and yes, cutting edge technology, has the potential for a revival, an unprecedented restoration.

To rebuild this iconic forest is within your hands. The righting of a wrong, that has been called the greatest ecological disaster ever in the history of America. We now can attempt to rectify our past mistakes. And we can do it with the least impact on the native tree, the animals and environment around it.

To meet the vision of the American Chestnut Rescue Mission, to bring the trees back to their mystical, abundant, unique dominance in the eastern half of the United States, I am here in support of this transgenic application request. Thank You."

Silvi turned the presentation over to Nita.

"Thank you for having me here today, I'm Dr. Nita Baldwin, from the College of Environmental Science and Forestry. Today I present three decades of my team's work and stand ready to answer all your questions. Skepticism about GMOs is justified, yet it is evident that most Americans who are aware of the blight, desire to bring back, from functional extinction, the majestic chestnut tree. It was a fast growing, valuable multi-use hardwood and it consistently and annually produced a crop of healthy nuts which were consumed by people, their farm animals and wildlife.

What killed, and continues to kill the tree, is an acid produced by the blight fungus. We have discovered a way to interrupt the effect of this acid, to prevent the death of American chestnuts. We have identified a gene that produces an enzyme called oxalate oxidase (oxo). It is inserted into the DNA of the chestnut to make this transgenic tree. The gene is common and found in all grains, and is consumed regularly by people, pets, and wildlife. This enzyme has been studied for decades and has been deemed safe in all the produce we eat.

The oxo enzyme detoxifies oxalic acid. This is the acid that damages the tree and causes fatal orange cankers. Our transgenic method adds just two genes from a wheat plant to the chestnut genome which passes on the blight resistance. No other genes are modified. We have cracked the code to mapping and understanding the DNA of the American chestnut, and the fungus that kills the tree.

She went on to say, "The method we have developed has the ability to render the fungus benign, so the American chestnut can mature to produce chestnuts once again and to spread and breed naturally throughout the forests of the Appalachian Range and beyond."

She finished with her evidenced based proof, "We have prepared a 300-page document that you all should have, that catalogues our rigorous and extensive testing. The results are assured, that the tree released into the wild is safe on all counts."

Nita drew attention to specific facts and figures, stories, and research, efficacy, safety, and demonstration results. She had decades of work to prove the methods and the conclusive results that had been documented meticulously through extensive investigation done to determine if these transgenic trees had any adverse effect on any animals, wildlife, or the surrounding environments. And they found none. Additionally, she declared that there would be no proprietary seeds.

"We want to be clear that these seeds will never be patented. It will give scientists around the world and homeowners, and institutions of North America accessibility to propagate blight-tolerant American chestnuts for their own use and benefit."

Nita closed her presentation and took questions.

"Yes, Sir with the blue shirt."

A scholarly looking gentleman in a corduroy jacket and glasses stood up, "Thank you. This has evidently been a decades long road for you. But I understand there are several methods besides genetic modification being studied to bring the chestnut back to its rightful range. Why do we need to use a transgenic approach?"

"Thank you for that question. Yes, that is true. There are several other methods. The first is propagating the few American chestnuts that somehow survived the blight. They obviously have some level of naturally occurring immunity. The problem here is there are so few of those trees in existence that it would require several thousand years, if ever, to repopulate the billions of lost trees of this species."

"I'll ask Silvina Hayes to reference the next method," said Dr. Baldwin

Silvi stood up and continued

"We have been working since the mid 1980's on cross breeding at the MeadowBrook experimental farms. There are also some backcross farms at a few universities in the U.S. and Canada. But I can speak to the work at MeadowBrook, in Virginia. It's been a long road and we have come a long way. We have thousands of trees in some stage of immunity but, we are just scratching the surface. We have developed a resistant chestnut by choosing offspring that include the gene for immunity from Chinese chestnuts. But it takes time to get from generation to generation, for trees whose lifespan is hundreds of years. This method is hopeful but as of yet, this method alone will not likely bring back the American chestnut in the timeframe that exists before the roots of the current trees diminish and die out."

Nita stood and explained that there was another method that involved binding a virus to the fungus and rendering the fungus neutral and incapable of killing the trees. But that this method was in it's infancy and alone would not likely save the American chestnut.

Nita concluded, "Science is always evolving and there may be other methods that we can't even imagine yet, but the most hopeful method we have today is neutralizing the blight with this gene implanted into the American chestnut to confer immunity, with the least change to the American chestnut or the fungus.

I'd like to leave you with one thought, as you reflect on your life, feel a sense of pride for the mark you left in safeguarding the Earth for future generations. We are entrusted with a duty to halt this destruction that we started 100 years ago. For the first time, we possess the technology and science to do just that. I firmly believe we have the power to bring back this keystone tree to its natural range. Let us unite in unwavering dedication to preserving the beauty, bounty and majesty of our planet, the precious jewel that we call home.

There was a period for public testimony and finally on October 19, 2020, the discussion was closed for comment.

By New Year's Eve in 2022, Nita heard that they were granted permission to continue their work. The guidelines allowed Nita's researchers and the Rescue Mission to disperse the transgenic seed into the wild and directly to the public, for purposes under the strict protocol they had requested. This gave the Rescue Mission many more points of diversification that would be needed for their survival.

It was a time for celebration.

Grandpa Tucker would've been so proud.

CHAPTER THIRTY-FIVE

Breeding Hope

January 3, 2055

Silvi's 100th Birthday

Right at the close of 2022, the Government regulators opened the way for transgenic American chestnuts to be planted and distributed throughout its native range of the United States, from the Atlantic Ocean, all the way to the Mississippi River.

It was a year of landmark transitions. Silvi turned 65 that year. Nita, at 82 was living at the farm. She retired from the College of Environmental Sciences and Forestry in 2011 and left Syracuse to spend her days side by side with Silvi creating a legacy. Nita never remarried after a brief nuptial in her youth, but instead found her companionship with her best friend; her cousin, Silvi. And with the volunteers at the Wild American Chestnut Rescue Mission. They were all bound by one big communal goal.

Twelve small rustic cabins were built on the farm which made for a highly intertwined community. Each cabin housed two volunteers. Some were committed for a year or more and some came for a semester on-site. In the midst of the cabins was a central gathering barn with a large kitchen that served as a social center. Each evening brought discussion and direction for the team. Most nights a crew of folks gathered for dinner and friendship. They all came with different skills and experience, but they all left with a camaraderie of purpose and resolve to the mission.

The ensuing 35 years saw successes and challenges. Imagination morphed and finetuned a serious reforestation effort of public and private lands all across the Eastern Seaboard. The project captivated the threadbare and gentry alike. At the tipping point, hundreds of public and private lands with backcrossed American chestnut trees from Silvi's "*Breeding Hope*" program started to produce nuts.

People far and wide planted hybrid and transgenic trees. Some of these were now fully reaching maturity and propagating spontaneously. Each tree was suited to that locality, climate, soil, and precipitation of the area. The diversity was vast, and clusters were beginning to thrive on their own.

This project was far from a smooth journey. There were many setbacks and failures. There were lots of lessons learned. Some were complete disasters and other experiments gave them hope. But through each they pushed on, adjusted, and learned. In some areas, the chestnut forests were maturing. Animals of the forest were flourishing again and dispersing the American chestnut across the range. After 100 desolate years, chestnut trees flowered, once again looking like snowcapped mountains in July. Homestead life was returning to the days of great-great-great-Grandpa Tucker Hayes. Silvi's dream of reforesting the American chestnut was starting to become real. Chestnuts again fell in MeadowBrook. A small amount, yes, but real American chestnuts, none the less.

It was exciting for volunteers, to be on the ground floor of the comeback tree. The base of support was growing by leaps and bounds. The chestnut project gained national attention. Documentaries were made. Conferences were held in all parts of the country. The Wild American Chestnut Rescue Mission became part of household vernacular across the land. Society ladies held fundraisers in big cities, and the foundation was featured on the front page of magazines and newspapers, internationally. Children learned about the Rescue Mission and the story of the chestnut plight in school. Children across the country were taught about responsibility in forest management, and their responsibility to all flora and fauna. There were far reaching groups wanting to partner with the Mission that were spontaneous and unexpected. Grade schools organized farm visits for their field trips. There were over 750,000 volunteers across the country and the evolution to "Save the American chestnut" became a fashionable philanthropic enterprise.

The awareness expanded outside the original range, to the entire country and into Canada. It became a movement. The Wild American Chestnut Rescue Mission and the "*Breeding Hope*" program became household names. People were passionate about the legacy of the chestnut forests and were bequeathing to the Mission in their estate plans for future generations. Once again, vendors roasting chestnuts on street corners showed up with their little carts in all major cities across America. The roasty, aromatic smells permeated downtowns, especially Manhattan.

There was a national contest and a little fifth grader from Pennsylvania won with the motto "We ain't messin, we need chestnuts for dressin." Another fourth grader from New York started a club called "New York is for Nuts." A fraternity at the State University in Kentucky changed their Greek house slogan to, "We are Chest- Nuts." The Junior League of Connecticut wrote a cookbook reviving old recipes from the 1800's, incorporating chestnuts into many culinary delights from soups, to breads, to pastries, to fish. All proceeds were donated to furthering research and the protection of the American chestnut forests.

After a couple of more decades, American chestnuts were becoming plentiful. The American chestnut trees once again took over a large portion of the Eastern forests. Their tall and broad canopies towered over the oaks and elms. Some of the original crossbreeds were over 80 years old now. They would soon be the dominant species in the once auspicious range. These boundless trees produced oxygen that helped clean the air and the waterways. They started, once again, to support animals that lived in and around these vast giants. Deer, elk, chipmunks, bear, squirrels and wild turkeys started to flourish again too.

Silvi's family also thrived, and grew. Her son, Sam developed into a wise man, and at 55 years old, was still serving in the U.S. Senate representing Virginia. His wife, Kim had retired and joined "Doctors without Borders," to work with children in underserved communities around the world.

Their Daughter Tessa, Silvi's beloved granddaughter, loved the farm life and followed in her grandma and grandpa's footsteps to become a PhD botanist. She joined the team at MeadowBrook. Tessa decided to dedicate her life to the plight of the American chestnut and the Rescue Mission. Which of course was to the greatest delight of Silvi and Luke.

Silvi lost Nita in 2035 at 96 years old. It was one of the hardest days of her life. They had shared everything. A part of Silvi died that day too. Nita was her best friend, her mentor, her family. Nita was the foundation in her life's work from the time she was a teenager. And she was her partner, for their purpose in life. Silvi and Nita each championed each other's dreams. Silvi leaned on Nita's wisdom and generous spirit until the day she died. Nita had now joined her grandpa, her mom and dad, her sister Lily and all the ancestors that came before her.

Luke passed away five years later, at 85. Luke and Silvi shared a long, beautiful life for 51 years. They built not only a life, but a legacy together. They were very proud of what they concocted and created together. From the earliest days, Silvi and Luke shared a life goal. They used their talents and skills to complement and support each other every day of their lives. Luke lived to see a breakthrough with the *Hypovirus*. He was able to produce a viably immune American chestnut by inoculating trees against blight. But he never saw the *Hypovirus* genetically pass that immunity to the next generation. That would take more time and more work, if it were possible at all. Work that Tessa was carrying on in her grandfather's footsteps. A new generation was carrying the torch now, as it should be, and they were doing a prodigious job.

There was great success with a growing scale of volunteers inoculating tens of thousands of trees, that saw maturity in producing vast masts of chestnuts in groves from New England to North Carolina. Luke knew on his dying bed that it was just a matter of time before there would be a viral remediation that would naturally pass on in the wild. That would be the next generations barrier to break.

Luke also discovered and had great success in cloning identical pure American chestnuts by capturing all the superior traits with great genetic variance, including blight immunity, and replicating exact duplicates in great numbers. Luke's work was innovatively radical. Without his years of dedication as a trailblazer with the *Hypovirus*, along with his vast store of knowledge, this project never would have blossomed. He altered the course of history for this planet and guided a future generation to carry on in his footsteps. Silvi was right by his side and held his hand until Luke took his last Earthly breath.

Tessa was educated in D.C. and grew to be a fine woman. She was smart and accomplished but she always felt her mom and dad were overachieving extroverts that made her seem like a slacker. Tessa liked politics from behind the scenes but, it wasn't her passion. Her dad, being the senior U.S. Senator from Virginia, would have opened many doors for her to an involved Washington D.C. life. But it wasn't what moved her.

Her mom became a highly successful philanthropic medical doctor who travelled the world. She admired her mom, but that also was not what motivated Tessa. Her days on the farm were her happiest. She loved the work that her family was doing to return the chestnut forests, and that nudged her connection to her roots with her Grandma Silvi.

Sam and Kim were very proud of Tessa and only wanted her to follow her dream. Although she loved her life in D.C. with her mom and dad, she spent every summer and every free holiday on the farm in Virginia with her grandparents, Silvi and Luke. It's where she felt she belonged. Silvi understood her passion, as it was the same pull that she had so many years ago.

However, in 2032 Tessa stayed in D.C. for much of the summer because her dad was running for re-election, and he needed her help. She always worked on her dad's campaigns, and this year would be no different. This race was contested in the primary and for the first time in over a decade Senator Woodbury needed to actually campaign, kiss babies and raise money.

A young college graduate named Jared Powell volunteered for Senator Woodbury's campaign on the fundraising side. In real life, he came from a prodigal East Coast family. He appreciated his parents' choices, but that decadent lifestyle did not resonate for Jared. Though he was a licensed financial planner, he chose to work for a small firm that had a contract with the government. That firm assisted the underprivileged and underserved community in Washington, D.C. His job was to help people in financial straits get out of debt. And teach them skills to get on a track for financial success. Jared had an empathy for those less fortunate, a trait so often lacking in the rich and famous.

Tessa and Jared met early on the campaign trail. It didn't take long for them to become inveterate twins. They shared the same values, the same passions, and similar goals. They were perfect for each other, and they fell in love. Senator Woodbury liked Jared, and after he won his election, Jared was included in the private victory celebration with the family.

The next year, Tessa and Jared married and soon after had a son. They named him after her great-great-great-grandfather Tucker, whom she had heard about her whole life. They named the boy; William Tucker Powell. It was important for Tessa to honor the man who was born and raised on the Hayes Hog farm and loved the land. Tucker passed the farm on to be run in perpetuity as a trust for the betterment of nature and the natural world. And mostly to bring back the wild chestnut forests of North America. Alongside her grandmother Silvi,

Tessa loved her summers in Virginia, and this is where she developed her love of nature and love of the land,; the land that had been in her family since 1883. She was determined to live out her days in the footsteps of Grandma Silvi, and those of her great-grandfather, Ben and her great-great-grandfather, Tucker Hayes.

After Tessa and Jared had their baby Bill, all three of them moved to the farm. Tessa worked in the lab doing research in her grandfather Luke's footsteps and Jared became the Chief Financial Officer of the Wild American Chestnut Rescue Mission.

Bill Powell was a smart and curious boy. He was inquisitive, unorthodox and had a gloriously funny sense of humor. Tessa and Jared loved that they could give their son this kind of simple and beautiful life in the country. Although he grew up on this old Appalachian farm, Tessa and Jared saw to it that Bill was well educated. He excelled in college and got a degree in plant genetics and forest management. He had a deep love of nature.

When Bill was 20 years old, Grandma Silvi had her 100th birthday. She lived to see her great-grandson fall in love with the farm all these years later. She loved this land, as her grandfather had before her. And it meant the world to her that her family also cherished the land. It stood for everything that she cared about in life. Silvi adored that her great-grandson, Bill, understood the value of the American chestnut. How the blight devastated life as they knew it. Through Silvi's and Tessa's influence, Bill had the vision to carry on and rebuild the culture and the lifestyle that his great-grandmother dedicated her life to. And for all his ancestors before Silvi .

Silvi lived to be 104 years old. When asked her secret to longevity she always attributed it to; "A purpose, a mission, and a deep desire to see my grandaddy's chestnut trees blossom in summer, and roasted chestnuts every fall. That, and a little nip of whiskey before bed," she would say with a wink.

Christmas Eve, 2099

Bill Powell grew up to be a man on that farm. His love for the forest was immeasurable. Bill's second passion was writing, and he became a well known author of historical fiction.

It was the year 2099, the turn of a new century. He was introduced at the Changing Hands Book Store in Abingdon, Virginia. It was a chilly and snowy evening but inside it was cozy and warm. Abingdon Village at Christmas was an erstwhile, sentimental portrait of American life. A slice of Americana, lost for most.

The book shop was bustling, people laughing and toasting their brandied eggnog topped with a dash of nutmeg. The welcoming Christmas tree glowed in the sparkling bay window at the front of the store, beckoning passersby in for a warm smile and holiday cheer. It was decorated in traditional white twinkling lights and large red and green checkered bows. It had glittering stars hanging from every branch. And a floating angel graced the top.

The turn of the century's Christmas celebration brought unusual crowds to this normally sleepy town. Abingdon had a picturesque small-town center, a perfect gathering spot for a white Christmas. It was also Bill's 65th birthday. The celebration was replete with caroling and local fare. The air was awash in the scents of the season. Especially the smell of chestnuts roasting on open fires throughout the town square. It permeated the air with a sweet nutty scent. Much like he imagined it would have been at the old homestead at the Hayes Hog Farm in 1883.

Bill took the podium at the very back of the bookstore and looked out over the crowd, there must have been 300 people packed into that small shop. The chairs were full, and people curled up on the floor, squeezed in together, to hear the reading of his new novel. He stood for a moment, a very reflective moment, took a deep breath, and thought about how he had gotten there.

He was deeply lost in thoughts about the ancestors that came before him. His mom, Tessa, who sat in the front row that Christmas Eve.

His Grandpa Sam: a great U.S. Senator that served Virginia until the day he died.

His great-grandma, Silvi Hayes Woodbury, who had the vision to rebuild an entire forest and save the Iconic American chestnut from the brink of extinction.

His great-great-grandfather Ben Hayes, who had a deep connection to the forests.

And his great-great-great-grandfather, Tucker Hayes, born at the turn of the 20th century, in a homesteaded cabin made entirely of chestnut logs, felled on their land. A cabin, his cabin, which still stands steadfast and strong today, at over two hundred years old.

He stood in awe, at how a fungus blight took down to functional extinction an entire species, a lifestyle, and the culture of millions of American families. And how his family, against all odds, with thousands of dedicated volunteers, had the heart, the tenacity, and the determination to rebirth that forest, as well as the culture and way of life of those rural Appalachian families.

It was a story that needed to be told, learned, embraced, and never, never forgotten. Now at 65 years old, Bill was committed to giving his family's story of hope, back to the world.

With a tear welling up in his eye, and a crack in his voice, he started reading his novel aloud…

"It was a stifling summer night in MeadowBrook, Virginia. My great, great, great grandmother Bessie Hayes was in labor. It did not come all at once but when it did, it was resolute and with abandon. Leaving destruction and bewilderment in its path……."

Bill read from his novel and ended with a quote from Thomas Jefferson.

"The American chestnut forest was so thick; a squirrel could climb to the canopy in Virginia and not touch ground again until he reached the Mississippi River."

His standing ovation went on for a full minute, as sweet roasted American chestnuts were passed around to every guest.

He stood in deep gratitude to all his ancestors, to all the pioneers, who had the providence and persistence to plant a seed, the resilience, and the triumph of the human spirit, so, it could flourish again on the Eastern Seaboard: The American Chestnut Range.

THE END

AUTHOR'S NOTES

THIS NOVEL IS BASED ON A TRUE STORY. IN 1904 A FUNGUS WAS discovered on the American chestnut trees at the Bronx Zoo in New York. The fungus had been imported on agricultural Asian chestnut trees. It infected the entire population of American chestnuts across the eastern United States, the tree's native range. It spread quickly, ravaged, and destroyed the predominant tree of the forests, four billion American chestnuts.

These are facts in our American history, yet as I started to write this novel one question nagged at me. How have I never heard about the demise of this significant tree species before? I grew up in New York, part of the American chestnut's native range. I'm a biologist, a hiker, a nature lover, and this travesty occurred in my parents' and grandparents' lifetimes! How could something this devastating have slipped the textbooks from which I was educated? Why was there no 'movement' like save the whales, or save the rainforests ?

I interviewed everyone I could connect with that was still alive from that era. Yet, no one I spoke to remembered it as more than a nebulous footnote at the dinner table.

My dad, currently at 100 years of age, lived on the east coast for ninety years of his life. He is sharp as a tack and when questioned, he had very little recollection of a devastating blight that wiped out four billion trees in his backyard. How could that be? He was born in 1921 in New York, right in the thick of the devastation.

An in-depth search turned up very little written or recorded information about the near death of the tree.

It turns out however, as the blight rampaged in the early 1900s, a lot of intervention was attempted by individuals and local, as well as federal governments, to save the American chestnut. Unfortunately, all the vigorous attempts and all the money spent did nothing to save it. The scientific technology needed at that time simply didn't exist. It would take another fifty years before there was a glimmer of hope.

On June 22, 1983, a group of scientists, from Minnesota, with the proper education, knowledge, and a vision, officially established The American Chestnut Foundation (TACF).

The organization's platform was the brainchild of Dr. Charles Burnham, a retired plant geneticist from the University of Minnesota, who was joined by one of his students; Dr. Norman Borlaug, (a Nobel laureate for his work involving the "green revolution"). They bantered about the hope of returning the American chestnut. They knew the dead tree stumps continually sent up shoots, so surmised many of the tree's roots were not "dead." This, they theorized, could be key in the ability to bring the tree back. But the sprouting trees held little hope, as they lay in wait for the dreaded fungus to once again attack, usually before the trees were old enough to produce nuts. The blight was still thriving in oak trees and in the soil underground, throughout all the forests in the range. But science was evolving, and Burnham had a plan.

As word got out, another student of Burnham named Phil Rutter believed that the work attempted by the government on the American chestnut was the wrong approach. He believed they now had the knowledge to breed a chestnut that would genetically carry the traits of the American tree, yet have resistance to the blight. Rutter organized a meeting with Burnham; Dr. David French, chair of plant pathology at the University; Dr. Ronald Phillips, professor of agronomy and plant genetics; Dr. Budd Tordoff, head of the university's Bell Museum of Natural History; Dr. Harold Pellet of the Minnesota Landscape Arboretum; and an attorney, Donald C. Willeke, who had served as president of the National Urban Forest Council.

This esteemed group met to determine if the American chestnut could be restored to its place in the forests of the Eastern United States. After much banter and discussion, they determined that it was possible, but would require a dedicated nonprofit foundation that could stand in perpetuity. They believed the goal could be accomplished within, give or take, 100 years.

This was the genesis of TACF.

Phil Rutter was elected by the board as the foundation's first president. He worked tirelessly and took on many roles as plant breeder, fundraiser, and development director for the organization.

Burnham, well into his eighties by now, was elected vice chair and was made senior scientific advisor. By 1987 the group knew that to accomplish their goal of breeding the genetic material for blight resistance in a tree that otherwise has substantially all the characteristics of the American chestnut, they would need a dedicated research center and land, preferably, in the native range of the American chestnut.

In 1989 their dream came true when they were offered by the Wagner family, a long-term lease on their farm in Meadowview, Virginia.

TACF has grown from a few Minnesota scientists to a premier environmental conservation nonprofit, whose goal is to produce a viable American chestnut using multiple pathways, including traditional breeding and biotechnology, and to return this iconic tree to its rightful home.

Since the time of the original board, the foundation established a national office in Asheville, North Carolina, and four regional offices in the tree's native range: New England, based in South Burlington, Vermont; north central, based in College Station, PA; mid-Atlantic, based in Charlottesville, VA; and southern, based at the national office in Asheville. There are 16 state chapters in these four regions.

The organization celebrates its many research partners, all of whom utilize cutting edge scientific technology to develop a blight-tolerant American chestnut tree.

TACF's mission is "to return the iconic American chestnut to its native range", and its vision is "a robust eastern forest restored to its former splendor".

Today in 2023, Don Willeke is still the foundation's legal counsel, and Lisa Thomson is the President of the Board and Chief Executive Officer.

If you are piqued by this immense effort, please consider exploring further and joining us on this bold mission at www.ACF.org. Membership includes a subscription to the foundation's award-winning magazine, *Chestnut,* which offers stories about the tree being revived through science and how it has been revered throughout history.

And please join us at www.TheTreeThatCalledUsHome.com for event announcements, book signings, blog entries, partnerships, movie screenings, speaking engagements, and news about the novel and progress of our mission to raise awareness of the story about the American chestnut.

IN GRATITUDE

So many people influenced the writing of this book that it would be impossible to mention them all, but I am deeply indebted to my friends and family who supported me through this adventure. Special thanks go to: Andy Anderson's red pen, Mario Valeruz's inspirational love of the land, Richard Ross's absolute attention to detail, unmatched sense of humor and the mug of Breeding Hope , Hal DeKeyser's endless patience, innate wisdom and guidance, Deb Gessner's generous heart and eye for beauty, all the dedicated staff and volunteers over the past forty years at the American chestnut foundation, and the ones who have shared their expertise with me; Sara Fitzsimmons, Jared Westbrook, Jules Smith and particularly, Lisa Thompson, for assisting me on this journey of enlightenment.

ABOUT THE AUTHOR

Robin Shaw is a naturalist with a deep passion for storytelling that dates back to her childhood. When she stumbled upon a *New York Times* article about an incurable blight that brought about the functional extinction of the American chestnut forests, she was moved and shocked. She wondered why generations of her family living in these forests never spoke about this incredible loss and why she had never learned about it in school.

It has taken a century, but today, science and technology exist to address this tragedy and turn back the hands of time. Restoring a functionally extinct species is no small task. The goal of this debut novel, *The Tree That Called Us Home* is to share a story based on true events, and disseminate that story far and wide such that every American, for generations to come, knows the beauty of sitting under a spreading chestnut tree and roasting chestnuts on an open fire.

Robin holds a bachelor's degree in biological sciences from Syracuse University, and for years taught traditional breeding methods as a high school educator. She also had a career as a financial planner, founded Advanced Marketing Concepts, worked as a ski instructor, is a lifelong organic farmer, and was elected and served as State Representative in the Arizona Legislature. Robin has two grown sons. She currently resides in Arizona.

Honorable Robin Shaw is available for select speaking engagements.
To inquire about a possible appearance, please visit
www.TheTreeThatCalledUsHome.com

www.ingramcontent.com/pod-product-compliance
Lightning Source LLC
LaVergne TN
LVHW020706110826
845149LV00012B/2133

* 9 7 8 1 9 6 0 5 0 5 3 1 6 *